PRAGUE:
Darkness Descending

Robert Tecklenburg

The contents of this book regarding the accuracy of events, people and places depicted and permissions to use all previously published materials are the sole responsibility of the author who assumes all liability for the contents of the book.

International Standard Book Number 13: 978-1-60452-153-5
International Standard Book Number 10: 1-60452-153-8
Library of Congress Control Number: 2020939192

BluewaterPress LLC
2922 Bella Flore Ter
New Smyrna Beach FL 32168

This book may be purchased online at -
https://www.bluewaterpress.com/prague

"Weep, for the light is dead."
--Friedrich Von Schiller

Chapter 1

Hoa Lo Prison, Hanoi, October 15, 1945

Major Charles Stanek jerked awake in the silent darkness, hearing only the sound of his own breathing. His whole body throbbed with pain. He raised his head ever so slightly to see a very narrow beam of light entering through a barred window above him. That reassured him that at the very least, he was above ground. Fighting a growing panic, he tried to consider his predicament, but unable to keep his eyes open, he again blacked out.

How long he lay there, he would never know. When he regained consciousness, he found himself in another place, a room in a house, not a dungeon cell. Its bright light flooded in from several windows to blind him.

He curled up in the fetal position and shielded his eyes. *Where...?* Charlie asked himself, his mind groggy. He struggled to focus his thoughts, to make sense of what had happened to him.

Very soon, a European-looking man entered the room. He was dressed as a soldier. Charlie forced himself to move, but his body would not obey. *Drugged*, he reasoned, as he lay helplessly while the soldier walked toward him.

Two other soldiers with rifles at the ready entered and followed the first man. The first soldier stopped and stood over Charlie. He nudged him in the ribs with his boot. Turning to look, Charlie recognized his uniform as that of a Russian officer, *probably NKVD*, he thought. He was familiar with Russians, from having to deal with them on the Eastern Front during the war. They were ruthless—enemy or ally—it did not matter.

"Where am I?" Charlie whispered, his blue eyes following the Russian soldier like those of a hawk. "Who are you?"

"You are in our mission in Hanoi, Indochina." The officer replied in poor English. "Now you will get up," he ordered. He again kicked at his ribs.

Charlie slowly struggled to stand.

"Sit in this chair, Comrade Stanek," the officer ordered in Russian and pointed at the chair in the middle of the room. "I am Colonel Andre Pavlov, Army of the Union of Soviet Socialist Republics."

He must know I speak Russian, Charlie thought. "I will not move until you tell me why I am here," he replied, still speaking English.

The officer smiled bleakly, turned, and motioned to the two soldiers behind him. They obeyed immediately. They both reached for their prisoner. Charlie backed away, fighting off their attempts. "Leave me, bastards. I'll walk on my own," he said, giving in to their demands. He slowly limped over to sit in the chair, but he never took his eyes off the three men, especially the older officer with his thin colorless lips, and large, protruding nose set in the narrow chalk colored face. Where the man's eyes should have been, Charlie saw only two dark shadows. Now, he knew evil.

"Tell me your name please," the officer said slowly, continuing in Russian.

Charlie recognized the dialect. *Urals*, he decided.

"My name is Charles Stanek, and I am an American citizen," he replied in English, refusing to speak the man's language. *Fuck him*, Charlie thought. *This Russian reminds me of a corpse, one of the many dead I saw in the Carpathians, who lay frozen in the snow.*

"You will speak to me in Russian," Colonel Pavlov said in Russian. "Now, tell me about your position and why you are in Vietnam."

"I am a representative of the United States on the Allied Control Commission. I am here to investigate the death of an American soldier," he said again in English.

Colonel Pavlov struck him hard across the face with the back of his hand. "In Russian, Major Stanek. Yes, I know you are an American soldier who speaks my language fluently. But where is your uniform, your identification?"

The blow surprised Charlie. He shook it off. "I'm on a diplomatic mission. My papers were taken from me," he said, but this time in Russian. *How do they know I'm a major? Donovan promoted me only before I left on this mission*, he thought perplexed.

"Oh yes, major, we know all about you," the colonel said, reading his mind. "Now, I want to know your real purpose for being in Vietnam?"

"I don't know what you're talking about."

"We must have certain information. If you do not tell us, we will kill you," Colonel Pavlov said slowly and directly.

"And if I tell you what you want to know?"

"Yes. Then we will take you to Moscow on the next transport."

"Why?"

"The Vietnamese people captured you. They say you are a spy. By taking you to Mother Russia and not allowing them to shoot you, we will be assisting you."

"I am not spying. The United States has an agreement with the Annamese, colonel," he said, staring directly at the Russian officer. "I must demand that you release me immediately. I have diplomatic immunity. You are violating an international treaty. And we are allies."

"You are a spy and have been a spy throughout the war. Now you are here in Indochina to receive important information from your agent," he said slowly, indifferent to Charlie's denial. "This, we know already. Give us the name of your contact. Tell us when and where you are to meet this traitor."

"What?" Charlie replied, growing more confused. "I don't have a name. I don't know any spy or agent. Who told you that?"

"We have our sources. They are very reliable, so do not lie to us. It will only make things worse for you." The colonel nodded to one of the soldiers who immediately stepped behind their prisoner.

Charlie turned his head to the right to watch the soldier.

"The spy's name, Major Stanek," his interrogator demanded, grabbing Charlie's head with both hands to force him to look at him. Pavlov's cold dark eyes chilled him. "I want the message he sent you."

"Where is Major Zerenowsky? He will explain who I am. He knows that I am not on an espionage mission."

"Major Zerenowsky? I think not," Colonel Pavlov said, slightly amused. "The major has proof that your agent has contacted you in Saigon."

"What?" Charlie stammered, bewildered. "Here in Indochina, thousands of miles from Europe? You are badly mistaken."

The soldier grabbed his arms and tied one wrist to a rifle barrel and the other to its stock, behind his chair. He then tore open the rough Russian tunic to reveal Charlie's bare chest. Finally, he pulled off Charlie's boots.

Charlie watched Pavlov take a deep drag from a cigarette he had lit only seconds before. He slowly exhaled, blowing smoke in Charlie's face. Charlie coughed and that reaction seemed to delight the Russian.

"We take our time, Major Stanek," he said, then touched the glowing cigarette butt against Charlie's chest.

Charlie gritted his teeth to keep from crying out. His face contorted at the drilling pain. The officer took the cigarette away and looked away from his prisoner to nod at the soldier behind Charlie. The soldier took firm hold of the rifle by the stock and by the barrel. Slowly, the soldier pushed and twisted the rifle, stretching and contorting Charlie's arms.

"Are you ready to tell us, major?" Pavlov asked, smoke billowing from his mouth. He again nodded to the soldier.

The soldier stopped twisting the rifle, but he did not loosen his grip. The faint smell of burning flesh permeated the small room.

"General Donovan, the man who runs your spy agency, has sent you to Saigon to receive a secret communique. He is working closely with your allies, the British, and we know you met with them. They brought the secrets here, acting as your courier. Major Zerenowsky has tracked it. Tell us who he is."

"I told you what I know," Charlie whispered through clenched teeth.

"Tell me again."

"I was sent here by the President of the United States on a diplomatic mission to investigate the death of an American soldier, Lieutenant Colonel Rolly Dixon. I don't know anything about your spy."

"Lies," the cold voice hissed at him. "We have information that General Donovan himself briefed you." The NKVD officer took another drag. "Donovan told you everything about this spy. Tell me." The cigarette ash glowed bright.

"Who told you that?" Charlie asked, now perspiring profusely.

"A highly reliable source in your government," Colonel Pavlov said, holding up the cigarette for his prisoner to see. "You do know what happens to Americans who spy on Russia, don't you, Major Stanek?"

"As you know, I worked with the OSS. Of course, I've heard stories. But spying is not my mission here. I am telling you the truth."

"The truth," Colonel Pavlov said, staring at the coal on the tip of his cigarette. "We're not fools. We remember that you hid in the mountains with our enemies and spied on us. Did you forget?"

"Spy on Russia? I worked to rescue American pilots. We were allies against the Nazi's, damn it," Charlie said, fear quickly turning to anger.

"We found no identification," the colonel replied. "And look at this," he said, still standing directly in front of his captive. "You are dressed in a Russian uniform. Why is that Major Stanek?"

"I have already told you," Charlie replied, refusing to look into Pavlov's lifeless eyes. He knew men like Andre Pavlov. The taste of death and suffering drove them on. They smelled it, like wild dogs sensing a kill.

Suddenly, the colonel coughed and hacked violently, his chalky face turning almost red. The interrogation stopped. Pavlov gasped for air, then spit. The pinkish colored spittle passed only inches from Stanek's face. But the soldier still held the cigarette firmly between his fingers.

The guards stood silently, frozen there watching their commanding officer sicken. Charlie had only one wish—*die you son-of-a-bitch, die*, he thought, watching the Russian cough and wheeze.

The colonel gasped for air. His legs grew shaky, and he leaned on one of his soldiers. Then, as suddenly as it had begun, the coughing stopped. The colonel seemed to regain his strength, but the coughing spell had obviously weakened him.

"Do not disappoint me. It will only make things worse for you," Pavlov continued in a much weaker state, but he refused to allow his medical condition to deter him. He lit another Camel—his favorite cigarette--from the butt of the first. Charlie watched as Pavlov, with careful precision, dropped the butt on top of his bare foot.

Immediately, Charlie lifted that bare foot and tossed the cigarette back at Pavlov before it burned his skin. *You evil bastard*, he thought.

"You have told me nothing, Major Stanek," the colonel said with a pinched smile. "But you will." His face was just inches from Charlie's head. The smell of strong tobacco and vomit was overwhelming. "Don't give me this nonsense about traveling halfway around the world to discover how one soldier died. We know it is a lie, eh?"

Charlie shook his head. "I've told you what my mission here is. I'm conducting an investigation. It has nothing to do with your country." Then he suddenly realized. To a Russian, his mission all the way to Indochina to investigate the death of one insignificant soldier did seem far-fetched. Now even he began to doubt its efficacy.

"Who is he?" the colonel demanded again. He prepared to touch the new cigarette to Charlie's bare chest.

Pavlov nodded to the soldier behind Charlie.

Charlie felt renewed pain deep in his shoulder sockets as the soldier again tightened and twisted the rifle. "No, no!" he hissed at the soldier. His head fell forward, but the Russian officer immediately pulled it back.

"Who is this traitor to the Motherland? Tell me!" He pushed the cigarette coal into Charlie's right breast, twisting it slowly.

Charlie went berserk, spitting at the officer. The spittle struck Pavlov square in the face and ran down his chin. The

Russian backhanded Charlie hard across the side of his head, stinging his ear. He followed with a hard slap across the cheek and mouth. Charlie's head flopped sideways and then backward. The force of the last blow knocked him out. Blood trickled from the corner of his mouth.

Pavlov looked at Charlie without expression. "I will leave you to think. Tomorrow, major," the Russian NKVD officer whispered to his now silent victim. "We will begin again. And again, the day after tomorrow, if we must." He turned and stalked to the cell door. "And the day after that. In the end, you will tell us everything."

The soldier released Charlie, pushing him to the floor. He followed the officer out of the room, with the second guard close behind him. The door slammed shut, and locked.

Charlie lay on the cold, damp concrete. Pain swept over his body. Blood from his mouth stained the floor. The minutes passed.

Slowly he regained consciousness and forced himself to think, to focus. *They must have me confused with someone else. Who are they looking for?* He recalled the partisans he had served within Eastern Europe and could come up with no one.

Skin so soft. Her large dark eyes...Marie. He closed his eyes, fighting to hold that singular memory to block the searing pain on his chest.

Thirty minutes later, the key turned in the wood door.

Major Zerenowsky entered the room. One soldier followed him. "Major Stanek," Zerenowsky said, taking a water-soaked rag from a bucket and kneeling to apply it to Charlie's wounds. "Major, Major, wake up." He continued to dab the water to his face and neck.

The soldier, armed with a pistol, stood over him prepared to shoot if necessary.

"Get away from me, you bastard," Charlie said, regaining consciousness.

"You did not tell them? You must, or they will kill you," Gregor said, helping Charlie sit in the chair. "Here, I brought you bread and some tea. Drink. It is good, strong Russian tea. You like it, eh?"

"The only way they knew about me was because you told them. Why? Why did you betray me?" Charlie whispered, suddenly feeling very tired. "I have no name. I know of no agent here or in Europe. You told him I was his handler, and going to receive something from him," he hissed at the big Ukrainian standing over him. He wiped the blood away from his mouth with the back of his hand. "You lied to them, but why?" he asked.

"To escape, comrade," Zerenowsky replied.

Charlie threw the tea in the big Russian's face. "Get the fuck out of here and leave me alone."

"You're still bleeding. No good," Gregor said, refusing to leave. He wiped the liquid off his face with the back of his hand, and then leaned over, his ear against him. "Aha!" he exclaimed to the soldier standing beside him. "As I suspected." He stood. "Quickly, get the doctor. This prisoner may be dying. We need him alive!" he screamed at the soldier.

The man ran from the room.

"Listen to me," Gregor said, grabbing Charlie by both shoulders. "Pretend you are dying. Stay on the floor and moan when the doctor comes. Tell him it's your stomach. I must get you out of this city."

"What are you talking about?" Charlie asked, more confused than ever.

"Trust me. You must trust me," Gregor said, kneeling close. "They will kill you, my American friend. This, I know. For us to escape this place, do as I say."

"We to escape this place?" Charlie did not understand but knew he had no real choice. Left here he would die at the hands of Pavlov.

"You can fly an airplane still, can't you?" Gregor asked.

"Yes, but…What are you thinking?"

"Good, then we can escape this horrible place.

Charlie nodded, still dazed, and confused. He had no idea what was happening, but anything was preferable to staying here.

Within minutes, Zerenowsky activated his meticulously planned operation to save Charlie and most importantly, himself from the clutches of the NKVD. He stealthily got them out of the Soviet mission through an open window. They avoided the guards to reach an old Citroen Zerenowsky had hidden earlier and raced to the airfield one-step ahead of Colonel Pavlov's soldiers.

The Russians were unable to reach the airfield in time to stop them. Colonel Pavlov stood beside his auto and watched the American plane lift off the tarmac flying south. His anger boiled deep inside and caused pain in his chest as he watched the plane bank east toward the South China Sea.

"Stop shooting. It is too late," he ordered his men, who stood a few feet in front of him.

"Capitalist spies," he hissed. "I will hunt you down, and you will tell me everything. I will have the name of the spy. Then, Major Stanek, I will send you to Siberia to live out your days, but for the traitor, Zerenowsky… He will die."

Chapter 2

April 1, 1946

Deep in the north woods along Lake Superior, in a four-room clapboard and log cabin, a large man sat in an overstuffed chair in front of a blazing fire. His stocking feet were propped on a wood stool, bottoms toward the fire. Cut logs and kindling were stacked neatly next to the great stone fireplace.

The cabin was sparsely furnished—a cast-iron cooking stove, a table, several wood chairs in the small kitchen, and an overstuffed chair and sofa arranged around a fireplace in the main room. A double bed and dresser were the only bedroom furnishings. A heavy quilt with a brightly colored pattern lay over the bed, and an Orthodox religious icon was the single item on top of the dresser. On the interior wall, near the bed, a few clothes hung on a wood dowel extended from rough wood paneling.

The sink was a single basin with a small pump mounted beside it to draw water from a stone cistern under the cabin. Cupboards lined one wall filled with cans. A teapot and heavy cast-iron frying pan with hardened bacon grease covering its bottom--what remained from his early morning meal—were still on the cookstove.

The man was dressed simply--a rough woolen shirt, open at the neck, and green wool trousers. He had neatly folded heavier outer clothes on one of the wood chairs, with a pair of heavy leather boots on the floor in front. A high-power Winchester .30/06 hunting rifle was propped against the log wall, within easy reach of the occupant.

In his left hand, he held a half full tumbler. An empty vodka bottle was on the floor, partially hidden beside the firewood. On the other arm of the overstuffed chair was an English/ Russian Dictionary. A floor lamp provided lighting. It was one of two light fixtures; the other was a naked bulb hanging over the kitchen in the next room.

The man appeared to be talking to himself. "What-is-your-mother's-last-name?"

"My-last-name-is-Zerenowsky," he said slowly, having repeated it for the hundredth time. He chuckled and took another swallow from the tumbler. "You-are-so-beet, bati...," he said, stumbling, then consulted the dictionary. "You-are-so-beau-ti-ful." He smiled. Gregor Zerenowsky was determined to master more than just a few phrases of the language.

Outside, a late-winter storm had piled snow high against the walls of the cabin, leaving only the roof and front door clearly visible to the outside world. Smoke flowed straight up into the deep blue sky. Pinewoods surrounded the small clearing and extended for miles in all directions. He had cleared a walkway to a space ten meters away where he had built a single hole wood privy. A '40 Ford pickup was parked next to it. The small truck had a snowplow fixed to its front. A single ice-packed lane that he had recently cleared led into the woods. The only indication that spring had arrived was a slight thawing of the snow and ice on the outer fringes of the piles in the cleared areas and on the roof of the cabin, burned off by the midday sun.

Ten-foot pine poles spaced one every ten meters, paralleled the primitive road with a single wire mounted on top that brought electricity from the world, which was the town of Iron River twenty-five miles away. That was the former occupant's major contribution during his four-year tenure there. He had tapped into the mainline running along Highway 2 and brought electricity two miles to this cabin.

Beyond Iron River—about forty miles—was Duluth. The current occupant was already known in the small settlement where everyone seemed to know everyone else's business. That concerned him. Zerenowsky knew how quickly word got around. How long before everyone knew a former NKVD agent was living near them?

He learned quickly that most of the recent Russian émigrés had pasts they would prefer to keep secret, and so no one spoke of the old days, before the Great Patriotic War. Now that victory over the Germans was achieved, everyone in the community was filled with hope that a new world would come to the Soviet Union. Gregor knew better.

He had managed to meet a young woman, whose family had come to America in 1919, having fled during the Civil War. Her name was Ilena. A beautiful name, he thought, filled with feelings he had almost forgotten he still possessed. She had hair the color of summer wheat, like his mother, and sparkling blue eyes. Ilena worked in Iron River's only restaurant, a small operation owned by an Irishman. The little eatery served a hot and hearty cuisine that reflected the diversity of its citizens. Gregor ate there often and would wait until she got off to drive her home.

Ilena had encouraged him to learn English, and so he practiced...for her. The fire's warmth felt good against his damp feet. He had spent the day clearing the lane to the main highway. It was hard work, but he enjoyed it. I am free to work, he thought. I work for Gregor only. Soon I will have a woman to sleep with me. He took another swallow from the glass, finished it, and smiled. The vodka made him sleepy.

* * *

A short time later, as the bright orange of the early spring sun touched the tops of the pines on the western horizon, a black '39 Chrysler slowly pulled up and backed in beside the Ford, its front end pointed down the lane. A small figure in a long, ill-fitting wool coat, and black leather gloves got out, scanned the area quickly, and followed the cleared path to the cabin. The snow crunched softly under his heavy black boots. Standing at the front door, the man knocked softly.

Unbuttoning the bulky topcoat, he slid his right hand in to rest it on something underneath. Hatless, the man had black hair cropped close, with bushy eyebrows over dark, piercing eyes. He had no other facial hair, and a thin red scar ran across his right cheek just below his eye to the corner of his mouth. It was a wound he received in the war while fighting with Marshall Malinovsky on the Second Ukrainian Front.

There was no answer, so he tried the crude latch. It opened, and he allowed himself entrance. "Gregor Ivanovich Zerenowsky," the man called in a high-pitched voice. He saw the feet still propped in front of the fire. He stepped lightly across the wood floor. Still, the boards groaned with each step.

"Who's there?" Gregor called in Russian, awakened by the noise. He jerked up and turned his head. "Who are you?" he said, reaching for the Winchester. But the small man quickly grabbed hold of the rifle before Gregor could get to it.

The man looked the weapon over quickly, admiring it, and then he worked its lever-action until it was empty. The cartridges hit the wood floor and rolled around. "It is a beautiful rifle, comrade," he said softly, also in Russian. He threw the weapon on the bed and turned back to Gregor before he could move from his chair. He pulled an American .45 from underneath his heavy coat and pointed it at Gregor.

"The American government has hidden you well." He looked around the cabin. "I was lost twice coming from Canada, but your friends helped me, eh?" His thin lips didn't seem to move when he spoke. His cold, lifeless dark eyes never left the other man.

"Who are you?" Gregor asked again, unable to move from his chair with the pistol pointed at his head.

"I'm called the messenger," the much smaller man whispered as if he expected to be overheard. "I've brought you greetings from Comrade Stalin himself."

"You're too late, comrade," Gregor growled. "I've already told the Americans everything I know. I'm no good to you, so get out, you bastard."

The man shrugged. "We already know about your treachery."

"Then why bother me?" But Gregor already knew the answer to that question.

"You have been tried, Major Zerenowsky," the messenger said formally. "Or should I call you Rasputin?"

Gregor stared at his intruder. Now sure of what would follow.

"You have been found guilty of the worst crime of all."

"Of wanting a better life for myself?" Gregor said, contemptuously.

"You have betrayed the motherland and the Revolution."

"I had expected that this day would come," Gregor replied, giving in to his fate. "But, unlike you, comrade," he hissed, "I have at least tasted my dream."

The man quickly snapped the safety off the .45 with a click. "Your sentence is final. Smert shpronam!" he shouted loudly. With that, the messenger aimed the automatic at the bigger man's head and fired twice. The shots went unheard in the snow-covered wilderness. The force of the impact drove the big man's head sideways. Gregor Zerenowsky slumped against the arm of the chair. His hand still firmly gripped the dictionary.

"Dos vidania, Major Gregor Ivanovich Zerenowsky," the messenger said, dropping the automatic on the floor near the chair. He saluted the dead man, turned, and walked out the door.

Chapter 3

For hours, Typhoon Anna churned across the South Pacific, creating havoc for the Oriental Princess, an old Sydney-bound freighter Charlie took passage on. The endless rocking and rolling motion of the storm was taking its toll on both crew and passengers.

For five dreadful days, Charlie hung between the living and the dead. Finally, when he eventually fell asleep after hours of torment, the howling storm suddenly pounded against the steel hull. A great wave had crashed against the port side where he berthed, throwing him hard against the bulkhead. He jerked awake. Already seasick and sore, he now knew sleep was impossible.

"Air travel was so much better," Charlie had mused to the ship's captain on the third day of the storm. He got no response, only a shrug from the old mariner. During the thirty-six days Charlie had been at sea, he had become acquainted with Captain O'Hara. Even a friendship developed as the captain invited Charlie to dine with him on multiple occasions, but the typhoon had finally forced everyone to stay in or close to their cabins. The captain had become much too busy to spend time spinning stories with Charlie.

On the first day of June '46, the U.S. Army released him, and after four years, he was a civilian again. He immediately went to Union Station and bought a ticket on the next train across the continent to California. Charlie had had enough of the dangerous and lethal world of espionage. Determined to make a clean break with his military past, he bought passage across the Pacific to Australia. As a child, Charlie had dreamed of one day seeing Australia. Now was as good a time as any, he decided.

He slowly and with great effort raised his head to peer into the shadows of the cramped steel-walled room, but even that slight movement nauseated him. He fell back onto the pillow and closed his eyes again. The fierce battle between wind and waves raged inside him with equal fury. His stomach had a hollow ache that refused to go away.

"Seasick mate?" the captain asked after day three. Seeing that Charlie was, he sent him to the small dispensary. The pills had at least kept him alive.

Those days offered him time to think. Lying in his bunk hour after hour, he constantly thought about his mission to Indochina, he ruminated over his torture at the hands of Colonel Andre Pavlov, but his commanding officer's deceit troubled him more.

The General had dispatched him to the far side of the world with his life already in jeopardy. He had not even informed him of the dangers that awaited him. In fact, his ignorance was a vital part of the General's risky plan. The plan cost the General nothing, and he believed the possible sacrifice of a top OSS agent was worth the gamble. That left Charlie with a bitter taste in his mouth; a taste he knew would never go away.

Lying on the thin, narrow mattress, as he had night after night, he stared up at the pipes that crisscrossed the steel ceiling in the small cabin. In the dim light, everything reminded him of his prison cell in Hanoi, but this cabin was paradise compared to that hellhole. *Colonel Pavlov, you bastard.* He shook his head in disgust, but the fear of the man and his methods stayed with him. Charlie felt for the scars on his chest

He would never forget Gregor Zerenowsky, who rescued him from the clutches of a monster determined to kill him. I must respect Zerenowsky for his courage and his selfless contributions to American security, Charlie decided. When I asked him why he was willing to risk his life to betray the Soviet Union, he simply stated that he was Ukrainian. Zerenowsky, like many comrades he had lost during the war, was just a memory, a part of who he was, that he could never forget however much he tried. He hoped the Ukrainian was living happily in Northern Wisconsin. That had been his dream.

What surprised Charlie most was that General Donovan and Zerenowsky meticulously planned Zerenowsky's rescue, but never briefed him, even though Charlie was the primary instrument for his escape. *Send me to Indochina and let Zerenowsky do the rest. That was the plan. He probably expected me to kill Pavlov while I was there.* "The bastard," he growled.

Zerenowsky was the double agent, Rasputin, he rolled that over again in his head, as he had done a hundred times during the last year, but he still found that difficult to grasp. He did not ever want to know the identity of the other agent for whom Colonel Pavlov searched.

Charlie blamed the Army and General Donovan for everything that had happened to him. Donovan had a job to do, an important job. He had to use his skills at manipulating others to complete the mission. Charlie understood. But did that have to include sacrificing him to the Russians? He was just a pawn in a brutal game, for them to use and discard like an empty chocolate wrapper after the party.

Major Hiroaka, his liaison in Saigon, was right. It is a world where justice is never certain, often decided by the latest victor in an endless struggle for power. Yesterday our enemies were the Germans and the Japanese. Today, the Russians are evil, and we must defeat them. Charlie had decided not to be part of that power struggle. That was why he was escaping, and hopefully, for a new life where murder, torture, and deceit did not exist.

The storm continued through the night unabated, with only the crew moving about topside. The water-drenched blackness of sky and ocean had merged into an ink-colored mist streaked with grey, with day bleeding into night. Charlie knew the other passengers hunkered down in their cabins like him, seasick and exhausted, worn out by the unrelenting wind and waves.

Charlie heard a knock at his cabin door. *Who the hell?* The night was late. He crawled from his bunk and slowly limped his way across the cabin to answer it. The boat continued to toss and pitch about in the storm like a small toy in a large tub of water as he made his way toward the door. He grabbed his .45 and checked the chamber and magazine. That had become a routine security precaution. Some things never change.

"Yeah? Who's there?" he growled, finally reaching the door.

"Michael Wallenski in the next cabin," was the reply.

"What the hell you want?" Charlie asked. Was he not aware of the time of day? Then again, perhaps the man was confused, lost in the darkness.

He opened the door. The man standing in the hall, one arm braced against the bulkhead, was a much smaller man with blond hair and blue eyes. Charlie guessed him to be about twenty-five years of age. Studying the man—slowly from head to toe--he quickly remembered that he had seen him come aboard in Honolulu. They had even exchanged greetings in passing but had never conversed. Charlie saw that he was dressed very much like an American, but more importantly, he saw that Wallenski was not armed.

Before speaking, the young man pulled a packet of Lucky Strike cigarettes from his shirt pocket, freed one quickly from the opened pack, and lit up. The smoke hung in the stale air of the small cabin and did nothing to relieve Charlie's nausea.

Charlie, not taking any chances since he did not know the man, held his .45 close. Wallenski looked at the weapon, but he did not comment. Charlie stuck it in his trouser pocket, his right hand still gripped it--just in case.

"The captain told me an American soldier was onboard going to Australia. A one-way ticket?" Wallenski asked. "That you?"

Charlie said nothing.

"What will you do there?" Wallenski continued, nonplused.

"I don't see how it's any of your business, Wallenski," Charlie told him, growing suspicious of his intentions. From his years in espionage, he sensed that something about this guy didn't hold water. His visit seemed neither friendly nor was it a need for companionship during a bad storm. "What do you really want?"

"I want to be friends. "I like Americans very much," Wallenski said.

Charlie did not believe him. "Everyone wants something. So, come on. Out with it," he demanded.

Charlie recognized the man's heavy accent. Slavic--Russian or Polish. He could not quite make it out. "Your accent? Russian?" he asked.

"Polish. I was born in Warsaw, but I've lived in Cleveland for the past year," Wallenski replied.

Charlie decided to set a trap for him. "Hey, how about those Cleveland Indians winning the World Series last year?" he said.

"Yes, I was very excited," Wallenski replied. "But I'm new to the sport, so I don't understand all of it."

The .45 rose from his pocket immediately. He pointed it at the man's chest. "You're lying. Cleveland was not in the World Series." Charlie had caught him in a lie, much like a rat in a trap. "Tell me who you are and what you want, or I'll shoot you right here and throw your body overboard," he demanded. "They'll call it lost at sea in a terrible storm." He was prepared to do precisely that.

"Very clever," Wallenski replied.

"Talk, buddy," he ordered. "I'm running out of patience." He began to suspect the worst—that the Russians were somehow involved.

"I know all about you, major," he said. "We know what you did during the war."

"I'm not in the Army now. I'm a civilian traveling to Australia."

"Yes? But what is your American expression? A tiger may lose his teeth but never its stripes."

He stuck the .45 in Wallenski's face. "What do you want from me? Tell me.

"Rasputin is dead, Major Stanek, but not the network of traitors he created. Our security has been compromised."

"Our security?"

"Security of the Soviet Union."

Charlie knew immediately he was Russian NKVD, or perhaps, Ministry of State Security. "What do you want from me?" he asked again, but he already knew.

"We've watched you and know how you helped Zerenowsky in Eastern Europe, how you assisted him in his betrayal of the motherland."

"What of it? I'm out of that business," Charlie replied. "Is that why you have followed me? To get even? Pavlov has sent you, hasn't he?"

"You have certain information that we need. It's very important to us. As I've said already: our security hangs in the balance."

"I know nothing of value to you."

"We will pay you for your information, and we will pay you well."

"You think I go to the highest bidder, that I can be turned for a buck?" Charlie asked him.

The fool really believes that I can be bought, and by someone as evil as Colonel Pavlov, Charlie thought with contempt, his eyes probing the man's face, searching out the deceit he was convinced was there. "And if I refuse?" he asked.

"We have other ways. And they are not pleasant for you," Wallenski said. "I think you do not want to suffer the same fate as your friend, Zerenowsky."

"You..."

Wallenski smiled cynically. "No major, an assassin found him, much like with the traitor, Trotsky. No matter where you hide, we will find you."

"I've heard those threats before," Charlie replied. "So, go to hell."

"If I fail to get the information, someone else will succeed. We have many who have such skills. We will not give up until we have what we want. You cannot hide. So, make it easy for yourself."

Charlie pulled the .45 from his pocket and flipped off the safety. "That's the way it is, eh?" he said, pointing the barrel at Wallenski's chest.

The ship suddenly rocked to one side, throwing both men violently against the bulkhead. The crash of the high wave sent tremors through the cabin and knocked the .45 from Charlie's hand. It slid across the deck. Both men dived for the weapon. They struggled, wildly throwing punches and rolling on the deck, each trying to reach the weapon. Each man extended his arm to grab hold of it, but having longer arms and greater strength, Charlie got there first. He wrapped his hand around the grip and squeezed.

Suddenly, a single gunshot exploded in the cabin. Wallenski did not move. Blood poured from his head.

Charlie was confident the storm outside had covered the gunshot. Acting quickly, he wiped the blood splatter off the deck with his only towel. That done, he tightly wrapped the dead man in a sheet he had pulled off his bunk. He hoisted the body on his shoulder, opened the hatch door, and looked around for any movement. Seeing no one about, he made his way topside. Struggling against the violent rocking motion of the ship, he lifted his bundle over the rail and tossed it into the turbulent sea. Michael Wallenski quickly disappeared under the high angry waves.

For the next few days, the wind gradually slowed to a howl, and the waves flattened. The typhoon had run its course. The forecast was for calm seas for the duration of the voyage to Sydney.

Charlie's physical health gradually improved, but his nightmares became worse, much worse. His dreams were not about the spy, Wallenski. For him, he felt no remorse. They were about Marie, his lost love from the war years, and they terrified him. Tossing and turning nightly on the thin mattress in the darkness each night, he relived them:

The roaring flames danced in the darkness, rising higher and higher. The red monsters separated him from his beautiful Marie. He felt the searing heat against his face.

"Here, take my hand," she cried out to him reaching, but she could not hold on. The flames separating them bit angrily at her hand. Turning away from the intense heat, Charlie saw a figure in the shadows watching.

Charlie called to the man. "Help! Please help us." But the man did not respond. He turned to disappear into the darkness beyond.

Charlie watched in horror as the inferno engulfed and consumed Marie in its blazing sweep.

"Marie," he whispered, wiping away a tear. "My beautiful Marie." His calls to her always went unanswered. He woke up bathed in sweat each night, alone, in the darkness of the ship's cabin.

The days and nights passed like this for the remainder of his journey. He began to feel, with a growing sense of dread, that the ship's steel walls were closing in, crushing him. He knew he had to escape its narrow confines before it became another torture chamber for him. He counted the days, one by one, until the ship reached Sydney.

Standing on the bow of the Oriental Princess one day before making his final port, froth from the sea washing over him, he began to feel hopeful again. His dreams of Marie grew less painful. Four years in espionage had taught him how to compartmentalize his life. Wallenski's death went in one drawer while his love for Marie went into another.

Returning slowly to his cabin, Charlie froze, feeling as if someone had punched him in the face. The man in the dream... He was the man Zerenowsky warned him of, the man Donovan was determined to root out—the Russian spy, the double agent Donovan called Attila.

He stood in the narrow corridor in front of his cabin, trying to visualize the man's face. Other passengers walked by him, but he ignored them. *Who? Have I met him before?*

Those thoughts racked his brain, but he could come up with no answer.

He entered his cabin to pack for a new adventure in Australia.

A month after disembarking the Oriental Princess in Sydney, Charlie stood on a dusty, deserted street in Alice Springs. *Truly, the end of the world*, he decided. *Such emptiness and solitude.* He smiled with anticipation. Charlie was tired of running from his enemies and his memories and believed he had arrived at the perfect hiding place.

After spending a couple of days wandering around the small settlement, he decided it was time to take action. He asked around for work, and town folk directed him to a sheep station about 10 miles outside of town.

Hitching a ride on a produce truck, he reached the sheep station by mid-morning, and the driver dropped him along the road. He walked up the long lane, saw a few outbuildings and corrals, but he was most impressed with the single-story, white house. It seemed like a mirage rising above the shabby, unpainted buildings scattered about the dusty yard.

He heard the wind blowing across the dusty plain and nothing else. He liked the empty quiet of it, and silence seemed to travel across the hot wind as it touched his face. He walked toward the clapboard house with the white picket fence surrounding a small yard of mostly sand. He heard the bleating of sheep in the distance as he neared the house. He smiled, knowing he had arrived.

He jumped up on the old wood porch that wrapped around the house and set down the faded green duffel he had been carrying. Hearing movement inside the house, he knocked on the screen door.

An older man suddenly appeared from another room. He greeted Charlie with a slight smile on his old, sunbaked face. He was short and stooped, more from hard work than age. Charlie knew the difference. The man was dressed in a white shirt, with suspenders holding up his khaki shorts. He was barefoot.

"I'm looking for George Russell," he announced.

"Ya found 'im," the' old man said, without hesitating.

Charlie had seen right off that the older man was straightforward, not complicated. George opened the screen door for him to enter. "What do you want here?" he asked in an easy-going way as Charlie entered the tidy living room.

"I need work, a good job." An old stuffed chair was the first piece of furniture he saw as he entered a brightly colored and well-decorated room. It was also very inviting. *The perfect chair to take a nap in*, he thought. Charlie hoped he had not looked too longingly at it.

George squinted at him, and then slowly smiled. "Ya got one. Mind ya, I'll work ya hard, real hard," he said. "But today be Sunday, and we rest 'round here on Sunday. Come in and make yourself at home. I'll fix ya somethin' hot."

Charlie noticed that the other rooms were as neat as the living room. They walked through the sparsely furnished room lined with shelves filled with books, and into a large kitchen. A table, half-dozen chairs, and pot and pans scattered about were evidence that he used the kitchen to feed a crew of hungry men. Strong aromas of frying meat and coffee permeated the room. Charlie would never forget those smells. They reminded him of his childhood in Wisconsin.

Chapter 4

Two years later

A small slim man with evil eyes emerged from the older, black British Rover as if rising from the underworld. Red dust swirled about him as he quietly closed the door. He looked down a long lane towards a small white house silhouetted against the glare of the early morning sun.

The man wore a cheap dark suit, much too warm for the climate. But it was all that he had brought. Get in, do the job, and get out immediately, was the plan. If all went well, the American spy would take the bait. The general had assured him there would be no trouble.

He pulled a Tokorov automatic from a shoulder holster under his coat, popped the magazine, touched the top round with his forefinger, and reinserted it. *I'm ready*, he thought with a grim smile.

He walked slowly and carefully up the lane toward the house while listening to the sounds around him. A sheep bleating in the distance, birds he did not know, but no dogs and no human noises. *Good, no witnesses*, he thought.

The man stepped up on the porch of the house, approached an open door covered by a slightly run-down screen door. Looking into the room, he saw the top of a grey head above a stuffed chair. From the deep breathing and snores, he heard, the man had to be sleeping. He knocked. No reply, so he knocked again.

"Yeah? Who is it?" a voice finally said, seemingly not threatened by an intruder surprising him.

"I come from Alice Springs...to ask you questions," the man said in broken English with a noticeable Russian accent.

"You ain't nobody I know from Alice Springs," George Russell said, standing and turning toward the stranger. With hazy blue eyes, he looked hard at the shadowy figure standing at his door. He stepped closer and looked again.

"I am looking for a man, an old friend from the war. I have to give him an important message," the man said. "Can I come in only for a minute?"

"Yeah, I suppose. You some type of messenger boy then?"

"Some call me the messenger," the man agreed. "The man I seek is called Charles Stan-yak, ah, Stanek. Do you know him?"

"What'd you say his name is?"

"Stanek. He work for you?"

"Hmm, never heard of 'im," George replied. He looked the messenger over carefully, and by the look on the old man's face, he did not believe the story. "Ya best try another station, mate, maybe over at Churchill station. They got a lot of foreigners working there."

The two men were now only a few feet apart, but, like two aliens from different worlds, there was a complete lack of connection. Each sized up the other.

"Think harder, old man," the man said. "My information he works here is very reliable."

"You be damn wrong and the hell with your information," George said. His eyes quickly darted to the corner where his shotgun stood.

He caught George's eye movement and turned to see the weapon. He moved quickly to grab it. "Why you want this, old man?" He held up the shotgun, broke it with one hand, and flipped out the shells. "Here, you want it?" He tossed it, and the old shotgun slid across the hardwood floor.

"Get off my land, or you have hell to pay. My mates are just over by the shed. They coming anytime."

The intruder smiled. "I think you're lying to me. I think you're all alone here."

"I'm not afraid of thieves like you."

"Why you call me that? You think I come here to rob you?" He seemed hurt. "Just a couple of questions and I go."

"Ya ain't gettin' nothin' from me. If you want this Stanek, you find him, yourself."

"You don't believe me?"

"Not a question of that. Out here, a man lives private-like. Maybe he got troubles, lookin' to get away, or just runnin'. It don't matter none to me. I just ain't talkin' to a stranger."

The messenger stared at the old man. "I have a message on an important matter," he replied, still trying to convince him.

"Don't care what you have," the old man said. "Just get off my land an' there won't be no trouble."

The messenger reached inside his coat and produced the Tokorov pistol. He pointed it at the old man's chest. "I've had enough of your trouble, old man. You are going to tell me what I want to know, or I will shoot you dead." He shoved the old man with his left hand, but George did not move an inch. "Sit down in the chair," the man then ordered.

George sat in the chair. "What you gonna do with that pistol? A messenger boy with a pistol. Ha! If that don't beat all."

The messenger stood over him, not speaking but considering something. The old man had insulted him, and no one does that and lives.

"You best git out of here before me boys come. They won't think kindly to this."

"I know Major Stanek works here. Men in town told me this."

"They don't know nothing. Just told you wrong."

The messenger knew his sources were accurate and complete; otherwise, the general would not have gone to the trouble to send him to the other side of the world. "Why are you protecting him? He's a dangerous man who left a family to fend for itself, and a small child. I think you people would call him a scoundrel."

"Leave your message and git out of my house."

The messenger pulled a sealed envelope from his coat pocket and handed it to the old man.

George took hold of it, examined it, and then looked up at the other man.

The messenger raised the Tokorov higher and stepped back from the chair.

He smiled, but it was more of a sinister smirk. "Too bad." He fired one round, striking George Russell in the forehead. The bullet threw George's head back against the chair. He was dead instantly, the note clenched tight in his hand.

"Dos Vidania, old man," the messenger said. He holstered the weapon and walked out the door. The screen door slammed shut behind him. He knew Major Stanek would find the message. His mission was complete.

Chapter 5

Charlie and the rest of George's crew found the old man sitting awkwardly in his ancient stuffed chair, his head slightly tilted, eyes wide open and staring at the ceiling. He looked as if he had seen a ghost. Stepping closer, Charlie saw the entry wound, a small hole in the middle of his forehead. A single bead of red had slowly flowed from the wound to touch his cheek. He saw no sign of a struggle and decided the killer must have surprised him. George had grown hard-of-hearing in the last few years.

Ambushed in his home. The thought saddened him.

Charlie immediately knew who had murdered George. "Why did they have to do this to you?" he said, whispering to the dead man. "It's me the bastards want."

Charlie had returned to the station only minutes before with the other hands from a week in the outback bush rounding up sheep. He always checked in with George for mail and a quick chat. During Charlie Stanek's two years at the sprawling sheep station, he had risen to become foreman—head drover and George Russell's most trusted right-hand man among the mostly ex-soldiers and Aborigines who worked there.

George, in a very short period, had become the only family Charlie knew.

A single tear streamed down Charlie's cheek. He had learned from two years of war, torture at the hands of sadistic pros, and the hard life in Australia's outback how to keep his emotions in check, but the grief he felt was almost unbearable.

Charlie was alone with George when another of the hands entered the house, the screen door slamming behind him. The dark-skinned man saw George in his chair, neither speaking nor moving. He froze immediately. "Somethin' wrong here, bossman?" the Aborigine asked with growing concern.

"Something's happened, Rusty?" Charlie whispered, still staring at the body.

"What's wrong, boss? Things not right."

"He's dead," Charlie said. "They shot him."

"Who shot him, boss?"

"The damn Russians. I'm certain of it." Then Charlie noticed a sealed envelope still clenched in George's fist. He reached down and pried it loose. He saw the addressee's name and knew. 'Major Charles Stanek.' Charlie gripped the envelope tightly in his hand. "The bastards," he growled, not yet prepared to open it.

"Why would anyone kill George, bossman? He a very good man." Rusty was Charlie's top man and most senior, having worked at the Alice Springs station for more than ten years. He was a thin man, sturdy but powerfully built, with short-cropped curly black hair and skin like leather. His eyes were dark and penetrating, but he always wore a smile that told the others life could be worse. Now the smile was gone.

"He was, Rusty." Charlie stepped back from the body and Rusty to open the envelope. He unfolded the paper inside, and read:

> *"Major Charles Stanek, I have your woman and your child. If you want to see them alive, you must come to Prague."*

Charlie looked for a signature, but he knew who sent the message. The man was his old nemesis—Colonel Andre Pavlov, Russian State Security. *Marie,* he thought. She survived. *And my child?*

Marie Benes. Charlie's mind immediately flashed back to those days in the mountains of Slovakia when the two lovers lay naked together under an oak tree that had become their secret place. Two years in the Outback and still he could not shake the memories:

The Slovak National Council had called a general uprising against German occupation for August 25. Marie, without hesitating, joined the First Czechoslovak Corps commanded by General Ludvik Svoboda.

"I must go, Charles. The Germans are retreating. Don't you see? This is our chance to drive them out of Czechoslovakia for good."

"It doesn't have to be you. The Russians are bringing up a division."

"It's my country. If I don't fight for it, who will, my love?" she replied.

"What about us?" he had asked. "Isn't what we have just as important?"

"Oh, Charles." She kissed him on the forehead. "You are my one love that is forever," she told him. "But the freedom of Czechoslovakia is much bigger than both of us. I must serve her in her hour of need."

That kiss was their last. He never saw her again. The next morning, she was gone.

Charlie sighed as those memories came flooding back.

Rusty watched him. "Bossman, you okay?" He knelt beside George to examine the body. "Not much blood. I think he die one, maybe two hour ago only. Shooter stand, Mista Russell sit, I think." He pointed at the dead man's position in the chair. "Bullet leave here." He pointed to a larger wound at the base of his skull.

Charlie looked where Rusty pointed but said nothing.

Rusty stood and looked around the room. "A real bad man. A murderer."

"An hour, you say?" Charlie ignored the comment. "Then the shooter might still be around."

"Bossman," Rusty said. "What we do now, eh?"

Charlie turned to look at the shorter man. "Get a couple of men to wrap him up and place him in the icehouse until we can give him a proper funeral." He turned and marched into the bedroom and returned almost immediately holding an old Webley revolver and a box of shells. "Charlie knew that George always kept the weapon under his pillow fully loaded. He had brought it back from the Great War." Charlie emptied the box of shells into his trouser pocket.

"What you do with that?" Rusty asked, his eyes moving quickly from the weapon to Charlie.

"I know who did this and he's still around. He couldn't have gotten too far. One road and the airplane flies in and out only once a day. I have to settle things, and it starts with the shooter."

Rusty stared at him. "No, you top man now."

"It's my fault that George was killed, Rusty. I have to settle it." They moved the body to the wood floor.

"Russians do this?"

"Yeah," Charlie replied. "We have to contact his daughter. She'll handle things."

"A city girl, bossman. She knows nothing about sheep."

"She has to get out here right away. I'll send a telegram immediately. Now get the car."

Jill was George's daughter and only living relative. She had recently completed her education and was practicing the law in Sydney. George beamed with pride whenever he spoke of her and what she had accomplished.

Charlie knew her, had met her several times when she came to visit her father. George would play the matchmaker, conniving to get them alone. He offered the car for Charlie to take her into town. "To a picture show," he said. Jill and Charlie had gotten along well, always talking into the early dawn hours. They even kissed once.

A beautiful young woman, he thought, *but she told me she could not live out here in "the wilderness," as she described the outback. I told her I could not leave my self-imposed exile to venture into the city. That's where it had ended.*

Wounded at Gallipoli during the Great *War*, George had settled this land after returning in 1919. When he came to Alice, he immediately fell in love with and married a local girl, Elizabeth Hoolihan. They began a life on land that her father gave them. He later bought more, expanding the sheep station into one of the largest in the area.

He told me he would never leave this place. He did not, Charlie thought sadly, looking again at the dead man on the floor.

George wanted to be buried right here beside his wife. Charlie looked out the window at the single tombstone in the back yard. He knew George's Elizabeth had died at childbirth, leaving him to raise Jill. He was devoted to his daughter and only child, sending her to the best schools in Melbourne and Sidney, and finally, to study law at Oxford. He once told Charlie that the most difficult thing he had ever done was send Jill away for her education.

"I'm going with you," Rusty said. "I bring the car around, and we leave."

Minutes later, all of George's drovers came to the house. Hats in hand, they solemnly walked single file into the room where George lay, as much to pay their respects as to take care of the body. Charlie told them nothing about who killed him.

Rusty pulled the car around to the front of the house and ran back inside. "I help you." He picked up the 12-gauge shotgun from the floor. "For killing a snake." He grabbed the shells and loaded it. "We go!"

They drove off down the long dusty lane. The others stood on the porch and with looks of bewilderment watched them disappear in a cloud of red dust.

The 20-mile drive into Alice was long. Rusty drove, and Charlie again ruminated on his "other life." His two years in the Outback, it seemed, had done little to extinguish his memories. He closed his eyes and thought back to 1944, to his early days behind enemy lines:

Dropped in the mountains of eastern Czechoslovakia, his mission was to rescue American pilots. His first contact with Czech and Slovak partisans came a few hours after he reached the rendezvous point. Their leader's name was Jürgen Benes, and three men and his daughter accompanied him. Her name was Marie.

With eyes that sparkled in the sun and rich, dark hair, she captivated him from the moment he saw her, even though dressed in men's clothes and carrying a rifle. He decided right then that she the most interesting and mysterious woman he had ever met.

That's where it all began, Charlie thought.

At the outskirts of town, Rusty slowed the old sedan. "I talk with Samuel. He knows if strangers in town." They parked behind a dilapidated building with a large sign on the roof that simply stated, General Store. "You stay here. I go find Samuel, and we talk private-like."

Charlie nodded.

Several Aborigines clustered around the rear of the store drinking beer and talking. When they saw the car, all conversation ceased. Rusty jumped out and marched through the group into the store without a word uttered. The men watched. Charlie sat quietly in the sedan and waited.

Two years had passed. Charlie had hoped his wartime work in the Carpathians was behind him, a part of his past. He thought hard, working his mind to figure how all the pieces fit.

Leaving his band of partisans had been difficult. He had grown attached to them. However, the war was ending, and he had to get out before the Russians arrived. He had had many experiences dealing with the Russians, mostly NKVD security.

"Never trust the Russians. Their secret police are ruthless. That is why you must go now," Jürgen told him.

"What will happen then, Jürgen? What of Marie?"

"I will keep searching. I am her father. It is my only purpose."

"Then I will stay and help you," Charlie said.

"No, you must go, my young friend. You do not belong here," Jürgen knew to stay was too dangerous. "It is for the Czech people to settle our affairs. Get out before it is too late."

There was nothing more for him to do. He turned and walked into the forest, to never return.

Rusty ran from the store, passing the men, still without saying a word. He jumped into the sedan and started the engine. "We go fast," he said. "Samuel say man flew here in his own plane. We can catch him now." He slammed the sedan into first gear, and the two-armed men roared off.

"No policeman," Rusty said. "We settle this, you and me."

"The plane is still here?" Charlie tried to comprehend what Rusty was saying.

"At the airport," Rusty said. "Get ready."

Charlie pulled the Webley from his belt and checked it. "I'm ready," he finally said.

Within minutes, they were on the airstrip, the only piece of pavement in miles. Rusty punched the accelerator, and they raced down the strip. They crossed in front of the single plane. There he slammed on the brakes to block any forward movement of the small aircraft. It did not move, sitting silently on the tarmac as if watching them.

Both men jumped from the sedan. Rusty carried his shotgun and Charlie held the revolver tightly.

"Cover me," Charlie said. "I'll get them out." Rusty stepped back, pointing the shotgun at the open fuselage door. Charlie carefully made his way up the steps, then into the open door. "Out! Everyone out!" he ordered loudly.

Soon, one man stepped into the doorway and down the steps. Charlie followed close behind, but he had lowered his weapon. The man was the pilot.

Seeing the confusion on Rusty's face, Charlie said, "An Aussie under contract with the Russian consulate. Don't worry about him."

"Sorry, mate," the pilot said. "But I think the man you're looking for is still inside the terminal."

Both men turned as one to look at the unpainted, one-story wooden building. The terminal tower rose up beside it. A single, part-time air traffic controller, having watched the proceedings, waved at them.

"Let's go," Charlie said, leaving the pilot beside his plane confused. Both men raced for the building. When they got inside, they found a small, dark-haired man sitting alone at the only table. He appeared to be waiting for something or someone.

Rusty stood in the door and raised the shotgun.

"Stay there!" Charlie ordered and proceeded to the table. He was prepared to shoot. "Do you speak English, you bastard?"

The man smiled through thin, colorless lips. "A little, Major Stanek."

"Who are you?" His green squinty eyes reminded Charlie of a snake, an angry, venomous snake.

"I am called the Messenger."

"The Messenger? Do I know you?"

"Your friend, Gregor Zerenowsky, met me once."

"You killed him," Charlie said. "It was you, wasn't it?"

"He was a traitor to the motherland."

"Why did you murder my friend? An old man. He did nothing to harm your country."

"We want to get your attention, Major. We want you to understand that we do not play games when it comes to Russian national security," he said calmly. "Come with me, and your family will live."

"If I don't?"

He looked down and sighed. "Major, there are no guarantees. They will probably die."

"What's to stop me from shooting you right here where you sit?"

"I know this may not mean much to you, but I have diplomatic immunity. You would not want to cause an international incident." He smiled through thin, dry lips. "Bad for you and for me, I think."

Neither man paid any attention to the third man in the room. Rusty walked to the corner and positioned himself only a few feet away. He held the shotgun at the ready.

The man ignored him, focusing completely on Charlie. "Please come with me. General Pavlov is waiting. I expect you are anxious to see your woman and your daughter."

Daughter? Charlie thought, not used to the idea, but he said nothing. "Pavlov's a general now? Son of a bitch should be dead or worse, rotting in Siberia."

"Now, Major Stanek." The man stood, raising his slight frame to look Charlie directly in the eyes. He reached under his cheap, dark-colored jacket. "I am Russian and not used to such heat," he said as if apologizing.

Before he could pull anything from his pocket, the shotgun exploded in the small room, the tight pattern of steel sending the Russian sideways into a wall, his head partially gone.

Charlie, ears ringing and reeling from the explosion, reacted immediately. He knew already that it had to end this way and had been prepared for anything.

He quickly moved to stand over the dead man. He searched under his coat, expecting to find a weapon where the man had reached, but found a single document instead. He stuffed the document into his shirt pocket and continued his search. He next found a small-caliber Russian automatic in a shoulder holster. With a handkerchief retrieved from his back pocket, he took the weapon and smelled it. The Russian had fired it recently. He laid it near the corpse, careful not to leave his prints on it.

"It was an accident. Self-defense. I saw the whole thing," Charlie said, looking at Rusty. "Let's get out of here. We'll stop by the constable on our way back to the station." He left the room as fast as he could walk with the Aborigine right behind.

Rusty said nothing.

The Alice coroner hastily placed the body of the man who called himself the Messenger in a crudely constructed coffin and shipped it by air to the Russian consulate. He wrapped the dead man's weapon in brown paper and placed it on top of the body with a note attached:

> "This man without any
> identification was shot in self-defense
> when he attempted to shoot a resident
> of Alice Springs without provocation.
> A witness to the shooting has stated
> such under oath. I have filed no charges
> against the shooter. Case closed."

Hoagie McGuire, Constable of Alice, signed it.

Chapter 6

They held the funeral at the station three days later. George's daughter, Jill, Charlie, Rusty, and the drovers were present. Charlie shared his thoughts with the small group of mourners:

"By the manner in which he looked at me, I knew I must have appeared to be a wanderer...or a man on the run. I wore a pair of khaki trousers and a sweat-stained white shirt, with nothing on my head. My face was already peeling from the intense sunlight, and I must have smelled from a couple of days in the heat without a proper bath, but he treated me like a long-lost son."

Charlie looked around at the small collection of mourners and tried to smile. "When I arrived here, I immediately felt like I had found a home," he told the group. He gazed out at the men and Jill, with tears streaming down her cheeks. They stood in the dusty backyard, surrounding George's coffin.

Charlie had gotten to know most of the drovers well during the past two years. He had learned that they were an interesting mix of people. Several were former soldiers home from the war, and others were Aborigines, born to the harsh land. The veterans were much like Charlie—lost souls running from their pasts. But there had never been any trouble among the mixed group, and they worked together day after day like a tight-knit family.

After the short service by an Anglican minister from Alice Springs, the only man of religion in town, George Russell was laid to rest beside his wife.

Later that evening, Charlie and Jill sat down alone to talk. "Charlie, how could this happen? My father had no enemies. You brought them, didn't you?" She asked, but it did not sound like an accusation to Charlie. He understood that she had a right to know what had happened.

He looked at her, carefully paused before speaking. "They've tracked me across the world, Jill. It took them two years, but they found me. I wanted to make a home here with your father. I had hoped that someday you..." He stopped, not wanting to make matters worse. "I expect you will be leaving soon, back to the city," he asked to change the subject.

She gave him a steady look. "I'm not going."

"Not going? What does that mean?"

"I'm staying here. This station is a part of who I am, and I'm not selling it."

"I'm confused."

She smiled, "Charlie, I expected you would be. I'm going to run this operation, so tell the boys to get ready for a new boss."

"But, but..." Something inside him glowed bright. "You're staying? That's wonderful. I mean you'll make a great boss here just like your dad."

"Thank you. I hoped you would say that," she said, trying to smile through the tears. "I want you to run it with me. My father would approve of that."

She is so beautiful, he thought, *with her yellow curls and soft blue eyes.* He watched the wet tears on her cheeks, but he also saw something he had never noticed before. A steely toughness, a fire simmering just beneath the surface. Jill was no longer George's spoiled little girl, but more like a woman of the Outback—tough and determined. It was if she was changing before his eyes. She was convincing him that she would endure her loss and recover even stronger than before.

"I've dreamed of such an opportunity, especially with someone like you, Jill, but...but I cannot. Something has come up. My past, it's come back, and now I must face it."

She reached over to touch his face. "No, Charlie, don't talk about such things. I've learned that out here most people have a past. Now, this land...you. I don't know, just don't know. Here you have a future."

"I will get the man responsible for killing your father, Jill. I must. It's my responsibility." He did not hear what she just said.

"Is it about revenge, Charlie? A life for a life?"

"You don't know the type of man he is. He will never quit until he has me."

"Oh, Charlie..." She began to weep, then as quickly stopped and looked directly at him. "I loved him so much. I just couldn't live out here. And now, you're leaving me?"

Charlie reached out to pull her close. It felt good. They held each other, and the seconds passed. "You must let me go. I will return as quickly as I can," he finally said. "Rusty will take care of things, but the place needs you. You're strong. I know you will do okay." He knew she understood how important the station was to all their lives. "We can talk about things when I return. Tomorrow I must leave."

His words frightened her. She jerked from his embrace. "You're leaving tomorrow? That soon?"

"I must." He could not look at her. "But I will return. Give me two months."

Jill considered his request. "Two months, Charlie. It seems like so much danger. Will I lose you, too?"

"I'll return."

"Will you?"

"I have contacts in Washington. I'll get the U.S. government to assist me," he said, trying to reassure her.

She looked at him, doubt in her eyes. "Charlie, stay with me tonight. I may never see you again."

Her offer surprised him.

She kissed him. "I want you to hold me close for one night. Will you do that?"

Charlie was surprised. "Are you sure you want that?" he asked.

"I want you to come back to me, to want to," she replied.

Jill pulled him close. "Daddy loved you like a son, Charlie. He wrote that to me many times."

"He always talked about his beautiful daughter. 'Her hair is gold, like her mother's, and she is very bright. I don't know where she got that,' he would say."

That brought a smile to her face.

"I will always remember his infectious laugh. It seemed to erupt from somewhere deep inside him. And his stories of Australia were endless. I only wish I could remember more of them," he said.

"Are you avoiding my offer?"

He wrapped his arms around her. It seemed natural, and they both knew that it was what George would have wanted. "I must take care of this. Before we can have any type of life free of worry, I must return to Europe. But tonight, is ours."

"Come with me." She took him into her bedroom and closed the door.

Charlie had never been in this room. He looked around at the walls awash in pink, her childhood dolls neatly laid out on a chair, with her knickknacks. He walked to the large window that opened onto the buildings and looked out at the open range beyond. A large moon in a deep sky lit up the room.

They embraced. He kissed her on the forehead as a brother would.

Jill could not accept that. She wanted more, much more from him. In her room's reassuring comfort, she looked into his tanned face, and began to undress. He watched speechlessly. Within seconds, she stood before him naked. "Treat me like a woman, Charlie, a woman who loves you."

Charlie reached out to her. "Jill, I...," he said, but Jill lay back on the bed, bringing him down on top. She had caught Charlie off guard but in a pleasant way. They both laughed.

She began to unbutton his shirt. He stood and quickly shed the remainder of his clothes, while Jill watched with pleasure from the bed. Enjoying the sight of his naked body in the moonlight, she touched him, and aroused, he lay next to her.

"I don't want to make any promises to you I can't keep." He had to say before things went further. His honor demanded it. "I could never hurt you."

"I'm my own woman, and I can take my chances," she replied. "I'm not some virgin who is offering herself to a man." She pressed her body against his. Charlie felt both her strength and the softness of her skin. He touched her, slowly moving his hands across her back and lower. It felt good for both of them.

"I want you now," she whispered, then touched his ear with the tip of her tongue.

"I've wanted this for so long," he whispered.

"I love you," she replied. "And I want you to never forget me...Tonight is forever."

Neither held back. Their passion and desire for each other heated the room like never before. His hands roamed over her slowly and gently, and she signaled each touch with a soft moan. They consummated their passion in an erotic explosion of lovemaking. The old wood bed creaked and groaned to their rhythm. For the first time in many years, the house was alive.

Afterward, they lay together. Neither spoke while he held her tightly in his arms, with their legs entangled. He felt intoxicated by the smell of her hair against his neck, and she felt safe and at peace in his arms.

"Since the first time I saw you, I've wanted you," she said. "Did you know that?"

"I've wanted you, he replied. "But it didn't seem like things would work out, and I'm so sorry for that."

"Me, the big city girl and you with such a violent past. Oh, Charlie, will it now?"

She fell asleep in his arms while he gazed out the window, at how the star-studded sky touched the rugged landscape of central Australia. Since the first time he laid eyes on it, he knew it was the largest sky he had ever seen. He turned to look at her, sleeping comfortably in his arms. He did not think he could ever get enough of her. Listening to the soft rhythm of her breathing, he smiled. He knew that soon he must leave. Very soon, he would have to give up the simple, innocent life here with her, of a life worth living, but he also understood that he had no choice.

Beyond the door was a world torn apart by violence and needless death, where tens of millions had died from world war, starvation, and political upheaval. He had thoughtlessly brought that world to Alice Springs. Now, he had to make things right, if only for Jill.

They sat at the kitchen table the next morning drinking coffee. "I must go. I wish I could stay here forever, but I can't," Charlie said. His packed duffel lay in the doorway.

"I think I understand." She took his hand and kissed it. "I don't want to know about the woman. Always remember that here you have a home. Charlie, please come back to me."

Chapter 7

Charlie had lied to Jill. He knew he could not go to Washington, even if someone there would help him. Those bastards are just as evil as the Russians are, he decided long ago. He also knew Pavlov's agents would be watching, and that would further risk the lives of Marie and the child. Jill *seemed reassured when I told her the Americans would assist,* he thought, *but who can I trust?* He considered his situation and finally understood that there was no one.

He was sitting among the sprinkle of passengers on the DC-3 flight to Singapore and felt utterly alone. Looking around the cabin at the faces, he wondered if one of them was watching him.

Singapore's dusty terminal lounge with its crowds of people offered even less respite as he waited for his next flight west to the other side of the world. That leg would take him to New Delhi. From there, he would fly to Cairo, then to Istanbul, and finally Geneva. Thinking about it, and he had a lot of time to think and reflect, he realized he had never been to Prague. Even though he had spent months in Czechoslovakia during the war when the Nazis occupied the country, he never made it to the capital city.

He removed the single slip of paper—the second he had taken off the Russian assassin--unfolded it and reread it for the hundredth time.

"Our American source has learned subject is in Australia hiding in the desert. We will locate. Prepare to travel. Bring him to Berlin or if unsuccessful, terminate with extreme prejudice."

What interested Charlie the most was the "American source." Could he be Attila, the double agent? Only the highest levels of American intelligence--in Washington--knew I had reached Sidney in 1946. Had this man infiltrated even them?

He looked around at the large ethnic mix of people in Singapore's air terminal, rebuilt by the British after the war. Chinese, Malay, and Europeans—he assumed most were Brits—crowded the lounge. He decided, seeing how most were dressed, that they were business travelers. The world had begun to rebuild.

He happened to notice from the corner of his eye a small Asian man standing in a far corner, his head in a newspaper. The man's eyes constantly darted about, scanning the large room. He noticed that, too. *Curious,* he thought, eyeing the man more closely. Something seemed familiar about him.

A loudspeaker, between crackles, announced the call to board his aircraft. Charlie grabbed his single duffel and walked toward the gate. Approaching the ticket attendant, he felt a tug on his arm and quickly turned, prepared for anything. The same Asian man now stood only inches away. Charlie stepped back, fearing the worst.

"You remember me, Major Stanek?"

Charlie looked hard at him. Then he smiled. "Khanh?"

"You call me Bob. You remember?"

"Of course. How's the taxi business in Saigon these days, Bob?"

"No good. The war...Business very bad." Bob looked around.

"What's going on? Why are you here?"

"We know of your business, major. The Russians order us to watch airports for the American called Stanek. We must report to them. They always want Vietnamese people to do their dirty work."

Charlie listened without uttering a word. Standing with the smaller Vietnamese, he observed Europeans looking at him. He considered whether he appeared out-of-place stooping to converse politely and intently with an Asian. He had heard there was tension between the races on the Malay Peninsula, with the colony demanding independence from Britain. Australia had only one race where governance was concerned. Aborigines were not even a part of the ruling equation.

The Europeans travelers stopped, politely tried to overhear their conversation, but when they could not, they moved on with a shrug of indifference. Charlie was aware of how elitist Europeans were, especially when traveling in Africa or Asia. Their behavior slightly amused him.

"Truin say, 'Warn him that the Russians look for him. Stay away from Europe,'" he said. "Big mess, like in my country."

"I appreciate the warning, Bob."

"I go now. I never see you. Good-bye."

"Send my regards to your cousin."

Bob quickly disappeared into the crowd, and Charlie boarded the plane. He found his seat, sat down, and buckled up. With too much time to think, he considered Bob's mission, ordered by the Russians. That made him wonder how large a net Pavlov had cast, and how wide the web of security he had to penetrate to rescue Marie and the child.

He studied each face among the ten other passengers on the long flight. They were all men, mostly European, as far as he could tell. He heard English, French, and Arabic spoken.

The second hour into the flight, an older man in a seat directly behind his, bald, overweight, with a neatly trimmed mustache, stood, entered the narrow aisle, and sat down beside Charlie, surprising him.

Seeing who had just sat down, Charlie decided the man reminded him of a protagonist in an Agatha Christie mystery.

The man carried a package, which he partially concealed under a light jacket. He looked hard at Charlie, at his thin, tanned face, brown hair tossed back, and dungarees and khaki shirt. "Your first trip in an aero plane?" he asked, obviously forcing conversation.

"My first," Charlie replied. He would not mention that the U.S. Army had trained him to fly C-47s and that he had logged many hours, including an escape from Hanoi to Saigon in a C-47 transport.

"American?" the man asked, knowing well that Charlie was. His eyes darted about at the other passengers.

"I am." Charlie began to see that the man wanted more than idle talk to pass the time. "You?"

"I also am an American," the man said. "But I've lived in Australia since the early days of the war. Part of the effort there. You know...to drive the Japs back."

Charlie looked at him. "You stayed on to work there?"

"I do many things," he replied. "When the general needs me, I provide my services. Same game, different adversary."

"The general?"

He smiled. "We work for the same man. Now, I've been ordered to assist you, Mr. Stanek." The man spoke in a whisper, his eyes constantly darting about.

"How did you know? Who...?" Charlie was confused and concerned.

"Once part of the family, always part of the family," the man replied. "We belong to a unique fraternity."

"Spies?"

"Officers in the United States Army." He corrected him, still speaking in a whisper.

"How did you know…?"

"I have an old photo of you given to me by the general. My job is to monitor Singapore's air terminal, as we suspected you would pass through there. The general is worried about you, so he contacted me personally. It seems news of your exploits gets around real fast."

"It seems that way." Charlie was cautious. "And to ensure I didn't get into trouble…or freelance my services?"

"That, too." The large man laughed, but even that sounded forced. He fidgeted with a package he had produced from under his jacket.

"Who do you work for? Army Intelligence?"

"Still getting organized, and the President just created a new agency called the CIA, but I don't know much about them. No one does. I'm U.S. Army all the way, just like you, and as you know, we have our own ways."

Charlie noticed the man continued looking around the cabin nervously, but he did not move from the seat. "Is there something more?" Charlie asked.

"I am authorized to provide you with travel information. It must be oral."

"Go on."

"You will have a delay of one night in Istanbul."

Charlie was shocked that the man knew his itinerary. "How…?"

"Not now," the man replied. "You will stay in the Hotel Turkey while in Istanbul, near the Blue Mosque. You are already registered. We have taken care of all expenses. There, a man named Henry will contact you. He can be trusted."

He had a package sitting in his lap. "You may need this." He handed it to Charlie, and without waiting for a reply, got up, and returned to his seat.

The conversation disturbed Charlie. *The Army? How do they know my business?* He held the package and knew by its weight what was inside. He carefully placed it in his duffel and then slid the duffel under the seat.

Charlie caught his flight from Cairo to Istanbul without incident. No one else contacted him, and the man on the earlier flight had disappeared into the crowds of people in New Delhi.

Charlie arrived in Istanbul and had no problems locating the hotel and checking in. It was in the center of the city amid the hustle and bustle of people and autos, but it was not a tourist hotel. He could tell by its rundown, rather shabby condition. The room was small but clean, with few furnishings beside a bed, one chair, and a dresser with a single lamp. Following a quick examination, he decided the lock and deadbolt were sturdy, and the sheets clean. One window opened onto the street below.

He threw the duffel on the single chair, unzipped it, and removed the package the American had given him. Opening it, he saw that inside was a small Colt automatic with about fifty rounds of ammo. He checked it carefully and stuffed it into his belt. He locked the door and wedged the top of the chair under the knob for added security.

Now I wait, he thought and lay on the bed with his feet hanging over the edge. He did not know if someone would contact him in person or by messenger. He did not know if anyone would contact him. He closed his eyes and tried to sleep.

An hour later, a single knock at the door woke him. Slowly, he got up. He pulled the automatic from his belt. "Yeah?" he asked. "Who is it?"

"A friend," the voice replied. "They call me Henry."

Charlie removed the chair and unlocked the door. He opened it to a small, thin, otherwise nondescript man who looked middle-aged, with flecks of gray in his hair and mustache. The man had removed a well-worn fedora and politely held it in his hand. He cautiously entered and then stopped, only a step from the door. He surveyed the small room, and his deep-set brown eyes seemed to miss nothing. Charlie was reminded of an undertaker.

Henry's scan of the room finally came to rest on Charlie's weapon, which he had pointed toward the floor. "You won't need that, Mr. Stanek," he said softly but not accusatory.

"I'll be the judge of that," Charlie replied. *Who is this man?* he wondered with growing curiosity. German, Slavic, Jew, Romani, Hungarian, more than a thousand years of Central European history crushed together. If tomorrow someone asked me to describe him, I could only say he reminded me of my grandfather who I knew only from old photographs.

"You are young," the man said. "Too young for this work." He walked into the center of the room and sat on the bed. Pausing first to stretch his legs, he then removed an envelope from his worn black suit coat.

Charlie continued to watch him closely but said nothing. He now had set his weapon beside him on the mattress.

"First, my young friend, I must brief you on the current situation in Eastern Europe."

"Why do you think I need your briefing?"

"Because you come from the other side of the world...and because I think you not a fool." Henry's eyes locked on Charlie. Neither man blinked.

The man appeared to Charlie to be probing, trying to look into his very soul, searching for something. "Brief me," Charlie said. He leaned back on the bed, giving into this man's subtle persuasion.

Henry nodded, still without taking his eyes off Charlie. "The Russians now control all of Eastern Europe, including part of Berlin, and soon will have all of Czechoslovakia. If the Americans let down their guard, I fear they will have all of Germany to the Rhine. The Communists are on the march in Greece and hold the government in France. The Labor Party, with its left-wing support, has thrown Churchill and the Conservatives from power in Great Britain. Mao Tse-tung will soon have all of China, I believe."

"Tell me about Czechoslovakia," Charlie said.

"Since the end of the war, the government has been composed primarily of the Communist Party, Social Democratic Party, and National Socialist Party. The Communists are by far the largest party. They moved quickly to control all key ministries in the government of President Edvard Benes. Only last year did Stalin begin to interfere in Czech affairs, and when the Communists under Klement Gottwald grew more radicalized, the Soviets become more overtly involved. They initiated a coup d'état earlier this year, deploying police and armed workers' militias, of course, manipulated by the Soviets."

"Finally, in February, they forced President Benes to accept a new cabinet list from his Communist Prime Minister, Gottwald. Then the Communists were in charge. They, of course, purged dissidents from all levels of society. Benes resigned."

"What of my friends? They were not Communists, but trade unionists, I think."

"Many were arrested, others fled to the West," Henry replied. "Your friends..." He shrugged. "The woman you seek was detained during the protests, but I think she was later released. I have no current information on her status."

"What of her father?"

"He has returned to the mountains of Slovakia."

"Who has sent you to assist me?"

"I was sent by Allen Dulles, but not through CIA channels, still too many commies from the war years in your intelligence services. Army sent me. "

"General Donovan have anything to do with it?"

"He's retired but keeps abreast of some things through his Army contacts."

"Not the CIA?"

"The CIA is still very young and understaffed, so Donovan uses his contacts from the war, like me. He has a keen interest in your personal mission, and believes that by assisting you, the Americans can benefit." Henry was careful with his words. "It helps to have old buddies from the war, doesn't it?"

"I guess." Charlie was trying hard to put it all together. "And I thought I was hiding out and forgotten. I told only the general I would be somewhere in Australia."

"You've been watched, but I have no idea why."

"I guess I'm just an important part of that unique Army fraternity."

"If you're lucky, that's all it is."

"What's their angle?"

"The West desperately needs intelligence on what is happening in Central Europe, what the Soviet role is, and what kind of troop strength the Russians are deploying," he said. "You are a fluent speaker of the language, as well as Russian, have contacts from the war, have an intelligence background, and can be trusted. But most importantly, I think you are highly motivated to get inside the country. To find the woman...yes?"

"I will become the very thing I've tried to avoid for two years—an American agent. An asset."

"You will be serving your country in the new war against the Stalinists." He paused as if considering. "The Americans look for a traitor among them, a very high-level double agent," he continued, feeling confident he was not revealing too much.

"Attila?

Henry looked surprised. "Yes, Attila."

"I am the perfect agent to uncover him. Is that what you're saying?"

"That is what I am saying."

"Did you forget that I am high on General Pavlov's list, and he is searching for me?"

"We have not," Henry replied. "Regardless of whether you live or die, the Americans believe they will benefit from your mission. We know that this man, Pavlov, tortured you severely and that you were never broken. I suspect he wants everything you know about American agents in Eastern Europe. Information you may have received from the Russian double agent, Rasputin."

"Gregor Zerenowsky."

"Yes, him, but much has changed in two years, and Palov knows this. I think he wants revenge more than information. So, keep your mouth shut on what you may know. Don't allow him to take you alive."

"I don't know anything worth the trouble of chasing me from the far side of the world," Charlie replied.

"From your work in East Europe during the war and from your relationship with Zerenowsky, I think you know more than you think about the Soviet and American networks, many of which were established during the war. So, I advise you to be very careful."

"The Americans think they have nothing to lose by getting me into the country. A cheap price for intelligence, eh?"

"The Army trusts your abilities, and they believe they will have another agent there to assist them during a very critical time."

"Until Pavlov catches me," Charlie replied. "Then I swallow the little pill. Is that it?"

"That's it," Henry replied. "Oh, by the way, keep this...just in case." He handed Charlie the pill, wrapped in paper.

"Thanks." He took it and placed it in a shirt pocket.

"We must be realistic."

My contact? Will I have a contact once I get into the country?"

"You will be contacted in Prague, and that person has been briefed on your arrival. I assume you will cross in the east, through the mountain passes. You are familiar with this region and have good contacts. Yes?"

"That is my plan."

"You will operate—on your own—like before."

"Before?"

"During the war."

"I understand. Yes, that's the only way I operate."

"Here are your papers, and a Czech passport, money. Good luck." Henry handed Charlie the envelope, stood, and offered his hand. "Until we meet again." He turned, left the room, and as quickly, disappeared down the shadowy staircase as if a ghost. Charlie continued to stand in the doorway, contemplating what he was doing, and for whom he was doing it.

Chapter 8

Conversing with other passengers on his flight to Geneva from Istanbul, Charlie learned that the best way to travel while carrying a Czech passport, if you wanted to avoid scrutiny, was through Austria. The post-war borders were still being redrawn, passengers told him, creating a chaotic situation. That makes it much easier to slip in and out of the country.

Traveling through Switzerland with its spectacular scenery and well-run railroads, was almost pleasurable. Austria was much more difficult because its roads, railroads, and cities were heavily damaged during the war. The country still lay in ruins from the war's terrible destruction. He saw refugees at border crossings, train stations, and along the roads, everyone fleeing to find a new future in the West.

Charlie arrived at a heavily trafficked crossing near Bratislava and entered Czechoslovakia without difficulty. After many inquiries, he found a room and paid up for a week. Settled, he went walking to learn more about the city. He had not been in Bratislava during the war but had heard many stories from his men. Jürgen and Marie lived there before. They fled when the Germans took control in 1939, following the great betrayal of September 1938, as Jürgen referred to the British and French sell-out and subsequent Nazi takeover. Sitting in an outdoor café near his room, Charlie thought about Jürgen and Marie, but still carefully scanning his surroundings. *State Security could be anywhere,* he told himself constantly. He sipped a cup of tea and crunched on a fresh Kolach pastry.

After several days of exploring the city, Charlie decided it was time to head east into the Carpathians to contact Jürgen. He located the bus station, checked the schedule, and purchased a bus ticket east, into the mountains.

Charlie carefully explained to the bus driver that he wanted to go only as far as Kosice, the town near where he had fought with partisans during the war. "No further," he said.

The driver nodded that he understood.

"Everything is changing," said Charlie candidly.

"The Communists run the government, and the Russians have taken part of our land in the east. The bastards gave it to the Ukrainians. Part of our homeland," the man growled.

Charlie listened carefully to the man's provincial dialect. He spoke very little himself, not wanting to reveal that he was not from the area. He knew the people here were suspicious of strangers. According to his passport, he was traveling as a mining engineer educated in Moscow. He hoped that would explain his dialect, but he also knew that coming from the Soviet Union made him more foreign to them...and disliked. *At least they don't think I'm an American,* he thought, knowing that being an object of curiosity and wonder could easily blow his cover.

The old bus passed through small villages, making its way higher into the Carpathians, where the borders of Slovakia, Ukraine, and Poland converged. He remembered what his father had told him once about his people: 'If a Czech had a dependable source of water, plenty of timber, and a mountain on which to look down on his neighbors, he had everything he wanted.'

The mountains brought back many memories of that horrible day—September 23, 1944.

The battle for control of Dykla Pass had been raging for days. The First Czechoslovak Corps, commanded by General Ludvik Svoboda and the Soviet 38th Division, at first held their ground against the better-trained and equipped German Panzer units. Then, even with both sides suffering heavy casualties, the Germans were able to outflank the Czechs and finally seize control of the battlefield.

From the partisan's high mountain lair in the Carpathians, Charlie heard the rumble of artillery day and night. Then as suddenly, it stopped. A profound silence fell over the woods. Soon they learned that the German Army had won the day, holding off and then counter-attacking the Czechs and Russians.

Victorious, the German Army established a strong defensive line running west to east along the River Drava, Lake Balaton, and the flanks of the Carpathians, 150 miles along the Danube from Vienna.

Charlie and his band of partisans tried to contact General Svoboda's army to find out if Marie had survived. At first, they attempted to make radio contact with the Czech and Russian units engaged in the battle and were unsuccessful. Finally, with only his most trusted men, Charlie made his way down the mountain to reach Svoboda's last known headquarters. The partisan team encountered German patrols before they even reached the lower forests, with the Germans driving them back into the higher elevations. Twice more they tried, but every attempt was blocked. Messerschmitt Me109s prowled the sky overhead, while German combat patrols swarmed through the valleys.

The Germans had ruthlessly suppressed the rebellion and effectively stalled the advance of Marshall Malinovsky's Second Ukrainian Front. The Red Army was unable to come to the aid of the Czechs. In two weeks of heavy fighting, Svoboda's Corps and the Soviets' 38th Division had suffered more than 80,000 casualties, killed, wounded, or captured, as history later recorded.

From the partisan's mountain hiding place forward of German lines, the men heard the loud whistle of their trains. Night and day, they transported prisoners to permanent camps still operating in southern Poland. Black smoke from the locomotives darkened the skies.

It was more than a week before the partisans of any of the bands could reach the lower forests around the pass. When they reached them and searched the battlefield, looking for survivors, they found few to tell their story. Marie was not among the dead who, Charlie discovered, the Germans had left where they had fallen. He could only hope that she had somehow survived and was fleeing with the remnants of Svoboda's defeated army westward or for the higher mountains.

"Where was Marie?" he asked all survivors he found. No one knew anything, and Charlie assumed the worst: The Nazis had killed her on the battlefield, or worse, they had shipped her off to one of their death camps.

The bus driver left Charlie along the road, and he covered the last five miles to the cabin on foot. With each step, climbing higher into the mountains, he took the time to look around at the deep forest and the high mountains. The memories came flooding back. He was amazed that he and Jan Novotny, his subordinate, had parachuted in safely and found their way.

After several hours walking, the altitude began to take its toll on Charlie, forcing him to take a break in a grassy clearing he recognized from before. He lay in the grass in the bright sunlight, and soon, he felt reinvigorated. He sprang to his feet, determined to reach the cabin before nightfall.

As he walked, a warm breeze touched his face and brought back memories of Marie. They had lain together under a great tree somewhere near here, Charlie was certain. He recalled the smell of the fall flowers in the meadow and the sound of the wind in the trees. Everything reminded him of her. He sighed and pushed on.

Standing on a slight elevation to get his bearing, he saw what he was looking for. The one-room log building rose up out of the meadow, a haunting gray against the deep blue sky. The first time he had been here, he had approached the building stealthily with his rifle at the ready. He and Jan had had no idea what they would find back here in December 1943.

Charlie followed a well-worn path this time. When he reached the door, he turned the knob with his automatic drawn. Finding the door unlocked, he entered. The place was deserted, but he could see that someone had been there recently. Empty cans were on the table. Charlie felt the warmth when he touched the coals in the old iron stove. *This morning*, he decided. He opened the one window for more light and continued his search. Rummaging through the cupboard, a storage locker, and a narrow closet, he found nothing that would indicate the identity of the recent occupant.

Sitting at the table facing the door, Charlie considered who might currently occupy the cabin. *Did it still belong to Jürgen Benes?* He wondered and decided to wait. He placed his weapon on the table, looked around the room. Within minutes, he heard heavy footsteps plowing through the high grass.

The door opened and in walked a man. He saw Charlie and halted, his eyes fixed on the automatic now in Charlie's hand. "Who are you?" he asked.

Charlie saw that the man was much younger than he was. He was short, well built, but most importantly, he was unarmed. He wore a cap and heavy shirt with the sleeves rolled to his elbows.

"I am looking for Jürgen Benes," Charlie replied. "Do you know him?"

The man smiled. "Yes. Why do you look for him?"

"We are friends."

The man's eyes moved beyond Charlie, to the window. Charlie turned his head quickly. "Jürgen," he said, jumping to his feet. "So good…"

"My young friend, Charles, it is so good to see you again," the older man said, recognizing Charlie immediately.

They embraced at the window. "Sit, sit," Jürgen said. "I will come in and join you. This is my nephew, Frank."

The three men sat at the table and talked through the remainder of the afternoon. Mostly, they spoke of the war, their families, and life in general. Charlie learned that Jürgen had returned to Bratislava and resumed his work after the war. He had searched for Marie and discovered the Germans had first placed her in a temporary camp for POWs. Later they moved her to one of the work camps surrounding Auschwitz. The Russians liberated the camps in January 1945, just before the war ended. Marie returned to Bratislava and Jürgen, but not for long. According to him, she had become politicized and furious. When the Germans were gone, and the Czech government was reestablished, she left for the capital. Jürgen did not say what she had been doing there for two years, and he did not mention a child.

Finally, the discussion turned to politics. Jürgen said he suspected Marie was involved in the protests against the government, and he hoped she was working with the more moderate trade unionists. However, he worried that her outspoken opinions and determination to keep all foreigners out of Czech politics had gotten her in trouble.

"What of her child?" Charlie asked.

"My grandchild?" Jürgen seemed surprised by the question. "How do you know of the child?"

"That is why I'm here, my friend." He watched the old man. "The Russian State Security. They tried to get me to go to Prague. As part of the deal, they said they would release Marie and the child. Tell me what you know."

"I know that General Pavlov wants you. He told Marie he was hunting you, that you still possessed secrets dangerous to Russia. I was in Prague to visit her and Anna two weeks ago. That is the name of the child. Marie told me that Russian security forces had spoken with her. Interrogated her was more like it. She feared she would be detained at any moment and told me to get out of the city quickly."

"Anna? My child's name is Anna?"

"They told you the child was yours?"

"Is that true?"

"I think she belongs to all of us, or perhaps as others say, 'to God.'"

Charlie had no idea what that meant, but he did not pursue it.

The trip back to Bratislava was circuitous and long. Charlie returned with Frank in an old truck while Jürgen took a different route by bus. They decided to meet later at Jürgen's house.

"Before we return, I must show you something," Frank said. He drove east along a rough two-lane path through a densely forested area. Suddenly, he stopped the truck. "From here, we must walk."

Frank grabbed a pair of binoculars from under the seat. He led the way, and Charlie followed as they stomped through a dense thicket into the forest. They walked for about an hour. When they came to the edge of the trees and into a small clearing, Frank stopped. "There." He pointed.

Charlie moved closer for a better look. Then he saw it. A grave with a rough wooden tombstone that faced them. He read the hastily scrawled words:

Lt. Jan Novotny, Hero and American Soldier, killed by German machineguns on March 21, 1944.

Charlie stood in front of the makeshift grave marker with his head bowed without speaking. "Farewell, my friend," he finally said.

Frank nodded. "Come, I'll show you more." He turned and walked carefully toward a sharp ledge overlooking a river valley. When he was about five feet from the ledge, he got down on all fours and crawled the rest of the way. He motioned for Charlie to do the same. Both on their stomachs, they looked out over the valley below them, with a ribbon of road running through it from east to west.

"Down there...under the trees. Look." He handed Charlie his binoculars.

What Charlie saw surprised him. "Russian soldiers?"

"They wait."

Under the tall pines, clustered around an armored vehicle, soldiers were standing or sitting, apparently waiting for something. Charlie looked further up the road toward the east, and what he saw worried him even more. An armored column, each vehicle with Russian markings, stretched as far as he could see. "Where is the Ukrainian border?" he asked.

"Maybe five miles east," Frank replied.

"Will they move toward Prague to defend the Communist takeover?"

"I think they are prepared to do that," Frank replied. "Stalin now has what he wants, and he will never give it up."

"There is no one to stop them. "*Now, I do have information the Americans want*, Charlie thought, still watching the column of Russian vehicles through the binoculars.

"I think Czechoslovakia is lost."

Charlie did not reply.

For most of the trip to Bratislava, both men were quiet, content to think their own thoughts. Finally, Charlie asked about Frank's family, and Frank explained that the Germans had killed his parents. He had come to live with Jürgen after the war. Charlie then mentioned Frank's right arm, having noticed earlier that a large chunk of muscle was missing from the forearm. "How did that happen," he asked.

"Shrapnel from a Russian bomb," Frank replied. "We were caught in the middle between attacking Russians and retreating Germans."

Charlie asked him many questions about Marie and the child, but Frank shared little.

"Who does she look like?" he asked.

"She is beautiful, like her mother," Frank said.

"That's good," Charlie said.

They both laughed.

They reached the city well after dark, and Frank dropped Charlie off about five blocks from his room. Charlie cautiously made his way to the hotel, taking note of his surroundings, but especially, he watched people walking or standing about. He still believed he could spot a Russian Ministry of State Security--an MGB agent--anywhere. Seeing no one around, he entered the old brick building and took the stairs one at a time, very slowly. His hand was on the automatic stuck in his belt.

He reached the door, inserted the key, and opened it. He had planted matchsticks, positioning them so that if anyone searched his belongings, they would alter them in some way. He had placed his few articles of clothing, toiletries, and stationery in the single drawer. Nothing had been disturbed. *Good,* he thought, hoping that meant they did not yet know he had arrived. He took his items, reentered the hall, and made for a small toilet and bath at the far end. He would prepare for his meeting with Jürgen later in the evening.

He considered how his evolving plan to rescue Marie would work. If she was locked away somewhere in a high-security area, he knew they could not just break her out in a gangster-style operation. He also did not know how useful Jürgen would be after they got him into Prague.

Deep down, Charlie believed that getting Marie out would probably cost him his freedom. Worse, to keep himself and Marie alive, Pavlov would force him to become a double agent.

First, he would squeeze every bit of knowledge Charlie had on the American espionage network in Eastern Europe out of him. Henry was right. It would be best to die before that happened.

The two were meeting late in the evening in Jürgen's small apartment, several miles from the city center. Charlie walked, not wanting to arouse interest. When he arrived at the small brick home, Jürgen greeted him with a beer.

"Now we talk. There are no ears to listen here, and we must make plans," he said.

"Don't you trust your nephew?" Charlie asked.

"With my life," he replied. "But if he knows nothing of our plans, he cannot reveal them."

Charlie nodded. "I must get into Prague without being detected."

"I will get you into the city and to a safe house."

"Do you have a plan to rescue Marie and get her out of the city?"

Jürgen, at first, said nothing. "If the police hold her, we can free her. You have money, yes?"

"I should have enough. What if the MGB has her?"

"Then, my friend, there is nothing we can do but pray."

"No, you are wrong. There is one thing to do. We must negotiate a trade. Her freedom and safe passage to Switzerland for me."

"I cannot ask you to do that."

Charlie shrugged. "We may have no choice. It's me he wants."

"Then it must not come to that."

"What of the child, Jürgen? Where is she now?"

"She is being taken care of by a family appointed by the police," Jürgen replied. "I know where."

"Good, good. We will rescue her first and return her to a safe place. Then she will not be harmed in any way if things get rough."

"I think our plan is a good one. We leave in the morning, very early."

On the walk back to his room, Charlie contemplated how he could get the child out of the country. *I will need a passport and more money. Would the Americans help?* he wondered.

He had taken the same security precautions as before. Slowly, he opened the door, so he would not disturb the matchsticks he had stuck upright in the old, well-worn wood floor before he had left. Stooping for a closer examination, he saw that several were crushed. Someone had entered while he was out.

He went to the drawer. Here, too, someone had moved the sticks around. He saw them scattered about the drawer, not as he had carefully placed them. *They found me out, and by someone who is very clumsy,* he thought.

Charlie packed his few things into the duffel, checked his weapon, and headed for the door. He knew it was too dangerous to stay in the room, but he wasn't sure where to go. At the foot of the stairs, he saw that the light in his landlord's room was still on. He knocked.

After the fourth or fifth knock, he looked through the window into the apartment and saw the old man shuffle to the door in a heavy robe.

Recognizing Charlie, he opened the door. "What do you want? It is very late," he said.

"Someone was in my room," Charlie told him. "Who was it?"

There was a look of surprise on the old man's severely wrinkled face, but he said nothing. He just stared at the floor.

"Tell me," Charlie said. "Was it the police?"

"You are a foreigner, a Communist, eh?" he replied. "I must know...to protect my family. I was in your room. For a day, I did not see you, and I worried. 'Is there trouble from this foreigner?' I asked myself."

"I explained to you that I am an engineer hired to search the mountains for minerals. I speak differently because I have studied in Moscow for many years. Do you think I'm lying?"

The man seemed nervous, and he kept looking outside to the street. "The times are dangerous, and we see many strangers here. And..."

"And?"

"If you are from Moscow, why does your passport say you crossed the border from Austria like an American or British spy?"

Charlie smiled.

"Come in before the police see us talking," the man said. "That is no good for either of us."

Charlie entered the man's apartment. "I fly to Vienna, to the Russian zone, and travel from there. It is much faster than going through Prague or Budapest. If you have already examined my passport, you know that a Russian stamp is also there."

"It is in order," the man said. "Please forgive an old fool. But I cannot trust anyone. I remember the Nazis, and now it is bad again with the Russians and Americans preparing for more war. They will fight it here, I think. Too much for an old man. Go back to bed."

"Yes, thank you," Charlie replied. "I must leave in the morning to give my report. Good-bye."

Chapter 9

ndre Pavlov knew he was dying. Maybe two or three weeks, a month at most, and the cancer would finish its job. *Thirty-five years of smoking has done what Stalin's purges, the war, and my enemies could not.* "Ha! The bastards!" he said. "One more job to complete for him, and I will be ready." He exhaled slowly on the American cigarette and smiled.

Stalin had posted him to Karlshorst in the Soviet sector of Berlin six months after the war ended. Stalin told him he should build a strong network of intelligence gathering in the occupied countries. "To protect the Revolution from the Americans!" the dictator exclaimed. The general accepted the posting. He had no choice.

Only several months prior to his posting, he had learned one of his own people had betrayed him. The American, Stanek, had turned Gregor Zerenowksy. Even though he was Ukrainian, Zerenowsky proved to be an invaluable asset during the war against the Germans. How Stanek had turned him into the dreaded Rasputin, he would never know. But the

Americans had stolen valuable military secrets, and Stanek's agents were still compromising operations in Eastern Europe.

He knew it had to be his agents. No one else the Americans had could have worked so effectively and on our doorstep. He was bright, skilled, and much too dangerous to be allowed to walk free. Pavlov had decided that long ago. *I will get the American and turn him or kill him, but I must learn everything about those traitors who worked for Rasputin.* He took a long drag on his cigarette, exhaled. The pain was sharp.

The general was confident the American knew the names of at least several traitors to the Motherland. Zerenowsky would not have told anyone but Stanek. He believed that was why Stanek had had to disappear in '46. He had become a liability for the Americans, too. He knew too much, but the Americans—capitalists with no fortitude or character. *They were weak, unwilling to terminate him*, Pavlov scoffed.

He smiled again, thinking, *The woman will bring him to me.* Then through pursed lips, he grabbed at his chest. "Not yet, Andre," he said. "You still have much to do."

"Major Andropov, come here," he called through the closed door. Sergei Andropov was his assistant, the man who had to do the work that he could not.

Major Andropov rushed in and stood at attention in front of Pavlov's desk. "Yes, general." He saluted.

Andropov was a tall, thin man with watery blue eyes and a slight tremble in his upper lip. Andropov reminded Pavlov of a Gestapo officer he had shot near the Polish border in late '44. "Yes, yes, yes, major. Enough." The general had brought Andropov on in the Far East. He was a young officer then, but as an MGB agent, he had come highly recommended.

After returning from Hanoi and the disaster with Zerenowsky and Stanek, Pavlov realized he would have to rebuild his team—from the ground up. Rasputin had devastated the ranks of Russian intelligence, especially NKVD.

Under Stalin's direct orders, he had purged and reorganized the service. The MGB would be in charge of all foreign intelligence, and Pavlov demanded loyalty above all else when he picked his new staff. Sergei Andropov was no genius, but he was loyal. Pavlov knew and appreciated this. Therefore, he ensured that Andropov rose quickly through the ranks.

The general pulled the crumpled cryptogram from his pocket to read again. He had received the message from Moscow five days earlier. Operatives in Asia informed him that the Messenger had failed. Stanek had killed him. That alone disturbed him because the Messenger never failed. The worst, however, was that Stanek's whereabouts were unknown. Agents in Asia and Europe had not spotted him. The American operative—their best double agent--was silent.

Pavlov had made it clear that capturing Stanek was a high priority. Still, his contact in the American CIA provided no useful information. The general was confident Stanek would go to Washington to solicit the assistance of the new Central Intelligence Agency or his former boss, William Donovan. His operative had been prepared. Pavlov had little respect for his American counterparts in the CIA, so he refused to believe they could act without his knowledge.

However, the question remained. Where was Stanek?

Andre Pavlov was not an evil man. He was a survivor, having learned his basic skills as a very young soldier fighting in the bloody civil war. He received his advanced education during the horrible purges of the '20s and '30s. The Great Patriotic War against Hitler had been his shining moment, allowing him to impress first Khrushchev and then Stalin himself with his loyalty and dedication. Pavlov was a committed Communist who willingly destroyed all enemies to the Soviet state, and his superiors immediately recognized that. During his long career, he had killed many and sent thousands of traitors and enemies of the state to Siberian gulags.

"Fetch the Czech woman, Major," he ordered. "I want her in Berlin in two days to speak with her. But do not frighten her, Sergei. We need her cooperation." He studied Andropov. "Do you understand my order?"

"I do, General." The soldier still stood at attention in front of the general's desk.

Pavlov, watching him, smiled. He had another thought. "Sit down, Sergei. Sit down over there. We must talk before you leave."

"Yes, sir." Sergei relaxed only slightly, turned, and sat down in the designated chair.

Pavlov watched him. "Smoke."

Sergei nodded, pulled a pack of Russian cigarettes from his tunic, and lit up.

"Listen closely," Pavlov said. "This is a very delicate situation. We are looking for information, so do not kill anyone. The Czechs are now our allies—partners—so do not push them around...unless you absolutely must. Do you understand, Sergei?"

"I must use tact," Sergei replied.

"That's correct," the general said. "And you may encounter American agents or their puppets. Take whatever actions necessary, but do not kill Major Stanek. If you locate him, remember: He is mine, and must be brought back here." He coughed. The sharpness of it hurt him, the pain spreading across his chest and abdomen again.

Major Andropov watched him, appalled by the force of it but feeling helpless to take any action.

Finally, the coughing ended, and General Pavlov straightened in his chair. "That is all major. Dismissed," he whispered, embarrassed. He lit another cigarette.

Major Andropov stood, saluted, and left the room without uttering another word.

The general watched him leave, wondering if he was up to the job at hand. Still holding the cryptogram in his hand, he tore it into little pieces, and with his cigarette, lit each piece. He watched the yellow paper turn black and brittle, then shrink into ashes.

Walking to the window, he looked out over what remained of the city. The Russians had constructed temporary quarters for their troops and housed many in surviving German military barracks, but much of the city still lay in ruins. Everywhere the general looked, he saw the same thing. He knew the Americans were investing millions of dollars in reconstructing the British, French, and American sectors, which they had combined. *Such fools to trust the Germans,* he thought. *They will never change, and the Americans obviously are not leaving the city, so we must strangle them, force them out. So, what if the German people starve because of the blockade? They deserve no better than they gave us.* The remainder of his cigarette trembled between his fingers as his anger grew.

Pavlov believed the American airlift would fail. It was impossible to believe they could supply a city only by airplane, but he worried that their temporary success was strengthening their resolve to succeed. *Even before the war ended, Stalin had decided that all resources and what remained of captured German infrastructure should be shipped east. And that's what we did.* He worried that there would be repercussions. Hungry people were unpredictable and very dangerous. Extremely hard to control. He had seen that in his own country many times.

We must observe the Germans carefully. They are a dangerous breed, and we should never allow them to rearm. He could not understand why the Americans and British did not see that. *But that makes my job even more important,* he decided. *We must be vigilant with the Americans and the Germans, and if that means taking extreme actions, then that must be done. We must protect the motherland from American and German aggression.*

For Andre Pavlov, things were not that difficult to grasp, and he quickly forced the worries from his mind. His immediate concern was shoring up the Soviet intelligence operation in Europe and preparing for a very long fight with the Americans.

Chapter 10

Charlie and Jürgen arrived in Prague in early evening one day later. They had packed carefully and left from Jürgen's house. Frank drove them in his truck. He parked his vehicle on a side street far from the city center in New Town. Finding his bearing from a map he had purchased, Charlie saw that they had parked the truck near a tram station on Anglicka Street. From there it was a straight shot into Old Town and across the bridge into Central Prague.

"The truck needs repairs," Frank said. "I will meet you later."

"My brother-in-law will take us. It has been arranged," Jürgen told Charlie.

Frank dropped the two men off near a side entrance to a handsome two-story house facing a small courtyard. They had encountered no problems along the way--no roadblocks, protests, or soldiers. *Things are too damn quiet,* Charlie thought.

"The home of my wife's sister. Beautiful, no? It was never damaged during the war," Jürgen said proudly. They stood in the street admiring the well-kept front façade with a small garden off to the side.

"I'm impressed," Charlie replied politely.

"We will rest here," Jürgen said. "They are expecting me." He knocked softly on the door, and within seconds, it opened. An elderly woman with a bright smile greeted them. She sat them at a large table, served drinks, and left the room.

"What do they know of our mission?" Charlie asked. They sat alone in the kitchen, each nursing a beer.

"They know nothing, and it is better if they do not learn of it," Jürgen replied. "If they know nothing, they cannot betray us," he repeated.

"Then how can they help us?"

"You are not sleeping on the street, my young friend." Jürgen smiled, his weathered skin around his lips cracking. "We must get into the city near Prague Castle. They will take us."

"When?" Charlie asked. "Soon I think the MGB will know I'm here and begin searching."

"Maybe around ten."

"When we get the child, how do we get out of there?"

"Frank will wait for us near Wenceslas Square. Not far," Jürgen explained. "Everything else is as we planned."

The woman returned with food. "Eat," she said. She set bread with sliced cheese and meat on the table. She reached behind her to get silverware and two plates. "It is all we have. Times are hard, and we know they will get worse." She smiled bravely and left the room again.

"Your sister is very kind," Charlie said. "I know she is taking a risk for me."

"Since 1938, we have taken many risks, and our losses have been great. But what are our options?" He did not wait for Charlie to reply. "Our options are few. Now, at least, we can live with ourselves if we know what we do is right. My sister only knows that what we do involves my daughter, and she approves."

Charlie nodded but said nothing.

Soon Jürgen's brother-in-law returned home. He greeted them politely but quickly disappeared into another room, only to reappear a few minutes later in different clothes. "We go," he said.

They crossed the Charles Bridge and turned south into Little Quarter, nearing the house where Anna was living on Karmelitska Street. Jürgen knew the location because he had visited her before when Czech government agents placed the child there. He knew the agents wanted her close so they could keep an eye on her.

They dropped Jürgen off in front of the ancient building. No one spoke. Charlie got out when they turned the corner into a narrow alley.

"Thank you," Charlie said. He quietly closed the door of the old car and walked to the corner to look out on the street. Just as he peered around the corner, Jürgen knocked on the door. Charlie waited in the dark, knowing that if Jürgen was unable to get the child, he would be needed to take her at gunpoint. Charlie turned back into the narrow alley, pulled his automatic, and checked the clip. He hoped he would not have to use it, but he was prepared.

He heard voices. Jürgen was speaking with a woman. He heard the door close. *That's a good sign*, Charlie thought. The last thing he wanted to do was shoot someone for refusing to give up his child. He kneeled there in the shadows and waited.

The minutes passed, and he grew nervous.

"Charles! Come!"

Hearing his name called, Charlie stood, turned the corner, and raced for the door. When he was almost there, he saw Jürgen standing on the threshold empty-handed.

"Please, I implore you to allow an old grandfather to take the child if only for a few days," he said to the couple.

Charlie did not see the child.

"No," the woman said. "It is not possible."

"We were ordered not to release the child to anyone, not even to her grandfather. Speak with the police," the man said. "You must get permission." He saw Charlie coming toward him and reacted, trying to close the door.

Jürgen was too quick. He stepped forward and blocked it with his foot. "Charles," he said again.

Charlie, as if on cue, stepped forward. With his weapon already drawn, he moved beside Jürgen. "Inside. Now!" They forced the door open. "Jürgen, get her."

Jürgen ran for the stairs. When he reached the top, he disappeared into the darkness.

"Sit down," Charlie ordered the woman. He produced a cord from his pocket. "Tie her," he said to her husband.

When the man had securely tied his wife, Charlie ordered him to sit in a chair across the room. He tied him and then gagged both with strips of cloth he found in their kitchen. He had just finished when Jürgen came down with the four-year-old in his arms.

"Come, my princess," Jürgen said. "We must go."

The child stared first at her foster parents then at Jürgen, but she did not utter a sound. Charlie saw that she was small for her age, and with brown eyes and dark hair, he did not think she looked like either him or Marie. However, with an engaging smile and a depth to her eyes, he had never seen in someone so small, she was beautiful.

They left the house and quickly made for Wenceslas Square, covering the dark streets in record time. Frank was waiting when they arrived, the truck engine running. The two men and the child crowded into the narrow cab. The vehicle reeked of grease and gasoline but jumped forward instantly.

"We will spend the night in the home of an old friend. We cannot return to my sister's home. The couple will alert the police. Early tomorrow, we get Marie, then quickly return to Bratislava."

"With luck," Charlie added.

"It's very strange," Jürgen said. "When I called the police earlier, they said Marie was not there, and that they knew no one by that name. They suggested we check with the workers' militia who work for KSC. They are near Zbraslav Castle. I do not understand what she is doing there. We must be very careful and not be seen together. We could be walking into a trap."

Charlie did not reply at first. He stared at his daughter. "Yes, I understand. Always be wary of the MGB." His eyes were still on the child. "Anna... Anna, I'm Charles," he said to her. He tried to smile, but anxiety muted it.

She looked at him and smiled. "Char-les," she repeated.

* * *

"Where is the woman called Marie Benes?" Major Andropov asked, standing in front of the police desk the next morning. He had entered the Prague police station accompanied by two Russian soldiers. "I have orders to escort her to Berlin. For special assignment." He showed the sergeant at the front desk his orders. "They have been countersigned by General Svoboda."

The police officer reviewed the document. He turned to speak with an assistant. "We have no woman by that name who works here," he said.

"You were ordered to have her here when I arrive," the major said. He was losing patience. He turned to look at his lieutenant. "Such incompetence," he growled.

"I never received such an order," the police officer replied. "I suggest you contact the workers' militia. They are headquartered in Zbraslav Castle." He looked at the Russian with a confused expression.

"What's the matter, sergeant? Do you not understand?"

"Yours is the second request I've received for the woman and her daughter, but the child was taken during the night by two men. I find this all very curious. She must be important."

"Direct me to this castle."

The police officer provided directions and watched as the three Russians marched out the door. He shrugged and went back to his duties.

"I know Stanek is here," Major Andropov said. "Be prepared. He has the child. Now, he comes for the woman."

* * *

Charlie and Jürgen took the tram into the old city. Frank stayed with the child at the house of Jürgen's friend. Charlie had directed him to return immediately to Bratislava with Anna if something happened to him and Jürgen. "If we do not return by noon, leave the city," Charlie ordered.

Getting off the ancient streetcar, they saw armed civilians milling about. "The workers have not been disbanded. Be careful. They are bored and look for any excuse to contribute and be heroic," Jürgen said under his breath.

"Untrained and worse than soldiers."

"Find a quiet spot where you can see the entrance and wait for me," Jürgen ordered.

"If you do not return?" Charlie asked.

"Then you must leave at once. Or they will capture you, too."

"Good luck."

Jürgen nodded. He walked toward the old castle.

Charlie stood and watched him. He carefully observed what was happening in the plaza that Jürgen was walking through. However, sensing no immediate danger, he scouted out a café where he would sit and wait.

* * *

"What is happening here? Are you in the Army?" Jürgen asked a young woman near the front steps of the castle. He explained that he was from Slovakia and had not read the papers. The young woman, who Jürgen decided could not be much older than Marie, stopped and looked suspiciously at him.

"We serve workers like you," she said. "The Communist Party of Czechoslovakia has liberated the country, and we are volunteers of the workers' militia who stay here to ensure the reactionaries do not return. Don't you know that Benes resigned months ago and is replaced by Klement Gottwald?"

"No, I live in the mountains. I've only come to Prague last night."

"Welcome, comrade," she replied. Then, with a machine gun slung over her shoulder, she moved on with a stiff gait that partially resembled goose-stepping.

Jürgen entered the medieval building and approached an armed man standing near the wall.

The man stepped forward to stop him. "What is your business?" He looked Jürgen over carefully.

"My daughter is here, and I must speak to her."

"Do you have any identification?"

"Only this." He pulled a card from his shirt pocket and handed it to the guard.

The man read it slowly. "Benes," he said.

"Jürgen Benes and my daughter is Marie Benes. I must speak with her."

"Comrade Benes? Of course. Why didn't you say so," he said. "Come with me. I will take you to her."

Comrade Benes. That surprised Jürgen. Now, he did not know what to expect.

The guard took him firmly by the arm, and they walked up a wide stone staircase. At the top, they entered a large room where many people were coming and going. Some wore uniforms, and others were civilians. Jürgen saw that most were young and armed.

"She is over there behind the large desk. I will leave you here." The guard turned and returned to the stairway.

Jürgen looked where the man had directed. He spotted Marie and walked toward her, trying to ignore the conversations going on around him among people mostly milling about. At the desk, he stopped and waited for Marie to look up.

After several seconds she did. "Papa?" The look on her face was more one of consternation than surprise. Her eyes darted from him to several men standing beside the desk. "You should not have come here."

"A father can't visit his daughter?" he said. "We must speak."

The men overheard, nodded, and moved away politely.

"Papa, you should not have come," she repeated. "It is too dangerous for you."

"There are things I must tell you...about Anna."

Her expression immediately turned to fear. "What about her? Is she well? It's the Russians. They've taken her out of the country."

"Not the Russians."

* * *

Charlie waited impatiently. He sat at a small outdoor table watching the young workers with their Russian weapons walk by laughing and chatting as if they had already found their utopia and had no cares in the world. *Young fools*, Charlie thought. *Soon, they will learn about their comrades, the Russians.* The minutes ticked away slowly.

A young woman sat down at his table, taking Charlie by surprise. "Comrade," she said. "Will you buy me a coffee?"

Charlie looked up at an attractive, well-dressed young woman. Not beautiful, with her short hair and chiseled features, but attractive. Charlie did not conceal his surprise. He searched her face for some indication of who she was.

But a mask—lipstick that was too heavy, mascara concealing dark circles under her eyes, and hair dyed with blond roots showing—disguised any facial clues to her identity. She wore a dress that, unlike the others, he saw around him, was expensive and very seductive. He decided—perhaps too hastily—that she was a prostitute. In addition, for some reason, she seemed to consider him the only one about who could afford her services.

At first, Charlie said nothing. Then he raised his hand to motion the waiter. Wearing a wool shirt and a jacket borrowed from Jürgen, he played the part of a Czech worker content to watch events unfold. He decided that would be best, not knowing who he would encounter.

"A coffee for the young lady," he said when the waiter approached. "And a kolache. She looks hungry." Charlie thought she took little interest in the young people engaged in their political activities. She acted as if she were almost aloof and she was definitely different from the others he saw.

The waiter hesitated, then nodded and turned for the counter.

"Where are you from?" the young woman asked.

"Bratislava," Charlie said.

She smiled. "What is your name?"

"Andres Vavrock," he replied, remembering the name on his passport. "What's yours?"

"Marta," she said. "Your accent...It's different."

"I have been gone a very long time," he said.

"Where?"

This conversation cannot happen, he thought with growing concern. "Moscow."

"Moscow?" She did not sound convinced.

"Yes, I studied engineering. Now I've come home to work in the new Czech government." He smiled.

She returned his smile. "You are lying, I think. But I don't care because you are very handsome, and I like you." She slid a folded piece of paper across the table. "Andres, I must go, but you can call on me at that address. I want to see you again." She rose to leave as the waiter brought her order.

"Good-bye, Marta," Charles said as she brushed by his side. "Don't forget your kolache." He saw that she carried only a small purse.

"Good-bye, Andres." She picked up the pastry, took a large bite, and was on her way. "Visit me," she said, entering the plaza. "You won't be disappointed."

The meeting struck Charlie as odd, almost contrived. *What can it mean?* he asked himself. He watched appreciatively as she departed through the crowd. She looked back once to smile at him. He saw that she was tall and very well proportioned, guessing her age at around thirty. *That confirmed it. She must be a prostitute,* he decided, *who may yet be of some assistance to me.* He stuck the slip of paper in his shirt pocket.

Finally, the large crowd in the plaza swallowed her up. She was gone as quickly as she had come. He looked. "Marta," Charlie repeated her name softly to himself.

He waited another fifteen minutes then decided he had had enough. He motioned for the waiter again and got up to leave. The young man sauntered over and presented him with the cheque. He paid it without speaking.

He began walking across the plaza toward the castle. When he was halfway, a vehicle pulled up, and two Russian soldiers jumped out. Charlie could easily tell they were Russians by their uniforms. With pistols strapped to their waists, he also knew they were officers—not a good sign.

He watched them enter the castle. Their vehicle with one occupant did not move from in front of the building. The engine continued to run.

Deciding the soldiers could be MGB, he walked around the plaza slowly, his eyes always on the castle entrance. Charlie was already on his second trip around when the Russian soldiers came out. He saw a third person between them. He increased his speed to get as close as he could while still unnoticed.

Reaching the steps, he turned and watched them. A young woman dressed in men's clothing, much like the others, was speaking to the tallest soldier. Her back was toward him. She was not struggling and did not raise her voice. It was evident to Charlie she did not like either soldier and was being coaxed into the vehicle. Finally, she turned toward him.

Marie! He recognized her immediately. She was older but just as beautiful. He took a step then caught himself.

She continued to speak with the tall Russian. Neither noticed him standing nearby. Not wanting to take any chances, he stepped back into the shadows but continued to watch.

Marie's voice grew louder. Bystanders turned to watch.

"Mind your business," the other soldier said to those who stopped. He had an accent far worse than Charlie's. That told him the soldiers had to be MGB. Only an intelligence operative would have bothered at all to learn the language.

Finally, all conversation stopped, and Marie got in the vehicle. The tall soldier got in the front seat and the other in the back with Marie. Charlie watched as the car disappeared around the plaza down a side street. He knew it would be a waste of time to try to follow. He turned, walked up the steps, and entered the castle.

The guard stopped him immediately.

"Comrade Benes," he said.

"ID," the guard replied.

Charlie offered his passport, and the man accepted it.

"Welcome home, Comrade," he said. "What is your business in Austria?"

"I'm a mining engineer," he said.

The man nodded and handed the passport back. "Comrade Benes is gone. Can someone else help you?"

"Take me to her desk, and I'll leave a message."

"Come." Charlie followed the man up the large staircase and into the room. "Here," he said, then turned and departed without another word. Charlie sat down, picked up a pen, and pretended to write as he surveyed the room. He did not see Jürgen, so he stood and slowly walked through the small groups congregating in the large room. He shook hands, politely smiled, and nodded his way back to the main entrance.

Where could he be? Charlie had to assume something went wrong. He suspected the guards were holding Jürgen somewhere.

Out in the corridor, he stopped a young woman. "I must find security," he said. "I have information for them."

"Through there," the young woman said, pointing to a door at the far end of the hall.

"Thank you."

She nodded politely and marched off down the stairs.

Charlie felt for the automatic as he walked slowly toward the door. It was unlocked. He entered, not knowing what to expect, but he had to take a chance that Jürgen was inside the room.

There, sitting surrounded by two armed men, was Jürgen. No one was speaking. The men turned to Charlie.

"What do you want?" the oldest looking of the two asked. He held a short Russian machine gun at his side.

"I wish to take the prisoner," Charlie said in Russian. Both men looked at him with empty stares, but he could see they recognized the Russian language. "The prisoner is mine." Not understanding, the men still nodded politely. *Good,* he thought. *They know to respect Russian.* "I have been ordered to take the prisoner," he now said in Czech. "He is the father of Comrade Benes, and he has been put into my safe care until she returns."

"What is your authorization?"

"I just spoke with the major outside, so the official release will arrive this afternoon from the Russian liaison."

One of the men said, "Major Andropov ordered us to hold him until further notice." The two men looked at each other. It was apparent to Charlie that they did not know what to do.

"That was before the major saw me outside. When he took the woman, we talked, and he ordered me to take the prisoner."

"Comrade Benes...Yes, they just left with her on important business. Where is your uniform? You say you are MGB. Prove it."

"I'm not military but sent from the directorate and General Pavlov personally. Here is my identification." He pulled his passport from his pocket and hoped they would accept it without looking. His other hand rested on his weapon.

"That's unnecessary, comrade. After all, we are allies, yes?"

"Yes." Charlie could see they were not soldiers. "Then what do you want me to tell General Pavlov when he learns this man is not in our custody, that he is not protected?"

"He is your prisoner. Take him, but we must have something in writing," the man who seemed to be in charge replied. "With your signature."

"Give me paper and a pen, and I will write it and sign it." Charlie wrote out the order in Russian and signed it "Andre Vavrock, Major." He neglected to say what army.

Jürgen watched the conversation unfold without uttering a word.

"Benes get up and come with me," Charlie said. He made it sound like a command.

Jürgen stood.

"What section of MGB are you with?" the man asked, looking at the order.

Charlie stepped forward and grabbed Jürgen roughly by the shirt to pull him along. "Sorry, I only know how to write Russian. Special Intelligence Branch, MGB, assigned to

General Pavlov in Karlshorst," he said. "If that is clear, we will leave now. Come." He shoved Jürgen.

As quickly as the two could move without arousing suspicion, they were out the door. "Walk fast, Jürgen. We must get out of this building." When they reached the stairs, they slowed down and took the stairs in an orderly fashion.

"A counterrevolutionary," Charlie said to a guard as they passed him. "We must talk with him."

The man nodded without a word.

The number of people milling about in front of the castle had increased as they exited the building.

"Where do we go?" Charlie asked when they hit the street.

"Down that narrow street, turn left." Jürgen nodded toward the street nearest the café where Charlie had sat earlier.

When they reached an alley, they stopped. "Where did they take Marie?" Charlie asked. "I saw the Russians leave with her."

"I overheard them say Germany, to meet with General Pavlov."

Hearing that, Charlie's heart sank. "We can't rescue her there. Where will they hold her before they leave?"

Jürgen said nothing.

"How do we get her, Jürgen?"

"We don't, my friend. She is gone."

Charlie could only stare at him.

"We must get the child out of Prague. We can't help Marie. She..."

"I think there is something you are not telling me," Charlie said, with growing suspicion.

"She went willingly with the Russian soldiers. They did not force her."

Charlie was stunned. "Did you tell her I was in Prague?"

"I did not have an opportunity. They came as I was about to tell her where her child was."

"She knows nothing?"

"I told her only that Anna is safe." Visibly upset, Jürgen spoke softly. "We must get away, meet Frank, and leave the city quickly while we can. Come."

"Jürgen, my old friend, I must stay and see this through. But you take Anna and go. In the mountains, you will be safe, at least for the moment. When I've done what I came to do, I will meet you there. Go!"

Jürgen did not move. "What can you do? You don't know anyone. The city...They will capture you. Or worse, kill you."

Charlie put his arms around the older man. "Don't worry. I am not without resources, and I have an address." He smiled but knew that Jürgen saw through him. "I must do this. If I do not return, raise the child as your own. Good-bye, old friend." He turned and ran up the alley before Jürgen could say another word. Just before he entered a street, he turned one last time and waved.

Chapter 11

Charlie just walked, not knowing where, but he tried to avoid political activities and armed workers he saw. He hoped to familiarize himself with the city—the section called Old Town—and come up with some type of operational plan. He saw no bombed buildings or rubble of any kind that remained from the war, and when he inquired, local citizens told him that neither the Germans nor the Allies had damaged Prague. It seemed that, for whatever reason, both sides had spared the city.

When it was finally dark, he started his search for the one address he had. Marta was a long shot, but something about their earlier conversation compelled him to seek her out. At a small newsstand, he bought a current map. Using it handily, he found his way to his destination on Ovocny Trh, between Wenceslas Square and Old Town Square, with little difficulty. It was an historic and well-preserved section of the city.

He placed the slip of paper in his jacket pocket and knocked on the door. He waited several seconds and knocked again. Finally, he heard footsteps. The old lock clicked, and the door opened. The young woman he had met earlier stood in the open doorway. She broadly smiled when she recognized Charlie. "Good evening, Mr. Vavrock. Please come in." She stepped back and opened the door wide for him to enter.

"You remembered my name." He saw that she was dressed casually yet attractively in slacks and a thin silk blouse, which Charlie found very revealing. Her small breasts pressed against the thin, almost transparent material. Now she wore no makeup, which did not change his earlier opinion of her. *She has been waiting for someone*, he decided. *A client?*

"I almost forgot," he said, smiling. "Here. These are for you." Entering, he handed her a bag he was carrying.

Surprised, she reached out to take it. "Thank you." She looked inside and smiled. "And they're my favorites." She pulled out a kolache and, without waiting, took a large bite. "Delicious." She was effusive in her praise. "Thank you," she said again.

Charlie looked around the large flat and was impressed. It was well furnished and had high narrow windows that looked out on a plaza three stories below. "Nice place," he said. "Business must be good."

"It belonged to my father. I inherited it. The Nazis killed him in '43." She said it matter-of-factly, without a hint of sadness. Please sit down, and I'll make coffee to go with the kolaches."

"That would be nice." He continued to look around at the paintings and sculpture lining the walls. "Very beautiful." Examining several, he realized that Czech and Slovak artists had done them. Charlie looked up to find Marta watching him. "They're beautiful," he told her.

"Yes. Art that Goring did not steal," she replied.

"What is it you do, Marta? Or are you just rich?" He was pleasantly surprised, having expected to find a place more akin to a brothel.

She laughed. "My husband is wealthy, as was my father, so I am taken care of, as the Americans say." She sat beside him and poured coffee.

"I wouldn't know what the Americans say, but I hope your husband does not take offense to me visiting you."

She looked at him mischievously. "I have not seen my husband in more than two years...since the end of the war. Please don't concern yourself with him. He was nothing but a fascist playboy and a collaborator. Now I spend his money as I want. But enough of my life. Please tell me about you."

Charlie told her about his studies in Moscow, his service in the Red Army during the war. Everything he knew from his college days studying Russian or from Gregor Zerenowsky, the Ukrainian. As he rattled on, he began to wonder if she was buying it.

At first, she said nothing. Finally, "You are a very good liar, Charles Stanek from Milwaukee, Wisconsin."

Charlie's jaw dropped. He stared at her without speaking, and then saying in an even voice, "Charles Stanek? I think you mistake me for someone else." He decided quickly; the woman would have to die.

"I don't make mistakes." She stood and walked into another room. Charlie felt for his automatic. *Another one of Pavlov's agents?* He was prepared.

When Marta returned, she carried a manila envelope. She looked at him with her deep blue eyes and smiled. "Don't worry, Mr. Stanek. You are among friends." She handed him the envelope.

"How do you know my name?" He kept his grip on the automatic.

"Please relax, and I will tell you." She was looking at his hand.

Charlie's hand eased off the weapon. He looked at her. "Talk."

"I was contacted by Henry. I think you know him and have met him. Yes?"

"We met in Istanbul."

Marta nodded. "Before the war, Henry lived in Prague. He was one of the very fortunate Jews to escape the death camps. He avoided Auschwitz by hiding in the forests with partisans, and later, in 1944, he went west to serve with the Americans. He worked for your government, I think. The OSS with General Donovan." She paused to collect her thoughts. "He was one of your experts on Central Europe, and he later served with Allen Dulles in Switzerland."

"Does he live here in Prague?"

"No, he has moved to Palestine. He only took this assignment because the Americans asked. He contacted me by messenger. The Jews have their own network here, but that is breaking up as most who survived the war have left for America or Palestine. Probably, you will never see Henry again."

"Your history lesson has been very interesting, but what is your role in all this?"

"You Americans are so impatient, and we Europeans love to tell our stories," she said. "He asked me to assist you, but only this one time. We cannot meet again, or the MGB will discover us."

"What do you know of my mission?"

She ignored his question. "During the war, I met many Nazis. Like I already told you, my husband was a fascist...and a philanderer, I must add. However, he gave me opportunities to meet the Nazis. I knew Eichmann. Reinhardt Heydrich was a lover before we assassinated him, of course. Killing him cost us dearly. Do you know of the village of Lidice?"

"I have heard."

"I even knew Goring. I avoided him. His sexual perversion was not to my liking." She smiled.

"You were an agent?"

"After the murders at Lidice, our underground resistance was changed, but we continued to supply the Americans and British with valuable information through Switzerland, mostly. Your work in the mountains was part of the information I personally supplied to Dulles. So, Charlie, we have worked together for many years. It's all about secrecy, yes?"

"How can you help me now?"

"Look around you. Is this not a comfortable place to hide while both Czech and Russians search for you?"

"Are you certain they know I'm in Czechoslovakia?"

She smiled broadly. "Oh, Charlie, you are so naive. Then it was Germans. Now I share my bed with Russians. You men never change. Nazi, Communist, or American, it does not really matter when it comes to the bedroom," she said. "You men love to talk, and I am a good listener."

"A Russian told you?"

"Trust me. They know you are in Prague, and they have taken the woman to Berlin."

"So, you are suggesting I stay here?"

"For the night," she replied. "It could be worse."

He looked at her, appreciating her beautiful, lithe body while considering the offer. "Yes, it could certainly be worse."

The time was growing late, and the long day was catching up to him, but he was still ready for anything the evening offered.

She reached out to touch his hand. "First, I have things I must give to you. Business before pleasure, eh?" She reached over for the envelope, opened it, and extracted the contents. A passport, American dollars, and a key fell onto the sofa.

Charlie picked up the passport and opened it. He saw that the name was again Czech, but different. Edvard Konacek from Pilsen. He held up the key. "For?"

"It is to a safe house in another part of the city. You can stay there. You will leave me information on Pavlov in a special hiding place you will find. This is the address." She unfolded a small slip of paper. "You must memorize it then I will destroy the paper. Give me your old passport, and I will destroy it as well. It has served its purpose."

"A thousand American dollars? Why?"

"That will take you a very long way. Everyone is now buying dollars. Rubles are worthless outside of the Soviet Union."

"Well, I guess we've taken care of our business," Charlie said, sliding closer.

Marta did not move. "I love foreplay," she said. "But first. One more piece of business."

"Yes?"

"Be careful when you find this woman called Marie Benes. We cannot verify where her allegiances are, but we do know that she is a Communist. Henry knew her, having met her during the war. At the time, she was with the Soviet Army in Slovakia. He has told me never to contact her."

That supported what Charlie already suspected.

"To answer your earlier question, I know only that you are an agent getting information about Soviet intentions. I want to know nothing of your personal business."

Charlie accepted that. "The two may conflict, but I can give you one piece of information you can pass on to Washington."

She moved closer. He did not know if she wanted him or was anxious to hear what he had to say.

"Please, tell me."

"While in the mountains, I saw a Russian armored column on the road."

"The Russian Army is everywhere."

"They were on the Czech side of the border and moving slowly west. I think they were preparing to move on Prague if they were called."

"They have my country, and it seems they are prepared to hold it," Marta said. "Regardless of who runs our government, the Communists or the Democratic Party, the Russian Army will cut us off from the west."

Seconds passed, but it seemed like an hour. Neither spoke while they sipped their coffee. "Are you married? Do you have any children?" Marta asked.

"No, but I do have a place I call home."

"In America?"

"In the Australian Outback, on a large sheep station."

She stared at him.

"In the central part of the country. It's mostly desert; still, there's something magical about the place."

"No wife. That's good." She took his hand. "Come, Charles Stanek, tonight is for love." She led him into her bedroom.

He began to undress in the shadows. Before he could get his shirt off, she stood before him, naked, her body glistening in the dim light. She reached out to help him with his clothes... and to touch him. Soon, both were naked.

"I like you," she whispered. Her hands were all over his body. They kissed.

Charlie wrapped his arms around her and lifted her. Marta groaned as he laid her on the bed, his body pressing against hers.

Suddenly, there was a pounding at the door, startling both.

"What?" Charlie turned and dove for his weapon lying on the floor.

"I will see who it is. Stay here." Marta got up, reached for her thin robe, and quickly left the room. She closed the door behind her.

Not bothering to dress, Charlie held his automatic tightly. He quietly opened the door an inch, kneeled, and watched in the darkness of the room, prepared for anything.

"Who is it?" She said without opening the door. "It is too late. Go away."

"It's Frederick. Open up! I demand it!" the voice from the hallway said.

Marta quickly looked back at the bedroom door. She saw the two coffee cups still on the table. "Wait! I must find my robe." She ran to pick up the cups and deposit them in the kitchen.

She looked around again. "I'm coming." She unbolted the door and opened it slowly.

"Who are you hiding here?" A well-dressed, older man forced his way in. "I know a man is here. Or is it a woman tonight?"

"What do you mean?" Marta stepped back.

"Whore! Someone is here, and I will find him. The bedroom?" He grabbed her robe and jerked. It fell open. "Naked. Did I find you in the middle of a little tryst?"

"Get out! Now!" Marta tightened the sash. She stepped in front of him to block his way. "You have no right to come here."

He stopped to look at her. "No right? I have every right, woman."

"I will call the police."

"You will not." He walked toward the bedroom. "Maybe you have a woman hidden there? I should have known. You are nothing but a rich, self-indulgent whore."

Marta grabbed his arm to stop him.

The man turned, and with his backhand, slapped her hard across the face. The blow knocked her to the sofa.

"No, Frederick, stop!" Her nose began to bleed.

Raising his hand, he prepared to hit her again as she lay sprawled across the sofa.

"Touch her and I will kill you." Charlie stepped out of the bedroom, naked. He pointed his weapon at Frederick's head. "I warn you. One more move and I'll shoot."

Frederick froze. Marta regained her composure and, with her hand holding back her bleeding nose, fled across the room to stand behind Charlie.

"Look at me and raise your hands high in the air," Charlie said.

The intruder, still wearing a fedora and dark trench coat, turned to see Charlie for the first time. He immediately saw his nakedness and smiled. "Whore," he repeated a third time. "Your lover?"

"Get down on your knees," Charlie ordered.

The man at first refused, knowing what that meant. Finally, he accommodated him. "You would kill me for my jealousy? Because this woman has betrayed me?"

Charlie turned to Marta. "Who is this bastard, and what shall we do with him?"

"He misunderstood my intentions," she said. "Please, don't hurt him."

Charlie thought for a brief moment. "Get out of here before I change my mind. Don't ever come back. This woman belongs to me now." He spoke only in Czech.

Frederick stood and walked to the door. "Whore," he called out again as he opened it. Stepping into the corridor without looking back, he soon disappeared down the darkened staircase.

They watched him leave, and then Marta ran to slam and lock the door. "Thank you," she said.

"Another lover?"

She sighed. "Men like Frederick do not understand that I cannot be possessed like a dog or piece of property merely because I sleep with them," she said. "Whiskey?" she asked. The question seemed to fit.

"A double." He still held the automatic in his hand.

She pulled a bottle of American bourbon and two glasses from a wooden cabinet. "For special occasions. I got it from an American colonel." She poured both glasses to half. He noticed her hand tremble slightly.

"A whore? Perhaps," she said, taking a hearty sip. "But I will live my own life, and I don't care who's running this country."

"I believe you." He took a long swallow also. "Will he create trouble for you? Go to the police and file a complaint against me?"

"No, I don't think so. If I did, I would have had you shoot him." She said it directly, without any display of emotion.

Charlie looked at her, struck by the coldness in her voice. He threw the remainder of his drink down in two gulps.

"Come, my American friend." She set her drink down and smiled at him seductively. "We have unfinished business." They walked hand-in-hand into the bedroom.

Charlie still held the automatic in his other hand.

"I love men with hard rods," she said, looking down at his gun, but you won't need it in here."

Chapter 12

The sun shone brightly through the high window, waking Charlie. He turned slowly and saw that he was alone. *What time?* He found a small dresser clock. 11 a.m. He rose to look around the room. "Marta," he called. "Marta." No response. He got out of bed, looked for his trousers, found them on the floor, and slipped them on. He saw his weapon on a chair, grabbed it, and headed for the other room.

"Marta," he called again. Still, there was no answer. That worried him. He sat in a stuffed chair and waited. *I must move, but to where?*

Soon he heard footsteps. They seemed to be coming from outside the kitchen. He got up and walked into that room, pistol in hand, and was prepared to greet anyone who came through the back door.

The door opened, and Charlie quickly slipped into the shadows behind it. The person entered carrying bags.

"Marta?"

She turned and smiled. "Always ready. That is good. However, you don't need to worry, and I've brought food."

"No servants for you? I'm surprised," Charlie replied.

"Ha! The workers are liberated now, and they are in charge. Didn't you see that in the square?"

Charlie laughed. "When they see they must still have a paycheck to live, they will think differently."

"Sit and eat. I will make coffee." She set the bread and jam on the table. Standing over the stove, she began to brew coffee.

"You've made things much too comfortable for me, but I must go and finish my work." He tore off a large piece of bread and smeared jam all over it. He was too hungry to wait for coffee.

She turned to look at him. "What is your plan? I think you have none."

"I will go to Berlin."

"Don't be a fool. You would walk into an MGB trap and be done. Nothing would be accomplished."

"What do you suggest?"

"Wait here with me where it's safe," she said. "I'll use my contacts. We will learn when the woman returns to Prague, and she will do so soon. I'm certain."

"How can you be so sure?"

"Because you are here, and they know she is the only way to capture you."

Two days passed. Charlie paced the apartment. *I'm trapped*, he thought. *I can't stay here, and I can't leave.*

"Patience, patience," Marta told him each day.

That afternoon she announced that she had to go out, which surprised Charlie. "Why?" he asked. "You never go out in the afternoon."

"I must visit a friend." She went into the bedroom, changed into a dress, put on makeup, prepared to leave.

"How long will you be gone?" He saw the makeup and knew it was for a man. "For the night?"

She stopped at the door and looked at him. "There are things you should not know about me." She opened it and was gone.

For the remainder of the afternoon, he was uncomfortable and felt anxious. His primary concern was that the woman had betrayed him. The automatic was never far from his side. *I must take a walk*, he finally decided. He looked at himself in his Slovakian worker's garb and decided he had to change his disguise. He remembered that Marta said her husband periodically stopped by, and he wondered if he left clothes in the wardrobe. He went into the bedroom and opened her wardrobe door. He saw several men's suits and casual slacks, but what surprised him was that the suits were of different sizes. Searching further, he discovered the same with women's clothing.

He smiled. Then he laughed. *Everything about the woman is strange.* He found a suit he liked and tried it on. A perfect fit. That was curious because from the photos in the apartment, he knew her husband was much shorter and heavy.

Dressed in the best of the clothing that fit him, he prepared to go out. Deciding he needed a coat for the evening, he found a trench coat and hat in the foyer closet. They fit. *Again, a perfect fit*, he thought. *I wonder how many guests she sees.*

Before he left, he hid his clothing, toiletries, and everything else that identified him. Most importantly, he unlocked the back door to get back in. With the automatic safely tucked in his belt, he was out the door.

Charlie had plenty of money, both Czech and American, giving him the freedom to go anywhere in the city. He hailed a taxi.

"First, across the old bridge to Zbrashav Castle, then to the government buildings. I want to see everything," he said. "I have the money."

The cabby nodded. "Bad times for a tourist, but I take you everywhere."

"Thank you. I have a new job here as an engineer."

The cabby took him around the old city, explaining what each building was as they passed it. "I've lived here for thirty years. I fight for the Emperor in Italy during the Great War. Then, after the betrayal, I take Nazi generals around town. Today it is the Russians."

"Do you see many Russians here?" Charlie asked. He was mastering the dialect, and this man seemed not to notice his accent. "I haven't seen any soldiers."

"They're here, my friend. I'll show you where they are. MGB, I think."

"In the old city?"

"Near the old bridge."

They crossed Charles Bridge. "I see them coming and going. Not many and mostly officers. Be careful of them."

Charlie filed that away. "I'll get out at the train station," he said.

Several blocks later, the driver pulled up outside a large but very old building.

Charlie paid him handsomely and jumped out. "I appreciate the tour. When I need you again, where I can I find you?"

"Same place."

He entered the train station and walked to the arrival and departure board. Carefully, he read the schedule. *Trains to Bratislava leave on the hour. That is good.* Next, he scouted out security. He saw police posted at each entrance but no soldiers or militia, and there did not appear to be ID checks on the platforms. Charlie bought a coffee, sat at a small table, and watched the people come and go. He saw that there were few travelers. When he finished, he got up and departed the station for where, he had not yet decided.

"You there," someone called.

Charlie turned and saw that the police officer at the entrance was waving at him.

"Come here," the police officer ordered.

He did as instructed. "Is there a problem?"

"No problem. I make random ID checks." The police officer looked Charlie over. "May I see some form of identification?"

Without another word, Charlie handed him his new passport.

"Edvard Konachek. Do you live in Prague?"

"Pilsen."

"What is your business here?"

"I'm an engineer. I am looking for work."

The police officer handed him back the passport. "There is no work. The Americans will spend millions on Germany, but we will get nothing. The Russians are to blame. They tell the rich Americans they want nothing. Stupid, I think."

Charlie nodded. He stuck the passport back into his coat pocket and continued walking. He had been gone from the apartment for several hours, and it was getting late. He decided to return by foot, believing that if he knew a place well, had walked it, he could master it and survive.

About halfway back to Marta's flat, he stumbled on a neighborhood near Old Town Square where there appeared to be some nightlife. Not Chicago or New York, but there were live music and loud talk. He entered a tavern where the music was very loud and made his way to the bar to order a beer. Standing at the mahogany, he casually scouted the place. Groups of young people congregated near where a band played Polka music. They were dancing and seemed to be having a good time. He wondered if they were part of the workers' militia he had seen on the square two days earlier. *To be back in Milwaukee again*, he thought whimsically.

Charlie sadly recalled his college days at the University of Chicago, when he would return home to Milwaukee on weekends. That was when his parents were both alive. He thought of his mother, a tall raw-boned woman with long golden hair always tied in a knot. She loved to dance, and he remembered that she would kick up her heels with great joy to every Polka tune. Sometimes his father joined her on the floor, but most often, she just got out there and danced with whoever was available. The thought of her dancing in a Milwaukee beerhall made him smile.

Those tragic memories were still so very vivid in his mind. He considered the terrible disease that eventually killed her. The doctors called it a woman's problem. Cancer, he knew. After his mother's passing, his father lost all interest in living. He died a year later during Charlie's senior year of college. He would always believe it was from a broken heart. He would never forget papa and mama.

His father's death left just Charlie and his younger sister, with no other relatives in the country. Charlie lost contact with her after Donovan sent him on the mission to Indochina in '45. Emma had married and moved to Omaha during the war. Home on leave following his return from Europe, he traveled to Omaha to locate her. He found her and her husband, who worked at the airbase, after much searching. He spent several days with her family, which then included two children—a boy and a girl. He was reassured to know that she and her family were safe, untouched by the insidious world of espionage in which he worked.

Charlie continued watching the crowd of young people. Marta? He saw her near a group of drinkers who caught his attention with their loud, boisterous behavior. She was sitting in a secluded corner with a younger woman. He was surprised by her choice of hangouts. Charlie watched them and saw that they were more than acquaintances. They were sitting very close, and the young woman had her arm around Marta. She leaned over and kissed Marta on the cheek. They embraced, and as far as Charlie could tell, passionately. Was the young woman a lover?

He finished his beer, paid his bill, and got up. He took one more look in Marta's direction and headed for the door. He had another thought. Was this woman one of her contacts? He turned again to get a better look at the young woman. At that moment, Marta turned. Their eyes met. Charlie quickly turned his head and continued toward the exit. The last thing he wanted was for Marta to think he was spying on her.

Outside, he took a deep breath of fresh air and began walking toward the apartment.

"Edvard! Edvard!" someone called. Charlie kept walking.

"Edvard, stop!" he heard again. Realizing this was his new name, he stopped and turned.

Marta ran toward him.

He watched her, and two steps behind her, the woman he saw Marta with inside the tavern. The woman was taller than he had initially guessed, and not as plump. She wore her hair short and was dressed much like the young people he saw in the square. He wondered what Marta was doing with her.

Marta reached him and stopped, out of breath. "Were you spying on me?" she asked.

"I was looking for a beer and some fun, so I stopped at the first place with music," he said. "I didn't intend to ruin your fun." He looked at the other woman and back to Marta.

She winked at him. "I can share," she said.

Charlie had no idea what that meant. "I'm returning to your flat," he said.

The young woman wrapped her arms around Marta as soon as she reached the two. "Marta darling, who's your friend?"

"Edvard from Pilsen," Marta replied. "He's an old friend who is staying for several days."

"My name is Louisa." She stuck out her hand.

"My pleasure," Charlie replied. The three began walking away from the tavern. "How do you know Marta?"

Louisa held Marta's hand and leaned on her for support.

Marta reached over with her other hand to grab Charlie's, and they walked three abreast down the street.

"We drink together and dance together," Louisa replied.

"I'm sorry if I disrupted your evening."

"Don't pout. We'll go to my apartment and have a drink."

Charlie looked at her, perplexed. "Is that safe?"

"What could be safer?" Marta replied. "Louisa serves with the workers' militia. She will protect us, eh?"

"I certainly will," Louisa said. "Does it bother you if a woman protects you?"

Charlie noticed she was slurring her words. "I would be honored. Will you guard our door all night?"

Both women looked at him. Marta smiled. "I don't think she has that in mind."

"We will lock the door. Will that be enough...Edvard?" She stopped to let Charlie and Marta walk ahead of her. She looked appreciatively at him. "I think I like you. We will have a night of fun."

By the time they reached Marta's apartment, Louisa was sober, or Charlie thought she was. "How long have you lived in Prague?"

"All my life," Louisa replied.

"How long is that?"

"Twenty years."

Inside, Marta poured everyone a drink from her bourbon.

Louisa coughed, not used to spirits stronger than beer. "What is it Americans say?"

Standing, she wobbled slightly on her feet.

"Down the hatch," Charlie said, steadying her by wrapping his arm around her chest.

Marta turned off the lights and lit a single candle.

Charlie easily felt Louisa's full breasts under her shirt while he steadied her. She wore no bra. They were large but firm.

Louisa looked at him and smiled. "Down the hatch." She threw the bourbon down in one gulp.

Charlie watched her handle the drink, wondering what would happen next.

She collapsed onto the sofa. "Sit beside me, please." She took hold of Charlie's hand and pulled him down beside her. "Did you like what you felt?" she asked.

Charlie nodded appreciatively. He did not know what else to do.

Louisa slowly unbuttoned her shirt, and then slid it off. "Do you like?"

Charlie smiled broadly, looking, but said nothing. Her breasts were large, he thought, firm with her nipples erect, staring him in the face.

"Want to see more?" Not waiting for a reply, she jumped up, undid her belt, and fumbled with the buttons on her slacks. She dropped first her slacks then her panties, kicking them across the room. Before he could react, Louisa stood just inches from his face. She was naked. She pulled him toward her while thrusting her flat stomach and broad thighs fully at him. Her lust both surprised and overwhelmed him. He stood, and she began to undress him. He felt her hands on his skin. They were warm and soft.

"What is this?" She held up his automatic.

"These are dangerous times. I bought it to protect myself."

"I like a man who carries hard steel. Like this." She reached into his trousers and roughly grabbed his penis, holding it in her hand.

Aroused, he kissed her on the lips while she tore at the remainder of his clothes. "We won't need those," she said, tugging at the buttons on his shirt.

Charlie enjoyed the hard foreplay—it was the perfect pastime to help him forget his predicament. He felt her soft, smooth skin. Beneath the bold exterior, he discovered a young, not unattractive woman with needs. Though she was clumsy and inexperienced, there was no doubt in his mind what she wanted.

She reached down again, this time with both hands to hold him.

He kissed her on the lips.

"Such a shy man," she said. They both laughed.

He did not notice that Marta had left the room earlier. She reentered to join the two lovers. She was naked. Playfully, she pushed Charlie and Louisa to the couch and jumped on top. Everyone laughed.

The three lovers, their bodies tied in knots, held each other close. Finally, they fell together on the floor. Their passion pulsated and heated the room. as they touched and explored each other's bodies.

The two women used their mouths and tongues expertly--in ways Charlie would never have dreamed of to enhance satisfaction for everyone. They were not selfish in fulfilling their desires. Knowing they had the whole night, they shared. First Louisa and finally Marta had her way with him, each allowing the other to feel Charlie inside her. With stamina that even amazed him, he held on and stayed upright, as only a young man could.

They awoke the next morning in the same positions they finally had collapsed in after their night of drinking and lovemaking. Charlie lay on his back with both women curled up along his sides. Everyone was still naked but under a heavy quilt. The temperature had dropped during the night.

"I think I will keep you," Marta said. She stood, looked around the large room to survey the damage. Charlie searched for his weapon. Louisa was still asleep.

"Now for breakfast." She walked into the kitchen and returned with two large pieces of bread. Charlie lay on the floor, just watching her. He was sad when he thought he would probably never have another night like the last.

"Is this the way things are done in America?" She handed him a piece of bread she had torn from a loaf. Louisa still slept, her breathing loud. Charlie looked at Marta and they both laughed.

"If they are, it's unknown to me."

"We have endured almost ten years of upheaval and war. If we did not find moments to hold and love each other, life would no longer be worth living. Those moments demand that we squeeze every second of passion and love into them. Please try to understand," Marta said. She sat beside Charlie on the couch. Louisa did not move from her position on the floor.

"I would never judge you. And you're right. I needed that time as much as you and Louisa."

Chapter 13

"Tomorrow, it will be time for you to leave," Marta told him that evening. They were alone again. Louisa had left earlier in the day. "I will have the information you desire. Then I will no longer be of service to you."

"Information on Marie?"

"No, not on the woman. I will have more on Pavlov and his men who come to Prague. That's all I can do for you."

"I'll be ready," Charlie said.

"You must forget that you were ever here. That is for my protection if you are captured."

"I understand," he replied. "We communicate through the safe house."

"You have everything you need. When you leave Czechoslovakia, go the way you came. It is the safest."

There was a knock at the door.

"Who were you expecting at this hour?" Charlie asked. They both looked at the door.

"You must leave. The back way," she told him, running into the bedroom in search of her robe. "Go to the safe house, and I will contact you in the morning. Go!"

Charlie grabbed his weapon, coat, clothes, and hat that lay on the back of a chair.

There was another knock, louder. "Marta," a voice said. Charlie, in the kitchen, recognized the accent—Russian. He looked at her.

"Andropov," she said. "Go!"

Charlie was at the back door when he heard her say, "Sergei, please, it's late. You must let a girl prepare herself." She looked at Charlie and saw that he was through the back door. She opened the front door to the Russian major.

"Sergei, my darling," Charlie heard. He quickly dressed and ran down the stairs, two at a time. When he reached the street, he walked in front of the stone building. There he spotted a vehicle parked along the street with a man at the wheel. Charlie walked slowly past and saw the man was asleep, snoring loudly.

Andropov...Pavlov's man, he thought, as he continued to walk. *Does that mean Marie has returned to Prague?*

Charlie had an idea. He found a tavern and waited there until the early morning hours, slowly sipping at mugs of beer, and killing time. Finally, he got up, paid his bill, and entered the deserted street, strolling back to Marta's building.

When he arrived, he saw that the driver had not moved the staff car from the location in front of Marta's apartment. The soldier was still behind the wheel and asleep. Charlie walked slowly by, turned, and made another pass. This time, he walked to the driver's open window and stopped.

He pressed the barrel of his automatic hard against the man's cheek. "Wake up," he said in Russian. "I must have this car. Get out."

"What? Who?" the soldier stuttered. He acted as if he could not believe what was happening to him.

When the driver, still half asleep, got out and stood, Charlie saw that he was about his size. "A perfect fit. Even better. Come." He pushed him along to an alley and ordered him to strip. He tore the soldier's shirt into long strips and used them to bind the man's hands snuggly behind his back. "This goes in your mouth," he told him. He stuck the remainder of the shirt in the man's mouth. He pulled him along back to the car, the man clad only in his trousers and shoes. Charlie opened the trunk. "Get in," he ordered.

The soldier hesitated. "No, no," he said.

"Get in now, or I'll shoot you dead. And if you make a noise, I'll kill you and your officer right here." He slammed the sedan's trunk, took off his shirt, put on the wool tunic and hat, and crawled behind the wheel.

Charlie did not have to wait long for Andropov to return. It was morning but still dark as he watched the Russian run from the building to the car. When he had almost reached the car, Charlie got out, intercepting him.

Andropov turned and recognized that this man was not his driver. "Who?"

Charlie stuck the driver's Tokorov pistol in Andropov's face before he could utter another word. "Get in. Behind the wheel." He quickly disarmed Andropov and pushed him into the driver's seat. He ran around to the passenger's side and got in.

"I know who you are. Stanek...," Andropov said. "What do you want from me?"

"Drive," Charlie said.

"Where?"

"You will drive to where Marie Benes is staying. Any tricks and I will shoot you."

"I don't know where..."

"Liar," Charlie said. He pressed the pistol against Andropov's head. "I saw you with her, so take me to her room."

They drove through the early morning shadows, over the old bridge, into the heart of the city. Charlie decided the Russian was one of the worst drivers with whom he had ever ridden. He ground gears each time he shifted and was constantly riding the brakes. Eventually, they reached their destination, or so Charlie believed.

"She lives here?" He looked around at the stone and brick buildings. "Who pays for this?" Charlie could not believe she lived in such apparent luxury.

Andropov looked at him. "Czechoslovakia has entered a new, exciting time, and she serves the people. Living quarters are happily provided for her."

Charlie laughed. "This better not be a trap, major."

They pulled into a circle and parked. "I'll get out first and come around for you. No tricks." He concealed his weapon, got out, and walked around the car.

"Let's go." He swung the door open and grabbed Andropov by the shoulder to pull him out. Just as they crossed the cobblestone street, two soldiers came out of the building. "You bastard," Charlie said.

Andropov said nothing.

"Open your mouth and I'll kill you right where we stand. Got it?" Charlie made sure Andropov knew his automatic was under his coat and pointed at his back.

The soldier nodded.

The two soldiers turned and walked in the opposite direction, paying no attention to them.

"Who are they?"

"I don't know. Czech soldiers. Maybe they live near here."

Charlie knew he was lying. He quickly recognized Russian uniforms. "Those were Russians, you bastard." He took

Andropov's arm and swung him around. "We're getting out of here."

"She's inside," the Russian said.

"I don't believe you," Charlie replied. He still held the weapon, pointed at Andropov's back.

Andropov purposely slowed his gait. "You cannot escape, Major Stanek. We have soldiers everywhere searching for you. Surrender now, and things will go easier. The woman and child will be safe."

"Shut up!"

They returned to the car and got back in. "Start it and drive."

Andropov did as Charlie ordered. "You will never survive this," he said.

"I said shut up." Charlie stared straight ahead. "You have one more chance. Drive to Marie Benes' living quarters. If you betray me again, I will kill you and your driver."

Again, they stopped in front of a tall brick building not far from the other. "She lives in a room on the fifth floor of that building, and she's there."

"Let's go," Charlie said. They repeated their movements. This time they entered the building. "We'll take the stairs."

"The building has an elevator and it's in operation."

"You would know, wouldn't you?" Charlie replied. "We walk." The two men climbed the steps to the fifth floor. When they reached the exit door, Charlie slowly opened it and pushed Andropov through, using him as a screen. The hallway appeared deserted.

"Which door?"

Andropov led him to a door halfway down the hall. Charlie listened through the door and heard nothing. He detected no sounds from anywhere. He looked at his watch—0530. *Surely, someone would be out of bed by this time of morning,* he thought, growing suspicious that he was walking into another trap.

He studied the Russian, looking for any sign that would betray him. Andropov's face was expressionless.

Andropov stared at Charlie, observing every move he made.

"Open the door," Charlie said. He would risk everything on a hunch that he had surprised the Russians and caught them unprepared for this moment. He stood directly behind Andropov, expecting anything.

The door slowly opened. "Who is it?" an older man's voice said from behind the door.

"Major Sergei Andropov. Let me in."

The door swung open. An old man dressed in a nightgown stood in front of them.

With Charlie pushing him, Andropov barged into the room. The old man backed away but said nothing.

"Get me Marie Benes. Now!" the major said.

The old man nodded and left the room.

Charlie looked around and saw no one else. He closed the door behind him and edged Andropov further into the flat.

"What do you want at this hour, major?" a female voice said. Both men turned to see a young woman enter in a robe. "Charles?"

"Marie?" His smile lit up the room. "It's really you?"

She ran to him. "Oh, Charles, I can't believe it is really you."

They embraced awkwardly, with the Russian watching.

"Fools," Major Andropov said. "You cannot escape me."

"You should not have come here. The Russians watch everywhere for you," she said.

"I came for you...and the child."

She looked hard at him. "Anna. Yes, my Anna. Where is she?"

"She is safe," he replied. "I will take you to her."

Marie looked at the Russian, then back to Charlie. "How?"

"I have a way. And the major here is giving me his car."

Andropov smiled. "How far do you expect to go?"

"Charles, you don't understand. I'm part of the government here. I can't..."

"A sham of a government. The Russians are now in charge of Czechoslovakia."

Marie did not reply but looked over at Andropov.

"Get ready now. We're leaving."

At first, Marie did not move, but when she saw how determined he was, she turned for the bedroom. "I will get some things. What do we do with Major Andropov? We can't hurt him."

"Why not?" he said. "If I shoot him right here, he will no longer be a bother for us. His plans for me are no better."

"If I live, I will find both of you," Major Andropov replied. "Maybe tomorrow or the next day, but I'm a very patient man."

"If you kill him, I will not go with you," Marie said. "I refuse to have his blood on my hands."

Charlie thought a moment, his weapon still pointed at the Russian's heart. "I'll tie him with the old man and leave them. Is there anyone else here?"

"No," Marie replied. "He is a widower."

"Bring me the old man, and then we'll get some rope."

Marie led the old man into the room. He said nothing, acting as if everything that was happening was routine for him. When they had secured both men with rope and strips of cotton, they prepared to leave.

"We must get out of the city," Marie said. "Where is Anna?"

"I will take you to her."

She looked at the two men lying on the floor, securely bound. "General Pavlov will be furious. He will hunt for us everywhere," she said.

"We'll deal with that monster later," he replied. "Let's get out of here." Charlie had no plan of escape, only get out of Prague, and go east toward the mountains. He figured he had maybe a two-hour head start at most, and Andropov would be on their trail. At some point, he would have to abandon the Russian's car.

They ran down the steps and into the car. Before they left, he dumped the driver in an alley. "This car is too obvious," he said. "We have to get rid of it now." He pulled over and they both got out.

Marie said nothing, content to follow his lead. Charlie thought that strange. "I know of a place, and I think it's near here. We can hide there for a couple of days," he said. "Let things blow over."

"Where is my daughter?" Marie did not move. "I want to go to her."

"She is close, at your aunt's, where Jürgen is caring for her. We'll get her in two days and go to Bratislava," Charlie lied. He knew well that her father and Anna had reached the mountains by now, but he thought if Marie believed Anna was in the city, it would make her compliance with his demands easier.

Marie reluctantly gave in and followed him down a side street. He was seeking out street signs to indicate where he was. He remembered the address that Marta had given him. "We're close."

"Anna is still in the city?" She seemed surprised. "With my father?"

"Why does that surprise you? He wouldn't leave without us."

"You have risked your life to get my child and me out of the country? Why?"

He stopped walking. "General Pavlov found me...Another story. He said he would kill you and Anna if I did not surrender to him."

"You have come all the way from America to rescue me?"

"Australia. I lived in Australia, but he found me even down there."

"Why does he want you so much that he would go to all this trouble?"

"He thinks I can identify American agents operating in Eastern Europe--the Rasputin network," Charlie explained. "Also, I escaped from him in Hanoi two years ago, and I think he bears a grudge. Bastards like him never forgive or forget."

"Can you identify them?"

"No, Zerenowsky never gave them to me."

"Tell Pavlov that. Plead with him. Then we will all be safe."

He stopped walking. "Do you really believe it's that simple?"

She stopped and looked at him but said nothing.

"To give him what he wants is to give him my life...and probably yours."

Marie did not reply. They continued walking. In a wealthier section of the city, Charlie finally located the address. He checked his pocket to make sure the key was still there. "Come, it's on the third floor." They entered the building and climbed the two flights of stairs. When they reached the door, he pulled his automatic before he inserted the key. He pushed Marie off to the side.

Charlie pushed the door open with his foot. After quickly scanning the room, he entered and carefully searched the other two rooms in the three-room flat. No one. He returned to the door and retrieved Marie. "It's clear," he said.

"Who lives here?" she asked.

"A friend," he replied.

"For your first visit to Prague, you have many friends. Americans?"

He did not reply. "Make yourself comfortable. We'll be here for a couple of days."

"Then what?" she asked. "Do you think we can escape from the MGB? Soon, I will be missed at my office."

He looked at her. "Just what kind of work do you do? Your father didn't seem to know. Or even who you worked for."

"I'm part of the government, the Gottwald government. We are the new Czechoslovakia. I do important work in security. They will look for me."

"Like what?" He sat down and set the weapon on a side table.

"I am the liaison between the prime minister and the Army."

"The Russian Army?"

"The Russians are our allies. When I must, we meet with them."

"Do you meet with General Pavlov?"

"We have met and spoken."

"About me?"

"About you. He says you are a threat to Russian and Czech security. You helped Russians betray their country."

"And they are all dead because of him," Charlie replied.

"Pavlov wants you badly. Are you certain there is nothing else he wants?"

Charlie could tell. Marie was probing him. "Like I already told you, I don't know anything. Never did."

"He said if you cooperate, he will help us, protect us."

"From who?" Charlie was amused. "He is my only enemy."

"No," she replied. "That is not true. Industrialists working with the West are our real enemies. Yours, too."

"Are you going to come with me to leave the country, Marie? I don't think that's on your agenda, is it?"

"You are still the love of my life, Charles."

"You didn't answer my question."

"I will go."

The way she said it made him uncomfortable. He wondered if he should trust her.

"What's your plan?" she asked.

"We will leave when it gets dark. Take the tram to the outskirts of the city."

"Then?"

"Then we will arrange transportation to Bratislava. If we can make the mountains, the Russians will never find us. I have passports to cross into Austria, and then Switzerland."

"That's not much of a plan of escape. I'm sure General Pavlov will have figured out where we are and what we're going to do by then."

"We have to stay a step ahead of him. We must move fast."

"What of Anna? When do we get her?"

"Soon." He felt uncomfortable revealing Anna's location just yet.

"What happens to me when we get to America or wherever you live? I mean nothing to them."

Charlie looked at her. He did not have an answer but had to tell her something. "You'll be free to do whatever you want. You can stay with me or not."

"Oh, Charlie... What about Anna? Will she be left behind?"

"Never."

Marie said nothing.

Chapter 14

General Pavlov listened patiently while Major Andropov explained what had happened. They spoke over the telephone. "Good, good. The trap is set," he replied. "I will go to Prague tomorrow and wait."

The general dialed another number and listened to it ring. Finally, a voice on the other end answered. "I must have my car ready in the morning," the general said. "And I need additional security. Order Czech intelligence to provide us with men and a location with lockup." He listened impatiently to the voice on the line. "Prime Minister Gottwald will authorize it. Yes, I'm certain." He hung up.

He struggled back to his desk to sit. The cancer was getting worse by the day, and the medicine the doctors gave him did not seem to work any longer. He coughed long and hard. Then, he lit another American cigarette.

How should I handle Major Stanek? He considered. *When I tell him, what will happen to his woman and child if he does not cooperate, he will accept my offer. If he does not agree, I will have to execute him. He cannot remain alive.*

The road from MGB headquarters in Karlshorst, near Berlin, to Prague, was rough, with places still not repaired permanently from bomb damage during the war. The Russian staff car the general rode in only made things worse. "Can't they build a comfortable automobile?" he growled at the driver. But he still made good time, arriving in Prague later that morning. They were alone, and no other staff or cars had made the trip with them. The general liked it that way. It offered him more flexibility and privacy.

"Stop here." He grabbed his hat and buttoned his tunic. Three soldiers ran to the car to greet him. He thought he saw Major Andropov among them.

A private opened the door for him while the other two saluted. "Welcome to Prague," Major Andropov said.

"Prague, yes." He returned their salute. "Are my quarters prepared as I've ordered?"

"Yes, general, everything is ready," Sergei replied. All four men fell in step. The two lowest ranking walked in front.

"And Stanek?"

"He and Comrade Benes will get the child and flee to the east."

"You sound very certain, Sergei. Why?"

"I have a tail on them. They spent the night in an empty flat. They departed early this morning, took a tram. The woman is cooperating as we planned and signals us whenever she can."

"Where did they go?"

"To the outskirts of the city. To get the child."

"When will you apprehend him?"

"We have a plan," Sergei said proudly, "A good plan."

General Pavlov stopped before they entered the building with the other soldiers. "Never underestimate this man. He is full of tricks and has many skills."

"I understand, sir." Sergei stood beside Pavlov. "When they pick up the child, we will make our move."

"Where is the child?"

"We are not certain. The child was taken away in the night, but Comrade Benes has an aunt in Prague. We believe she is there with the grandfather."

"You believe she is there?"

* * *

Charlie, with Marie in tow, took the tram to the train station. The time was midday and pedestrian traffic crowded the streets. A light mist fell.

"Are we leaving the city?" she asked.

"Yes." That had thrown her off balance. He could tell she did not expect to be leaving the city this quickly and without Anna.

"What about Anna?" she asked. "We cannot go without her."

"She is safe outside the city, in the country."

She stopped. "In the country? My father."

"Jürgen has Anna in a safe place. When it is time, we will get her."

"What do you mean?"

Without answering her, he bought two tickets for Pilsen.

"Why Pilsen?" she asked.

"We must get out of Prague." He took her by the arm, threw their single piece of luggage on, and lifted her into the tram. He found them a seat near the exit. "Stay here." He got off on the other side and walked around.

Something had been bothering him since they left the flat. Leaving lights on, they had gone down a back flight of stairs, through an alley, and walked to the station, avoiding the main streets. He did not see anyone, but still, he felt the MGB was watching him. They were close. He was sure of it.

He stood in the shadows and waited, his hand never far from the automatic under his coat.

Within seconds, two men came around a corner. They were dressed as civilians, but Charlie could tell. The way they walked—always marching. They were looking for someone—him. He followed them. The tram began to move.

The two men jumped on, but in another car. Charlie ran around that car to return to Marie. He could only hope they did not see him.

"We have to get off," he said. "Now!" He grabbed her and the small bag. He jumped onto the platform, pulling her along. "Run." They got up and ran for the nearest street. A block away, they rounded a corner of a large building. Charlie turned, looked back at the platform, and waited. He heard Marie's breathing behind him. "You okay?"

"What's going on?" she asked.

"MGB following us." He turned to her.

"How could they know?"

"I was about to ask you the same question."

"No, Charles. I would never betray you."

"They think we're going for Anna. How did they know that? Tell me." He grabbed her by the shoulders. "Tell me."

"I told Andropov my child will be staying at my aunt's. That's where my father would take her. He knows I would never leave the city without her."

"Why tell that monster anything?"

"You don't understand because you live in a different world. Here, we survive the best we can. I don't like the Russians, but I must work with them. They are our comrades. That is the new Czechoslovakia I live in."

"Comrades...?"

"Yes, comrades," she replied. "Here, you are the enemy, not them."

"How can I trust you?"

"I told you I would go. I will not betray you."

Charlie thought for a moment turning to look again at the platform. He did not see the two men. *She already has betrayed me*, he thought, distrusting her. He tried desperately to come up with a new plan.

"There is only one way to be free of them," he said. "You must go to Bratislava." He turned to Marie. "Alone. Find your father. I will stay here. They won't suspect that, so I have the element of surprise on Andropov."

"What about my Anna?"

"She is with your father...there."

Her surprise quickly turned into a smile. "Oh, Charles."

"Go, but travel on the roads. Stay off the railroad. They will be watching there."

They embraced. She kissed him on the cheek, then on the lips. "You are the love of my life. I never lied about that."

"Good-bye," he said.

Within seconds, she was gone. Charlie stood, staring after her. He wondered if he would ever see her or the child again.

Charlie needed to locate Andropov, and he hoped he could find him alone. *He must sleep, but where?* Suddenly, he had an idea. Marta. She would know his habits. After all, she was screwing him. He jumped on the next tram to return to central Prague.

Charlie knocked on Marta's door, not knowing who he would find with her. On the first rap, there was an answer.

"Who is it?" a female voice asked.

"Open up," Charlie replied. "I must speak with you."

Slowly, the door opened. "What do...?"

He forced his way in. Partially clothed, she backed up and hid behind the door.

Charlie looked her over, one breast exposed. "Expecting a lover at this time? You are a busy lady."

"What do you want?" she said. "I told you it was too dangerous for you to return."

"I need information...on Andropov."

Marta tightened the sash on her robe and walked to the middle of the room. "I can't help you."

"You will," he replied. "I must know where he stays when he's in Prague. Tell me, and I'll leave."

"He stays here. I don't know of any other place."

He took a step toward her and grabbed her sash, pulling it slowly until the robe hung open. She was naked underneath. "You will tell me."

"You don't scare me. I've been threatened by the best." She allowed the robe to slip off and fall on the floor. "But try. I may enjoy it."

"Andropov and I will meet at some point. Do you want me to tell him you're a double agent as well as a whore?"

She stared at him. "You wouldn't. You would risk hurting the Americans. They need my assistance."

"If they must rely on you alone to track Soviet activities, they're in big trouble. And remember, I'm an independent operator. I don't give a damn about the Americans."

"Sit down and I'll get us a coffee." She picked up the robe and walked into the small kitchen. "You are a very dangerous man, Charles Stanek."

"No, I just have nothing more to lose."

"The child...and woman?"

"They are gone. Hopefully, where it's safe."

"You've been busy."

She returned with two cups. "This is the last of my coffee, so enjoy it."

"Talk to me."

"He stays near MGB offices in the center of the city. It is well-protected."

"A room? Apartment?"

"When not with me, he stays in a small room on the third floor of an old building. I'll get the address for you."

"Does he stay alone?"

She smiled. "There, as far as I know."

"When is the best time to pay him a visit?"

"You're crazy."

"I have no choice."

"Evening, after dark. He arrives late to change, I think."

"Then that's when I talk with him."

"I have more information for you."

"What?"

"His superior, General Pavlov, has arrived in Prague just to interrogate you."

"Where does he stay?"

"You really are crazy," she replied. "I don't know, and a visit to him would be extremely dangerous, but not suicidal. Right, love?"

"Finding Andropov is the next step." He finished the coffee. "I'll go."

"As long as you're already here, stay until evening. We can find something to do until then." She set down her cup and slid closer to Charlie. "Anyway, it's too dangerous for you out there in daylight. I'm certain everyone is searching for you."

Feeling refreshed but still without a plan, Charlie did not take Marta up on her offer and instead left her flat by the back door. Darkness was descending on the city when he crossed the alley and began to walk. He carried his automatic and still had Andropov's pistol. Halfway down the block, he remembered the taxi driver from several nights earlier.

He retraced his route and found the cabby parked at the same location. "Hey, I need a ride," he said, waking the driver.

"Yes, yes, at your service, my friend."

Charlie threw open the door and jumped into the back. "Take me into the old city. I'll tell you where to stop."

"Yes, sir," the cabby replied. The old French Citroen jumped into gear and they were off.

Charlie noticed that there were far fewer armed civilians about. Evidently, the crisis had passed. He saw more soldiers and wondered what that meant. He handed the address to the driver. "In an alley near this place," he told him.

The driver looked at the address. "Here, not good," he said. "Too many Russians."

"I must get around without them noticing me."

The cabby nodded. "I know how," he said, smiling at his ingenuity.

He dropped Charlie in an alley beneath a steel fire escape. "Here."

Charlie got out, tipped the driver, and looked around studiously, trying to get his bearings. "Wait for me at the corner. I'll pay you double."

"I will wait one hour, my crazy friend."

"That's good." He walked to the street and saw where the driver was parking. *Good,* he thought and returned to the darkened alley. He pulled the steel-framed steps down and began to climb. One, two, three floors. He tried the window and it opened easily to a long dark hallway.

He carefully closed the window, pulled his weapon, and walked down the corridor. Room 306. He knocked and knocked again, but no answer. He tried the lock, shook the door, and noticed the play. *Old and weak,* he decided, remembering the old doors from the family apartment in Milwaukee. He raised the knob and shoved. The lock gave way and the door swung open without damage.

He entered and immediately locked the door again. He quickly looked around the room—an old bed covered with a dingy spread, a stuffed chair, a table. There was no indication that someone was living here--no clothes in the wardrobe, no cup, not even a toothbrush. Pulling out both weapons and setting them on the table within easy reach, he sat in the old stuffed chair. *Now, I wait.*

Charlie did not have to wait long. Thirty minutes later, he heard the creak of old wood, then a key turned. He waited in the darkness for the door to open.

Chapter 15

Robert Johnson stood in the open door of the DC-3 military transport. He was a small yet well-built man of middle age. He looked much younger, but the greying above the temples and crow's feet around his brown eyes betrayed his age. He felt the cold biting wind as sleet peppered his pale, hatless face like grenade shrapnel. The plane had just landed at the Frankfurt airport, and Johnson was the only passenger among the many-crated items destined for the Berlin airlift.

Johnson had flown directly from Andrews Air Base outside Washington after Army Command had directed him to wrap up the affair with Charles Stanek. They ordered him to bring in "Outlaw," as they had tagged Stanek, to be de-briefed, if he escaped the clutches of General Andre Pavlov. *Then I am to assist with deep cover to protect him. Those are Donovan's orders, but who is he? He is no one now that he has retired,* Johnson decided. He also knew that Stanek was a threat to both sides, a rogue operator who could ruin everything he had worked to set up. Johnson could not allow that to happen.

The mission was clear. Johnson smiled. He knew Charles Stanek, had worked with him on missions during the war, and saw him in action—a competent and dangerous man. Still, he did not expect trouble.

In the darkness, Johnson scanned the tarmac lined with military transports. He looked for his ride. In Washington, the Directorate briefed him that a Captain Josh Lipton, Army Intelligence, would be picking him up. As he stepped onto the wet tarmac, he saw headlights of an approaching Jeep. *"Must be him,* he thought. *I hope he's alone.*

His mission had to be top secret. Johnson and only he must take care of Stanek. National security was at stake. He hoped Lipton had been briefed.

The Jeep pulled up in front of the plane, and an American soldier jumped out and rushed over to where Johnson was standing.

"Captain Lipton as ordered, Colonel," the much younger man said, saluting.

Johnson smiled. "I'm a civilian now, Captain...since the war. Just address me as Robert.

"Yes, sir," the captain replied. "To the hotel, sir?" He automatically picked up Johnson's grip, his only piece of luggage, and placed it in the back of the Jeep. Both men got in and the Jeep roared off.

"First, I need all the latest intel on Outlaw's movements in Czechoslovakia. I need our contact there. You got that?"

"Yes, sir. Got it," he replied with a smile. Everything we have on Outlaw is in the sealed bag.

Johnson looked down at the small bag. "Good," he said. "Also, captain, when I go to the hotel, I want you to forget you ever saw me. I've arranged everything I need so I will no longer need the assistance of the US Army."

"I understand. A staff car is parked near the hotel for your use."

They arrived at the hotel within minutes. Johnson got out. "Good-bye captain," he said, grabbing his grip and the bag.

"Sir," Lipton replied. They shook hands and the Jeep roared off down the partially lighted street.

"You have a room reserved for Ronald Esp?" Johnson asked a young German woman behind the desk of the Hotel Bavaria.

The young woman looked through a register quickly. "Da, Ronald Esp," she said. "Velcome to Deutschland." An even younger man stepped forward, wanting to take the grip and bag.

"That won't be necessary," Johnson said. He held out his hand for the key.

The woman handed it to him.

"Dunka," he said with a smile, turned to leave, soon disappearing in the shadows of the dimly lighted corridor.

In his room, he sat the grip on the single bed and unpacked it—a single set of clothing, paper, pen, address book, and a holstered .38 Colt automatic with extra ammo. He laid everything out neatly on the bed. He slipped the weapon from the holster and examined it. Seeing that it was in order, he slipped it back into the holster. He then picked up the pen, paper, and his address book.

He sat down and began to write a note. "Have arrived to track target," he wrote. He then encrypted it to a special code, placed it in a small envelope, and stuck it in a hidden pocket. *The trap closes,* he thought grimly. Robert Johnson was not a killer, just a man with an important job to do.

He opened the bag to examine the few items in it. He looked at an earlier photo of Stanek in uniform, quickly reviewed several short communiques—one from Australia and another from the embassy in Prague. *Not much on him. More on his personality, contacts in Eastern Europe would have helped,* he thought, but he had only limited contact with

Donovan, who was not briefed on his mission. No one in Army Intelligence Services seemed to know much if anything about Stanek, so all Johnson had to go on was his own experiences with him during the war. And that contact worried him most.

He walked into the bathroom to the toilet, pulled matches from his trousers, took out the items individually, and burned each, allowing the ashes to fall into the toilet bowl. Finally, he pulled a long chain, flushing everything down.

He heard a commotion in the corridor outside his door. Quickly, he placed the holster with the weapon in his belt. The address book he inserted under the lining in his grip. He carefully walked to the door, listened, and then opened it just enough so he could see down the corridor.

"Hey, American?" someone called. "Hey, join the party." Johnson saw that the man was dressed in a US Army uniform.

"Yes, thank you," Johnson replied. He closed the door, looked around quickly to ensure everything was in order. Satisfied, he re-opened the door.

"You an army man?" a young GI asked, drink in hand.

"Colonel mustered out in '45," Johnson answered.

"Here take this," the young man said, handing him a glass. When Johnson had it, the man poured him two fingers of American Bourbon. "Cheers," the man said, raising his glass.

"Cheers." Johnson lifted the glass to his lips but did not drink.

"So, what you do in the war, Colonel, if I may ask?" The young GI staggered and finally leaned against the wall. "See any combat?"

"No," Johnson replied. "I mostly worked in support of the troops...London, then Paris."

"Doing what?"

"Admin stuff. You know...getting bullets and bread to the boys." He smiled, purposely vague.

"Gottsha," the GI replied, too drunk to continue the conversation.

Johnson nodded to the young man, turned, and walked down the corridor.

Frankfurt had suffered heavy destruction during the war and was only starting to rebuild. Still, thousands of refugees crowded into the city seeking whatever assistance they could not get out in the country. Like everywhere in Central Europe, displaced persons were a serious problem, but in the espionage business, the chaos this situation created was helpful.

Johnson left the hotel to search out a contact, a man indispensable in his mission. He had received the name before leaving Washington. The world of espionage was also a small one where everyone operated secretly, yet secrets were almost impossible to keep for long. Johnson knew well this world. He had been operating in it since 1941.

Chapter 16

ndropov entered and immediately froze. "Who's there?" he asked, sensing something was amiss.

"Close the door," Charlie replied. He waited patiently for the Russian to do what he had ordered. "Sit down."

"Major Stanek, what a surprise." Sergei walked slowly to the only other chair in the room—a wooden chair—and sat down. "How did you know I stayed here?"

"Research."

"Please put the gun away. I think we can converse without it."

"I'm not convinced...So I think I'll just keep it close."

"Where is Comrade Benes? Has she served her usefulness already?"

"I was hoping you could tell me. I turned my back once, and she was gone. Whose side is she on?"

Andropov shrugged. "I can't keep track of your women."

"But your spy, eh?"

"Is that why you're here?"

"I want to know where General Pavlov is. I heard he might be in Prague."

That surprised Andropov. "Who told you that?"

The smirk never left the Russian's face, and Charlie hated it. He wanted to get up and smash his fist into it. "Tell me about Pavlov."

"The general has a great interest in your well-being. If you give yourself up, I would be more than obliged to take you to him."

"I'll bet," Charlie replied. "Where does he stay while in Prague? It would have to be somewhere very nice. You know… befitting a murderous general like him. Do you find him whores? Is that your job?"

Andropov did not reply.

"I'm waiting, Major. Give me the information I want, and I may allow you to live. Then why should I? There are too many bastards like you in the world." Charlie thought he could detect anger, just a hint that he was getting to him. "Which knee do you favor?"

"You'll never get out of Czechoslovakia alive. We will hunt you down, and when I get you, I'll cut your balls off and nail them to my door…to remind me why my work is so important."

"But who has the gun now, Major?" Charlie smiled. "Where is Pavlov?"

"You cannot get to him. Security is too tight."

"You forget who you're talking to. Tell me where he is. I'm losing patience and time."

"Your time ran out long ago."

"If you want to walk out of this room, you will give me the information I want." Charlie stood and walked over to Andropov. He held the Russian Tokorov tightly in his hand. "I will shoot you with your own gun, first in the knee, then maybe in the balls. Do you have any?"

"You're bluffing. There are other Russians here, and they will hear the gunshots."

Charlie grabbed a pillow from the bed and pointed the weapon into it. "I don't think so."

For the first time, Andropov looked concerned. "What do you want from me?"

"I told you. I need to know where General Pavlov is staying."

"Near the government buildings."

"A private apartment? Guards?"

"Of course."

"You will take me there. Now."

"Go to hell." He spit at Charlie.

Charlie backhanded him with the butt of the Tokorov. "You will or die." He backed away from the chair but held the pistol in Andropov's bloody face. "Your nose doesn't look so good," he said. He lowered the weapon and stepped back, smiling.

The Russian lunged at him, pushing him back against the stuffed chair. Charlie kneed him in the groin, but Andropov kept coming. The single lamp crashed to the floor. Andropov reached for the gun, but Charlie held on. He struggled to throw him off, feeling the full weight of the tall man.

"I have you," the Russian said. He rolled on top, trying to pin Charlie to the chair.

Charlie, with his one free arm, threw a punch into Andropov's face, striking him hard in the nose, and another across his cheek in rapid succession. Blood poured from Andropov's nose and mouth. He raised one arm to stop the blood flow.

Charlie took advantage of the move and slid out from under the Russian. Free, he turned and drove his shoulder hard into Andropov's chest, forcing him against the chair leg. Successfully escaping the larger man's hold, he rolled away from him. Once clear, he raised his pistol and pointed it at Andropov's chest. "Stop, or I'll shoot you. You hear me, you bastard?"

Andropov refused to concede. He fought to get to his knees, and succeeding that, he quickly stood. He was trying with all his strength to gain an advantage. Blood covered his face, but even that did not deter him. He prepared to pounce on a dangerous prey.

Charlie saw the man's dark eyes red with rage, like a big cat in the darkness focusing all its might on accomplishing one thing—kill him.

"Don't move," Charlie said again. He still held the weapon on Andropov as he crawled across the floor to get more distance from the other man, who now was towering over him.

"I will kill you," Andropov said. He lunged at Charlie.

Charlie fired point-blank, and the bullet struck Andropov in the chest. But it did nothing to slow the taller man. He fell on Charlie, grabbing at his hair, ramming an elbow into his midsection.

Charlie moaned as the Russian's full weight submerged him. He struggled under the larger man, still holding his gun tightly. Andropov reached out to get it from him. He tried in vain to knock it from Charlie's hand.

With all the strength Charlie could muster, he turned the weapon in toward the Russian. He fired. This time the bullet did serious damage, smashing into Andropov's brain. His body went limp, collapsing over Charlie. Blood from the Russian's wounds splattered him.

He heard footsteps in the hall.

I've got to get out of here, Charlie thought, struggling to free himself from the dead man.

There was a knock and another. "Major Andropov…"

"Go away," Charlie replied in Russian. "It's nothing, just an angry woman."

His lie did not work. The door began to rattle and shake. "Let me in!" the man demanded from the hall. Charlie knew it was just a matter of time before they were upon him. He looked around for an escape. The window. He rushed over to open it, but the old sash would not budge. He ran back into the center of the room and grabbed a leg from the broken chair. With one swing, he smashed it against the window. The glass shattered. He began crawling through the open space. It was tight, but he managed to squeeze out without cutting himself on the sharp edges of the ruptured glass panes.

Standing on a narrow ledge outside the room, he heard pounding on the door, then kicking. Finally, the wood splintered and gave way. The ledge was just wide enough for him to balance himself and sidestep toward the corner of the building. He had no other options. The soldiers had entered Andropov's room and were searching for him. Only a matter of time before they figure things out, he knew.

Chips of mortar broke away, but he slowly made his way along the narrow lip. At the corner of the building, he grabbed on to a broken telephone cable hanging along the side of the building.

He heard voices from inside the room growing louder and moved as quickly as he dared. The voices grew louder. "Doctor! Get a doctor!" he heard. Using the cable to keep from falling, he reached out for a steel upright on the fire escape.

Charlie was certain they had found his escape route, but he saw no one in the window. He crawled down to the second floor, and then he jumped the last ten feet into the alley. Hearing their voices above him, he pulled out his automatic and fired off a couple of rounds to force them to keep their heads inside the room.

He ran across VoFrank Park to Letenska Street. The taxi was still sitting where he last saw it. He jumped in. "Drive!" he ordered. Charlie looked back but saw no one in the street. He hoped that was a good sign.

In the backseat of the Citroen, he tore off his blood-soaked jacket and threw it out the window. Charlie had no idea where he was going, but he felt relieved just to be going anywhere away from that building.

The driver watched him. "I have a friend. You can stay at his place for a couple of days."

Charlie was surprised. "Why do you take that risk?"

"Because I like Americans. My brothers go to America twenty years ago. They live in Chicago."

"How did you know I was an American?"

"Because you always know what you're doing. You have a mission. We Czechs are drifting and searching for our destiny."

"You're correct. I have a mission."

"And I hate the Russians. They will treat our country no better than the Germans did."

Soon, the taxi pulled up in front of an old stone residence. "Here we are in the suburbs we call New Town. It will take the police a while to get out here to look for you. I will talk to my friend. Wait in the car." The driver got out and ran to the house. He knocked on the door, and almost immediately, it opened.

A man about the same age greeted the taxi driver. Charlie watched as they talked and pointed. He saw the homeowner nod. *Good*, he thought.

The driver ran back to the taxi. "It is okay to stay here a couple of days. Enter the side door. That room is yours." He extended his hand. "Good luck, my friend."

"Thanks." Charlie handed him a hundred-dollar bill. "Until we meet again."

"In a free, independent Czechoslovakia," he replied, more hopeful than determined.

* * *

General Pavlov was stunned when he heard that Stanek had murdered Sergei Andropov. "How could something like that happen?" he demanded to know. None of his staff had an answer.

It was late. Andre sat and stared out the window into the old city of Prague, into the darkness of the thirteenth century. His dismay and surprise slowly turned to anger. *I have invested so much into capturing Stanek. Now, I must change my plan. Stanek must die.*

Andre exhaled from the cigarette. The smoke hung in the air, distorting his view of the city. He tried to force any negative thoughts from his mind but failed. For one of the very few times in his life, he was bereft of a plan of action. He began to pace about the room, puffing on his cigarette. Only the over-present cough halted his movement.

There was a knock at the door.

"Enter," Andre said. He stopped the pacing and turned toward the door.

A young Russian soldier entered with a Czech police officer. "General, this is Commander Bergdorff with the Prague police."

"Bergdorff...? That sounds like a German name."

"I am Czech, sir. My family came from Sudetenland many years ago."

"Does he understand our situation, Captain?"

"He has been briefed, sir."

"We are searching for a very dangerous criminal, a spy for the Americans. He goes by many aliases, but his real name is Charles Stanek. Find him and bring him to me. Do you understand?"

"I understand, General."

"Go," Andre said. A fit of coughing suddenly seized him. The pain shot through his lungs and up his throat, like a hot knife.

The two men left the room, closing the door behind them.

* * *

Charlie slept for ten hours, surprising even himself. It had rained that night, and a thick ground fog stretched well into daylight. Charlie felt the gloom in every pore of his body.

The rain never falls in Alice Springs. The sun baked down on man and beast almost every day, but in those two years, I never wished for rain. He stared out the single window in his room. He estimated the time at around noon.

Charlie slowly rolled out of bed. He searched for his automatic and found it under his pillow. He stuck it in his belt while dropping the Russian weapon into a side pocket. His personal business concluded, he walked to the door. *The place is quiet, too damn quiet,* he thought, after opening the door.

He ventured into the hall and looked around carefully. Seeing no one, he found the small bathroom and used it. He looked into the mirror and hardly recognized himself. His hair and beard had grown, and he smelled. *Personal hygiene is important. It says that in the U.S. Army Manual,* he thought forcing a smile.

Searching for anything he could use, he found a clean cloth near the single basin sink. He washed up and brushed his teeth with his fingers. Reentering the room, he searched through a wardrobe until he found a shirt and trousers that fit.

When he realized he did not really know where he was, he went to find the owner. Seeing that there was no stairway to the next floor, he walked around the house to the door facing the street. He knocked. People on the street turned to stare. He smiled and nodded at them, but doubted if it erased the look of confusion on his face or his slightly disheveled appearance. Finally, the door opened.

A child stood looking up into his face. "I must speak to your father," Charlie said.

The child turned and ran back into the house. Soon, an older man came to the door. Charlie recognized him as the man he saw last night with the cabbie. "May I come in?" he asked.

"No, too dangerous," the man said. "The police search everywhere for you. You killed a Russian soldier. It is broadcast."

Charlie read the fear in his eyes, and he understood—first the Gestapo and now the MGB. "But...," he tried to explain.

"Go away. I have a family to protect. Run for the mountains."

Charlie said nothing. He turned to walk away, stopped, and turned again to the man. "Tram? Where is the tram?"

The man pointed right down the street, and then turned, closing the door behind him with a loud thud.

He walked in the direction the man pointed. Several blocks later, he discovered a small bakery and entered. Realizing he was famished, he ordered coffee and pastry. He bought a newspaper and saw the front-page headlined, "American killer loose in Prague." *At least, they don't have a photo,* he thought.

Charlie quickly finished his meal and resumed his walk to the station. When he arrived, he looked around carefully to make sure no one was watching him. Confident that no one was, he stepped up to the window and purchased a ticket back into the heart of the city. *I came here for a reason,* he decided, *and I am not leaving until my mission is complete, or I am dead.*

Chapter 17

Marie tried the door, but her father had locked it, and she did not have her key. She went next door and knocked. Through the window, she saw an older woman shuffle to the door. Upon seeing that it was Marie, the old woman smiled. They had known each other since Marie was a child.

The door opened, and the woman stood in the shadow staring at her visitor. "Marie, so long, and you've grown so." Because of a widow's hump that severely stooped her, the woman's breathing was loud and labored. Cataracts cast a haze across both eyes and severely limited her vision, but she had quickly recognized Marie. She beamed from ear to ear, partly because it was Marie, but also because she was lonely with few visitors and welcomed conversation.

"Baba, it's been months and I've missed our talks." She grabbed the old woman's arms.

Baba looked up and tried to focus on the person standing in front of her. Suddenly, her wrinkled face lit up. "Come in, my darling," she said. "So long," she repeated. The old woman's ancient blue eyes, limited as they were, stayed on Marie while she held the door for her to enter.

Inside, they embraced.

"Baba," Marie said. "Where is my father? Have you seen him?"

Baba clutched Marie's hand and held it tightly. "Oh, your child is so beautiful. And well mannered. You can be very proud." She examined Marie closely. "You're too thin. Don't you eat in Prague?"

"Thank you, Baba. No..." She looked at herself and realized that she had not slept or changed her clothing since the day before. She noticed a tear in her long skirt, and there were stains on her white blouse.

"You have left your work?" the old woman asked.

"I've come on holiday and must see my baby and my father. Will they return soon?"

"They have gone to the mountains, my dear. They left yesterday, and Jürgen said they would not return for a week. I am to watch his house while he is gone." She laughed. "But I cannot see much these days. You see the clouds there?" She held an eye wide open and tried not to blink.

"Yes, Baba." Marie looked where the old woman had pointed. "Where? Did he say?"

"I ask my son to watch your house. Do you remember Michael?"

"I remember him." Marie got up to leave.

"You can't leave so soon. I will fix us some tea, and I have pastry, baked fresh this morning." Baba stood. "He did not say where he was going...and I did not ask. I think if he wanted me to know he would tell me. He didn't."

Marie did not speak. She knew where he was.

"I can let you into the house if you want, my dear."

"Thank you."

While Marie slowly sipped her tea and listened to Baba speak about all that had happened in their neighborhood since she left, two men pulled up in a nondescript sedan and got out. Both women, sitting behind curtains, watched. Hearing the car, Baba stopped speaking. She placed her finger to her mouth and motioned for silence.

One man knocked on Jürgen's door. The other looked in the window, and then he walked to the side of the house and tried to see into a room. Satisfied that no one was at home, the two men got back in their car and left.

"Police," Baba said. "I know the type, but they are not from here. They are state police. I know the police here. They are my neighbors.

When it was dark, Marie entered the house with Baba's key, quickly bathed, packed a few things, and departed. She was off to the cabin and was determined to get there by morning.

She made excellent time, catching rides first on a bus, and later with a farmer in an old truck. She walked the last few miles on foot, feeling exhilarated by the fresh mountain air. *So much better than the soot-filled air that often hung over Prague from the steel mills,* she thought.

She reached the meadow several hours after daylight and stopped there to take in the view, but mostly she wanted to remember the last time she had seen the cabin.

It was after I made love with Charles under the large Oak tree. There I told him that I had decided to join General Svoboda's soldiers to drive the Nazis from Slovakia. The plan was that Russian General Malinowsky's 38th Army would reinforce us. I fought alongside my Slovak brothers in the Dukla Pass, and the battle was horrendous. The Germans drove the Russians back under the onslaught of Hitler's

Panzer Divisions, and we were overwhelmed. They killed or wounded more than 80,000 patriots.

They captured me before I could escape into the hills. Along with hundreds of others, we lined the roads for miles guarded by German soldiers with their machine guns, watching and waiting for someone to escape so they could shoot him. They first marched us to large camps and gave us nothing to eat or drink. Then the trains arrived. The Gestapo loaded us into boxcars for shipment to death camps. The trains never stopped. Finally, one came for me. Every minute of every hour, I thought of Charles, how much he loved me. That thought kept me alive.

The camps changed me forever. I am not the woman you think I am, Charles, and I can never be that person again. She accepted that, but the thought of what she had lost still made her sad. For some reason, she needed Charles to accept that she was not that girl anymore.

"Papa," she called when she reached the cabin door. "Are you here?" She heard a sound from inside. Slowly, the door opened.

Marie looked into the dark interior and saw no one.

"Mama," a small voice said.

She looked down and smiled. "Anna, my Anna," she said.

The little girl wrapped her arms around her mother's legs. "You've come."

Marie kneeled. They hugged.

"We've been waiting for you," another voice said from the darkness in the cabin. "Where is Charles?"

Marie stood. "Father, it's you. I'm so happy."

"Did Charles come?" he pressed, his voice clouded with worry.

"No," she replied. "He said he would come when his mission was complete. I don't know what he meant."

"He is determined to kill the Russian MGB officer," Jürgen answered.

Marie, holding Anna's hand, squeezed hard when she heard, frightened for Charles. She quickly entered the small cabin and closed the door. "He will not succeed. The Russians are..."

"He believes he has no choice. For him, it is kill Pavlov or run from him for as long as he lives."

"If Pavlov dies, then another will take his place," she said.

"Why does he want Charles so badly?" he asked.

"It's because of Zerenowsky."

"The Ukrainian NKVD officer?"

"He was discovered to be an American agent called Rasputin." She watched her daughter while she spoke. "Pavlov still fears Rasputin's agents and is determined to hunt them down."

"Charles knows who they are?"

"Pavlov believes that he does."

"You and the child must leave Czechoslovakia. It's not safe here any longer with the Russians moving in."

"No, Papa, I must return to Prague. I must save Charles."

Jürgen looked at her then at the child but said nothing.

Chapter 18

Charlie had to change trams several times, but he was able to ride all the way to the government buildings west of the Vitava River. In a large plaza near the Ledebour Gardens, he found an outdoor café and sat down. He decided this was a good place to wait and watch. He hoped the police would not think to search for him this close to the scene of last night's deadly encounter with the Russian MGB officer.

Across the street, Russian soldiers came and went, always entering the same building. They were few in number, but distinctive in their brown uniforms. Charlie stood, paid his bill, and started walking. He decided he needed to get closer and see if he could somehow see Pavlov.

"Edvard! Edvard Konacek!" a voice called from behind him.

At first, Charlie paid no attention, and then he remembered his new name.

He turned and looked. He saw a young woman run toward him.

"Don't you remember me?" she asked when she was beside him.

"Louisa. Of course. How are you?" She looked different, dressed in a fashion much more feminine than the gray slacks and shirt she had worn several days earlier. He must have been more preoccupied then. Now, she wore a dress and lipstick. Her ample breasts filled out the dress, pressing against the light fabric with its floral design. Her hair fell to her shoulders. "You look, ah, different from our last meeting."

Louisa laughed. "I guess that's a compliment, coming from a man."

"I think a woman would say the same thing."

She was flattered. "What are you doing here in the government plaza? I thought you were an engineer?"

"Yes, I'm sightseeing," he replied. "My job search is going so poorly I decided to see the city." He felt her eyes on him, studying him.

"You don't look well. Are you still staying with Marta?"

"No, that was only temporary. I had a room last night, but tonight..." He shrugged. "Perhaps I will return to Pilsen."

"Edvard, you must not give up. We have begun a new world, a socialist world. I'm certain there's room for you. Come with me." She bubbled with enthusiasm. "And I will find you a job." She grabbed on to his arm.

"A job? Where?"

"I will take you to the place where I work. In the government palace."

"I would like that very much," Charlie replied. "Do you know important government officials?"

"I'm only a minor worker, but I'm around many important people."

"Do you work around Russians?"

She looked at him. "A few. Why?"

"I studied in Moscow. Perhaps I will run into a friend."

"Russia is a very big place, and there are only a few here."

"Of course."

They walked across the plaza and talked as she led him toward a large gray building, the same one he had seen Russians entering and leaving. They entered with ease. The single guard at the door nodded when he saw Louisa.

"What kind of work do you do here?"

"I type correspondence, important letters, and memorandums."

"Do you ever see the Prime Minister?"

"Often. I even type many of his letters." She seemed proud of her work.

"The new Czechoslovakia will do well if all its government workers are like you."

She squeezed his hand tightly.

They strolled down a large corridor. Just when they reached her door, two Russian soldiers came out of an adjoining office. Charlie immediately put his head down and stepped into her office.

She looked at him. "Do soldiers frighten you?"

He looked at her, pretending embarrassment. "I think they're some type of intelligence. In Russia, everyone fears NKVD. Everyone stays away from them."

"I was told they are MGB, but they are few. Don't worry, I'll protect you."

He smiled. "Thanks."

When she left work several hours later, Charlie was waiting for her at the outdoor coffee shop. She greeted him at the table. "Come," she said. "I don't live far."

"Tomorrow, when I've cleaned up, I'll go with you and talk to people in your building about a job...like you suggested."

"That would be good. Then we could take lunches together."

"I would enjoy that." *Her life seems so peaceful and pleasant,* he thought, putting his arm around her.

Two police officers walked by but paid no attention to the young lovers. Charlie bent over to kiss her on the cheek when they passed.

Charlie could not forget what a tremendous sexual appetite Louisa had. Later in the evening, when he returned to her room from a bath in the communal tub down the hall, she was waiting for him.

She approached him in her robe, the sash tightly drawn. He was dressed only in trousers with his weapon wrapped in his shirt, and she caught him by surprise. Standing in the middle of the room, Louisa undid her sash and allowed the robe to drop to the floor. She wore nothing underneath. "Hold them, please," she said, her large breasts exposed, nipples upright.

He set his bundle down on a chair and reached out with both hands to caress them. Then passionately, he bent to kiss her. She unbuttoned his trousers and reached down.

"You are ready, yes?"

"On the bed?" Charlie felt her insatiable passion. It was contagious.

"No, here on the floor," she said, kneeling. "You still have the pistol, I see."

"Yes, does it frighten you?"

"No. Not at all."

They made love where they lay.

The next morning, she woke him. "Coffee, my love?" she asked. Before he could move, she pulled off the blanket, and covered his naked body with her own. and kneeled over him. She pressed her lips between his thighs. Again, they made love, but in the early morning darkness.

"I will take you to a man who hires people. He is very kind and will help you," Louisa said, as the two walked hand in hand to her workplace.

I will try the office next to the Russians first," he told her. "Their work is city sanitation, my specialty." They embraced at the door. When she looked away, he quickly slipped his passport into her bag. *It will be safer with her*, he thought.

"Good luck, my love."

Charlie waited for her to enter her office. He moved his weapon to his belt for fast access and buttoned his jacket to hide it. He opened the door and looked around. Workers turned to look at him. No uniformed people were present, nor did he see any doors to connecting rooms. "Sorry, wrong office," he said and exited the large room.

He stepped into the wide hall just in time to see three Russian soldiers enter the adjoining office. The leading man looked much older than the other two—stooped and unsteady on his feet. *Pavlov*, Charlie hoped. He followed close behind the three, placing one hand on his automatic.

One soldier turned and blocked Charlie from entering. "No entrance," he said, extending his arm to push him away. That did not deter Charlie. He forced his way into the room, shoving the soldier back.

"Stop!" the soldier said. He reached down for his weapon.

Too late. Charlie drew his weapon and pointed it into the man's face. "Move, and you're dead," he said. The man froze.

"Pavlov. Andre Pavlov."

An older man, standing in the large room with the others, stopped and turned, surprised to hear his name called in that manner. When he saw Charlie, he smiled enigmatically. "Major Stanek," he replied. "So, we meet again. Finally." The other Russians in the room took notice and moved to apprehend Charlie. He put the automatic to the soldier's head. In Russian, he said. "If anyone moves, I will shoot this man and General Pavlov."

"Your Russian is still very good, Major Stanek." The general motioned for everyone to stand down. "Come. In my office we will speak, eh?" He turned to lead the way.

Charlie followed, still holding the soldier as his hostage.

In the office, General Pavlov turned to Charlie. "Please, let him go. I will be your hostage."

Charlie paused for a second, suspicious. "Get out of here and close the door," he finally said to the young soldier.

"You know that you cannot escape this place. Everywhere there are MGB and Czech Secret Police," the general said. "Your life depends on keeping me alive." He laughed. "That must disappoint you."

"You forget that I'm an expert at finding my way out of such predicaments. And I'm certain they would not risk the life of their general."

General Pavlov coughed. It sounded like two dogs doing battle inside his chest. The force of the episode drove Pavlov to his chair. When he was finished, he laughed a cold raspy gargle. "Hand me a cigarette."

Charlie threw the package at him.

"You would be a fool to be that certain. I may not even leave this room alive." He lit up and exhaled slowly. "My death warrant is already signed. I think they call it cancer."

"You are a dying man. Why did you go to so much trouble to get me here?"

"Do you think I should spend my last days fishing? When Rasputin's spies are dead, then I can..." He began to cough again. This bout was even more violent than the last. Pavlov gasped desperately for air.

Charlie watched without emotion. "I told you in Hanoi, and I will tell you again. I don't know anything."

General Pavlov fought to get his breathing under control. "You will tell me everything about your conversations with

Zerenowsky. I must know what the traitor told you in his debriefing. Then I will decide."

"You will decide? Remember, old man, who has the gun."

The general was struggling to breathe, but he looked at the gun. "What will that pistol do for you?"

"I will tell you nothing." Charlie saw droplets of blood trickle from the corner of Pavlov's mouth.

"You are here, Major, and you will never leave this place. Look outside my door. Those men know who you are and have orders to stop you." He tried to stand but failed.

Charlie knew it was too late to call for a doctor. His situation concerned him far more than whether Pavlov lived or died in this room. He walked to the window and looked out, contemplating a route of escape.

Pavlov saw him and laughed. "The irony." He was whispering, trying to force each word from his mouth. He knew they could be his last. "You came here to kill me and get your freedom, but very soon, I will die, and you will be imprisoned for the rest of your life."

"I don't give up that easily, General."

"The men outside that door are the very best. I trained them. They will get everything from you. Then they will send you to Siberia where you will live like an animal. A life worse than death, I think." He watched Charlie. "But is that place where we found you any better than Siberia? Hiding in the desert among the sheep? You have nothing. Your country has abandoned you. Alone with your woman and bastard child." He laughed. "You don't even have her."

"What do you mean?"

"She is mine, works for me, not you. So, I think you are all alone. That is truly tragic, I think. I am dying, but for you, it is much worse because you will live."

"Why, General? Why do you care? One man who is crazy as hell runs your entire country. You spent your entire life serving a ruthless dictator who would put you to death without blinking an eye," Charlie said. "My life may be over, but at least I didn't waste it, like you."

"Captain!" General Pavlov called. "Captain, come in at once!" He expended every ounce of strength he had left. His head hit the desk. General Pavlov gasped one last time and was dead.

Charlie ran to block the door with a file cabinet, and then he went to the window. There was pounding on the door, and the cabinet slowly gave way. He threw the window open. Knowing he had nothing to lose, he looked out over the narrow ledge. Too high up to jump, so he had to step back. When he turned, two Tokorov pistols confronted him. Like the dark vacuous eyes of a snake, they stared him in the face.

Russians and Czechs rushed into the room with weapons pointed. They immediately saw Pavlov, his head face down on the desk.

"Drop the gun, Major, and I will not kill you," one of the Russians holding a gun at his head ordered.

Without a word, Charlie dropped his weapon. The other Russian grabbed him and slammed his face into the wall. Blood trickled down his cheek. "That was for Major Andropov," he said. The soldier slammed his elbow into Charlie's kidney. "For my general."

Charlie felt the pain shoot up his back but refused to cry out. Using as much brutal force as they could get away with, the Czech soldiers dragged Charlie from the room, followed by Russian MGB.

They followed the stretcher bearing General Pavlov. A coat covered the general's body. With Czech secret police—one on each side and two MGB officers behind--he was escorted down the long corridor. They had handcuffed him, not wanting to take any chances.

The offices emptied, everyone wanting to see the American spy the Russians had captured. Louisa watched as they marched the prisoner past her. She was shattered when she saw that the spy was Edvard. She wanted desperately to act, but she was confused.

Charlie looked up when he passed her. He saw the hurt in her eyes. He knew that her conflicting emotions would trap, and even paralyze, her, but what he saw there was worse. It was a look of betrayal. Of that, Charlie was certain. Louisa's eyes said it all. They screamed, "You used me!"

Chapter 19

"The MGB has him. Do we try a trade, or do we terminate?" a young man in a dark suit asked. In his mind, he already had the answer. "What does he know about our current operatives in Eastern Europe?" He stopped to gaze out the large window that opened on the central section of the city. "Hell, how much do we really know about them?"

The two men were meeting privately in a small office in central Frankfurt in a nondescript building the American Army had requisitioned. The men sat facing each other. The older man did not reply, content to examine the other.

"No one has told Stanek about our other contacts, but he may have figured out who the major players are," the younger man said. "The Russians may have gotten that out of him already."

"At this stage of the game, I don't think anyone expected him to be still alive," the older man said. "I figured he would have died in a blaze of glory, shooting it out with Pavlov to get the woman."

"He has provided some useful information on Russian troop movements. And, what about loyalty?" the younger Jonathan Grey asked. "Don't we owe him something?"

"The game doesn't work that way, and we have too much at stake here. The damage he will cause just being in the country could be irreparable. He's a loose cannon that we can't control," Robert Johnson said. "Washington worries he could eventually talk."

The younger man said nothing.

"You're right. It is about loyalty," Johnson said, returning to an earlier comment. "Stanek has no loyalties, not to us, anyway. He's a lone wolf out there, and we can never tolerate that. Understand?"

The young agent stared at him, not understanding the other man's meaning. "I read the report from his debriefing of Zerenowsky. I don't understand why they want him so badly. I didn't see much that would really hurt us."

"Pavlov was looking for revenge as much as information. No one ever escaped from him and lived...until Stanek, that is."

"But Pavlov is dead. The old bastard finally died," the younger man replied. "From the information I received, Stanek was there, witnessed it. Hell, he probably killed him."

"Others, just as ruthless as Pavlov, will take his place and carry on his work. They know about Stanek. Hell, Pavlov trained them. They'll learn quickly enough how much Stanek knows about our operations. He did much of his work in Eastern Europe, and some of those boys he worked with are still there. Collateral damage."

"I hadn't thought about that." Grey felt uncomfortable. "Where will they hold him?" Jonathan Grey was new to the world of espionage. As a Foreign Service Officer in the State Department, they first placed him in London where he was to gain experience, and then finally, they reassigned him to the Czech Embassy.

"I think they'll move him to Karlshorst. The Russians like familiar surroundings, and they won't want to rely on Czech Secret Police for assistance," Johnson replied. "They probably already have him in solitary confinement, no food, that sort of thing, to soften him up. It will take that and more. The man is famous as one tough son of a bitch, and remember, he has his people there who may help him escape before the Russians can move him."

"I understand."

"We may have to use our own resources to silence him, but only if we are forced to. So, prepare for the worst-case scenario. You may have to get your hands dirty."

Grey nodded, uncertain of what exactly his superior was asking of him.

Johnson lit a cigarette and exhaled slowly while looking hard at the younger man. "The Directorate of Operations doesn't want a loose cannon working for the Russians. They've given me free rein to dispose of Stanek as I see fit. 'The Stanek problem,' I call it." He knew Grey did not have the information to challenge him.

He waited for Grey's reply but hearing none continued: "The Soviets are on the move, and we cannot afford any breach in security. Do what must be done. If he escapes from the Russians and we cannot retrieve him, he must be silenced." Johnson knew he had to be persuasive. He neglected to tell Grey that the Pentagon disagreed and by utilizing all means wanted Stanek brought safely back to the U.S. The Army was willing to trade to get him and was prepared to approach Moscow. The old man has insisted on that, Johnson, thought, but he knew things happen beyond anyone's control. He smiled to himself.

The young agent nodded, thinking he understood his boss. "But he's a war hero."

"Get a message through to Raindrops. He could be of invaluable assistance."

"What?" The younger man was unnerved. "We can't risk getting Raindrops directly involved. We lose everything if he is compromised. That's our most vital link, and he's been supplying us since Zerenowsky recruited him in '45," he said. "He is so anonymous his name wasn't even revealed to Donovan when Zerenowsky recruited him to build a network of agents. That's the way they wanted it."

Johnson rocked back and forth in the creaky chair. "Get him involved. That's an order." He watched Grey for a response. "And Washington insists on knowing Raindrops' identity...to better track his movements.

Grey looked at Johnson, irritated by the constant noise of the chair. "Security around Stanek will be tight, damn tight for us to get him back to the West. I think the Russians got him good."

Johnson sighed. Grey still resisted. He butted the cigarette, only to light another. "If it comes to that, so be it," he said, now knowing the younger man was agreeable to his demands. "If we must silence him, get it done as an inside job. Get a Czech or German shooter and leave no trail. Remember: this is only between us—no one else must know. If the Russians can get him to Karlshorst, it's too late. Then you must call off the hit. Understand? No loose ends."

"I understand," Grey replied. "I'll do all I can. That's all the assurance I can give you. How much money have we got to spend?"

"On this job, resources are unlimited," Johnson replied. "Get a message to your contact immediately. Tell him we will pay top dollar to anyone who does it."

"I'll leave for the Embassy within the hour."

Johnson stood. "Good luck, Jon, and remember, there are no war heroes in this game. Can't be," he said, offering his hand.

I'll get Stanek either way, Johnson thought, pleased with his thoroughness. He had concerns about Grey's inexperience, but he had another plan if Grey failed—his fail-safe.

"Thanks, and I'll try to remember that." He shook Johnson's hand.

When Johnson was alone again, he reached down to the lowest drawer and pulled out an unopen bottle of Four Roses. Johnson thanked the army for that. He broke the seal and poured a three-finger shot into a tumbler on his desk. He took a deep swallow, felt its burning. The heat billowed up from his insides.

He remembered the bad parts of his job, how much he hated himself for the decisions he had to make. *It is a brutal game where someone often has to die. I have worked this job long enough to know that.* He told himself that often and threw down the remainder of his drink. *Taking unnecessary risks only makes me more visible, and therefore, more vulnerable. So, it was better if Grey completed the mission I assigned him. Grey was, after all, the perfect fall guy.*

* * *

They had recruited Jonathan Grey right out of Yale. He had completed ROTC and planned to receive his commission in the U.S. Army. A recruiter for the Central Intelligence Agency then approached him. That was only twelve months earlier. Congress had just created the agency through legislation to try to pull together the various intelligence services under a single umbrella. His recruiter was a former agent of General Wild Bill Donovan who had run the Office of Strategic Services during World War II. President Truman had moved him aside after the war ended.

The man painted a glamorous picture of espionage-type work, but he never mentioned assassinations, torture, and payoffs. *The lying SOB,* Jon thought, having declined the offer to work with the CIA. He learned before he signed up what the work entailed. He chose the Foreign Service instead, but still wound up in the intelligence field.

Able to speak fluent Czech, Jon was the ideal choice for duty in the American Embassy in Prague. He liked the cloak-and-dagger stuff but killing a good guy and a war hero was difficult to swallow. No one had ever asked him to do anything like this. He thought it rather strange that Johnson was willing to risk Raindrops' cover. The operative was the most important intelligence asset the U.S. had in Central Europe.

Jon Grey returned to his posting at the Embassy in the DC-3 supply run, ruminating over how he would handle this. He knew he had no choice but to follow orders if he wanted to keep his job.

That evening, Jon contacted the only person he knew in Prague who could help him with his assignment. Marta Sturnburg was the richest whore in town, and she knew everyone worth knowing. She was the first person outside the Embassy that Jon had met when he arrived. She had introduced herself at a dinner party for the Russian Ambassador. He had already heard the rumors about her, that she had no love for the Russians. He had used her services several times to gain information on the change in government, once to corroborate Raindrops' documents, but mostly as a courier. Now, he needed her for an entirely different reason.

He had sent her an encrypted note, her preferred method of communication, and she had agreed to schedule a meeting. He took the tram across the Charles Bridge from the American Embassy, always trying to lose himself in the crowd. He worried about the Russians, but he knew there still were not many in Czechoslovakia, and Czech State Security was not overly cooperative with the NKVD. They did not appreciate the Russian encroachment on their turf. That issue would leave assassination as the only option before they took Stanek across the border to Germany.

He walked quickly through Old Town Square near the old Jewish Quarter to the Church of Our Lady Before Tyn, where he was to meet Marta. The church's courtyard was large and private, a perfect place for a clandestine meeting. He strolled through the gardens, taking time to enjoy the flowers and observe if someone had followed him. After carefully scrutinizing the park, he knew he was alone.

He found a bench in the far corner of the courtyard, sat, and tried to enjoy the morning. Fifteen minutes later, he heard movement behind him.

"Mr. Grey," a female voice said, "How nice to see you again." She sat down beside him but did not look at him. "I think we are quite alone," she said. "It isn't often that I meet secretly with an employee of the American Embassy."

"I've come to discuss an issue of utmost importance...to the United States."

That immediately piqued her interest. "Yes?"

"If I can speak to you in the strictest confidence," he began. "I know you have been a very important supporter of the United States throughout the war, and now with all the troubles in Central Europe..."

"Please, Mr. Grey, get to the point." She looked around the grounds as casually as she could. A priest walked through the gardens and passed them.

"It's about your last house guest."

"I delivered the items you gave me."

"Yes, thank you, but now I need your assistance on a matter...uh, that's more involved and unseemly."

"Yes?" She looked at him, waited for him to continue.

"He has become a grave threat to American operations here. He is an outlaw with no allegiances," Jon said. "He must be eliminated."

"You want him killed."

"And we will pay generously to have it taken care of."

"I am an assassin now?"

"No, of course not. I just thought you knew of someone who will take the job," he replied. "It must be done now before the Russians make him talk. While he's still held in Prague. Perhaps you could find a way to involve Raindrops. To ensure success, I mean."

"I have no ability to contact this Raindrops."

Jon nodded. "I understand. Do you have information on where Stanek is now?"

"I've heard he's being held in the old castle, guarded by Czech police. MGB are monitoring him or, as you say, softening him up. They may have begun their horrible interrogations." She looked down and closed her eyes. "Much like the Gestapo."

Jon looked around. He knew it was time to leave. "Can you help?"

"I know someone. It will be expensive for you. Half now and the remainder when the job is finished."

"Done," he said. "How much?"

She wrote a sum on a slip of paper and handed it to him.

He looked at the figure and nodded. "The money will be at the usual drop this afternoon." He paused briefly. "One more thing. I would like it done quickly and quietly. Today. And painlessly, if possible. Find a way to get by the Russians." *I sound nervous and weak*, he thought.

She nodded. "It will be taken care of," she said directly. The meeting ended. They got up and went their separate ways.

Jon walked the entire distance back to the Embassy. He would not use Raindrops and felt relieved that he could protect his best agent. He could tell Johnson that he had tried to involve him but was unsuccessful. *The fool. What was Johnson thinking?*

Chapter 20

Charlie sat silently on the stone floor in the damp darkness. He was naked. He no longer felt chilled, but only because his body had grown numb. He did not know how long he had been there. The hours passed slowly, giving him plenty of time to think...and think.

He reflected on his childhood in Milwaukee, growing up in the Czech and Slovak neighborhood. As a child, he felt alone much of the time. The world was bleak and hard—the packinghouses, breweries, foundries. Everyone had the same thoughts and the same dreams. He had decided as a teenager that he would escape that world, and then the war came. Everything changed. He was recruited into the world of intelligence and espionage while he was training to be a pilot. "We need your language skills," they told him. Soon, he was parachuting behind enemy lines to work with anti-Nazi partisans. Everything that has happened since is because of that service in Eastern Europe.

He estimated that about every two hours, two Russians came in to interrogate him. One watched while the other asked questions, the same questions repeatedly. He always provided them with the same answer— "Fuck you, I don't know anything." He knew their tactics, had learned them first-hand from Pavlov in Hanoi a lifetime ago. He knew their treatment would soon change, become more brutal. Now they were merely assessing him, and his stamina, much like a man would gauge the training of his fighting dog. They were in no hurry.

He did not remember the last time he had eaten or even had a drink of water. His throat was parched, but he had lost his hunger. In the darkness, he searched for anything he could use as a weapon, but there was nothing. It was if they had swept the cold, stone room bare before his arrival. Not even rats wanted this place. The prison reminded him of the one in Hanoi where Pavlov had thrown him two years earlier. At least now, his captors had not chained his ankles to the damp concrete.

A plan. I must have a plan, he thought, pacing. The movement around the cell helped, keeping the blood flowing and allowing him to focus his thoughts. He heard a noise at the door. Charlie quickly positioned himself against the wall next to the door and waited.

The door slowly opened, and two men entered. Immediately, he saw they were dressed differently from the others. The man with the revolver carried a bundle, while the other, having holstered his weapon, carried what looked like food and water.

"Comrade Stanek, where are you?" the first man asked in the darkness. He held his weapon in front of him as he cautiously entered. "We have brought food and clothing for you."

"Who the hell are you?" Charlie asked. He stepped away from the wall, realizing that attempting to escape was futile.

"Police. We are Prague police."

"Where are the MGB agents?"

"We have been sent by the court," the second man answered. "Before the Russians can take you out of the country, the judge must approve."

"I will have my day in court?" Charlie asked. "Justice?"

"Of course," the same man said. "We are going to take you. Here." He handed Charlie a container of water and half a loaf of bread. "Eat the bread. It will make you feel better."

He smelled the water, decided he would take the risk that it was not bad. He tipped it up and gulped it down. Water ran down his chin. He placed the container on the damp floor and picked up the stale bread, prepared to bite into it. Then, while the guard looked on, he put it down in a far corner of his cell. "I'll save it for later," he said. He did not know why he decided not to eat.

The other cop walked over to him, lowered his revolver, and handed him a bundle of clothing. "Dress quickly."

Charlie put on the shirt and trousers. They had even brought his shoes. The two cops stood in the lighted doorway while he dressed. They watched but did not speak. When Charlie was finished, they handcuffed him, with his hands behind his back. One man grabbed each arm, and they marched him out of the cell and up the ancient stone stairway.

When he reached the top of the stairs, one of his MGB interrogators confronted him. "Nothing has changed," he said. "I hope you ate well. That's all you'll get for a very long time."

"Fuck you," Charlie replied.

The two Czech cops chuckled under their breath. "Things aren't good for you," one of them said. "This is only a formality to make us feel important to the Russians. They don't care about you."

"How long before they take me to Germany?"

"Tomorrow, maybe the next day," the cop said. "You will never return to Prague."

Then I have nothing to lose, Charlie thought. "Where are we going?"

"Across the plaza. Our government wants to present you to the Russians...like a dutiful child who always tries to make Papa happy. Because you are such a famous prisoner, you see?" he said. "Otherwise, you probably would have been shot already."

"I feel honored."

The three marched across the large antechamber to the exit. Bystanders turned to watch as they passed. Charlie looked up and thought he saw Louisa standing among them. Before they reached the doors exiting the large room, three men in civilian clothing intercepted them.

"We will take the prisoner from here," one of the men said. He was older than the other two and appeared to be in charge.

The police officers were surprised. "Who the hell are you?" one asked.

"Czechoslovak State Security. We are working with MGB on this matter," he replied. The other two grabbed Charlie and pushed him along.

"Wait!" the police officer replied. "How do we know who you are? Do you have papers? And I want to see an ID issued by the new government."

The StB agent reached into his jacket and produced an ID. He shoved it into the face of the police officer. "Frank, show him our orders," he said.

The second StB agent produced a single sheet of paper from his coat. He waited patiently for the police officer to finish reviewing the ID before he shoved that into his face. "Can you read?" he asked.

The police officer stared at the agent but said nothing. "Who signed this? I don't know him. Do you know this man?" he handed the order to the other police officer.

"Nope," he replied. "We'll have to telephone the boss and get it approved."

"What? You're wasting our time. We must get this man to the chief magistrate."

"Sorry."

The other police officer strolled over to a large desk and asked to use the telephone. The other four stood in the middle of the large room with their prisoner, waiting.

"Cigarette?" the police officer asked. "I seem to have run out. French, if you have them. I hear StB agents only smoke French cigarettes."

"Go to hell."

While the men stood there gridlocked, a young woman approached. "Perhaps I can be of service," she said. "I work for the Politburo."

As one, the four men and their prisoner looked at the woman. "How?" the agent in charge asked.

"Prime Minister Gottwald surely has an interest in the prisoner and his disposition. If this must be expedited, he can facilitate the exchange, so he is handed over to our Soviet allies quickly."

Charlie watched quietly, masking his surprise at seeing Louisa. What was she trying to do?

"Good, good," the chief agent replied. "What is your name, comrade?"

"Comrade Povik," she answered. "If you will wait, I can make a telephone call."

The agent looked at the police officer, who shrugged indifferently. The other cop had not yet returned.

"Go," the agent said.

"I must use the restroom," Charlie said. "It's an emergency."

The agents stared at Charlie, then at the police officer.

"Take him," the agent ordered the cop. "And be quick. Keep the gun on him at all times. He's dangerous."

The number of onlookers had increased dramatically while the four men, the woman, and their prisoner stood there.

"What has this man done?" someone asked from the crowd.

"He is a political prisoner. Keep still," Louisa Povik said. "It is not your business."

Her statement affected the onlookers. "Appeasing the Russians?" another called out from the back of the group.

"Mind your own business," Louisa yelled.

Charlie stood there, head bowed, not uttering a word.

Seeing that Louisa was having a negative effect on the crowd, the head agent stepped forward. "Please, this is a police matter. Do not alarm yourselves. The Russians are not involved."

"Liar!" a man yelled.

"Quickly," Charlie said.

"Let's go," the police officer who had fed him said. "I will take you." He pushed him along through the crowd. People opened a path for them. "Stand aside," the cop said.

The banter between the agents and the crowd grew heated as Charlie and his guard found a toilet. They entered a small dingy room off a side corridor. "Can you unlock these?" Charlie asked. "Where do you think I can go?"

Without lowering his weapon, he retrieved the key from his pocket and threw it at Charlie. "Here, relieve yourself."

Charlie bent down, and with his hands behind his back, picked the key off the floor, unlocked the cuffs, and turned toward the urinal. Before he could unbutton his fly...

"Run for the door," the cop said suddenly. "Go, it's your only chance to escape."

For a second, Charlie considered it. He took a single step toward the door. From the corner of his eye, he saw the cop raise his pistol. In midstride, he turned. With all the effort he could muster, he threw a hard right into the cop's face. The blow was glancing, but enough to jar the cop's aim. The gun fired with the round hitting harmlessly into the ceiling plaster.

The cop staggered, turned toward Charlie, and prepared to fire again.

Charlie was on him. Grabbing the gun with one hand, he rammed his forearm into the man's throat.

Charlie's sudden assault caught the cop unprepared, but he tried to fight back. Quickly, Charlie pinned him against the wall. Still holding the hand with the pistol in it, Charlie thrust his knee repeatedly into the man's groin.

The cop's grip on the pistol loosened. Charlie took hold of the gun barrel, finally twisting it out of the cop's hand and into his own.

Gripping the weapon firmly, he said, "Don't move or I'll shoot."

The cop froze.

"Why did you want to kill me?" Charlie asked, confused. He held the man against the wall with all his strength, while pointing the weapon in his face. "You know the Russians want me alive."

"The money...for my family," the cop said. "I received a message with five thousand American dollars in the envelope."

Charlie stepped back, holding the pistol in the man's midsection. "Keep talking."

"The message said, 'I know about your collaboration with the Germans. If you want to live, you must kill the American prisoner you are guarding. Another five thousand will be sent to you when the job is done.' I don't know who sent it, but I do know it was from the partisans. The same people who fought the Nazis. They wanted me to wait to see if you would escape, but I need the money...and your life is gone no matter what happens."

"All for the money?" Charlie said sympathetically. "Betrayal is a mark that stains your life. The war does not go away so easily, does it?"

"I only worked with the Gestapo to protect my family. I'm a poor policeman."

"Take off your clothes...quickly," Charlie said. "And put these on." He began disrobing. "Hurry."

The police officer at first stood and watched, a forlorn look of failure darkening his features.

"Quickly or I will shoot you and do it myself."

The man did as ordered and Charlie dressed in the police officer's uniform.

"If I were you, I'd take the money and run for it," Charlie advised him as he finished dressing. "The MGB does not forgive betrayal or ineptness."

"Please hit me. Hit me hard in the face," the man said. "It must look bad, or it will go bad for me."

Charlie, without hesitation, struck him in the face and the midsection. When the man doubled over, he kicked him in the ribs. "Good luck," he said, stepping quickly to the door.

Chapter 21

Charlie was gone before the man could get off the wet tile floor. Back in the main lobby, he saw that a swelling group of onlookers were still shouting and crowding in on the cops, distracting them. He decided that was his break and ran for a side door. Once outside the building, he looked for the tram and then remembering he had no money, he began to walk. *As a police officer*, he told himself, and adjusted his step to one of marching, nodding and politely bowing as he passed pedestrians.

He knew he could not go to the American Embassy. That was too far. Marta. Her apartment was close. He figured she was involved or, at the very least, knew something about the attempt on his life. Nothing happened without her knowledge or cooperation.

Taking side streets and avoiding public venues, he was still able to cover ground and reached her apartment in good time. Along the primary streets, he saw police cars and army trucks roll by. They were looking for him. *I wonder how they posted my escape. An American spy? An American killer on the loose?* He also wondered about the police officer but felt no guilt.

Within minutes, he stood at Marta's door. He knocked. No answer so he tried again. It occurred to him that it was better if she did not answer. *I will surprise her, try to unnerve her by waiting for her in the apartment.* The more he considered it, the more he thought that she knew the cop who just tried to kill him. He knew she was working both sides. That was how she survived.

Charlie left the building, walked down the street and around the side to the fire escape. He knew the route well. Standing at Marta's back door, he tried the lock, prepared to break a window if necessary. But the door was unlocked, so he entered and decided to make himself comfortable. He poured himself a glass of her American bourbon.

He decided he needed a change of clothing. He rummaged through her closets for a suitable fit. Half an hour later, he walked out of the bedroom in a pair of slacks, white shirt, and casual jacket, still sipping the bourbon. He smiled, thinking he had not looked this good in years.

He waited. The hours ticked by slowly. The sun passed overhead, and then he saw it begin to cast long shadows across the wood floor. He grew restless and hungry, and finally, driven by a need to eat, he scavenged through Marta's cupboards. Just as he found cheese and fresh-baked bread, he heard noises in the hallway. The key turned. He set his food aside and stepped back into the kitchen.

Marta entered alone. He heard the door close. She switched on a bureau light. He decided it was as good a time as any and stepped out of the kitchen.

"Marta, welcome home," he said. He pointed the revolver at her. "I've been waiting for you."

"Who? What are you doing here?" She forced the words out, in obvious shock.

"You thought I was dead, didn't you?" He walked into the formal living room. "Please, sit down so we can have a nice chat." He watched her sit then sat across from her.

"Why are you pointing that gun at me? Me, your lover."

"I want to talk about that. It seems someone paid a cop to kill me this morning. Know anything about it?"

"Oh, love, you know more than most that it's a very dangerous world we operate in. Friends today, but enemies tomorrow."

"Don't give me any of your double-talk. I want the truth. Who hired the cop to kill me? Was it you?"

"You're such a handsome man. Did I tell you that before?" She began to take off her coat but kept her eyes on him.

Charlie smiled. "Did I tell you before that you're a conniving, dangerous bitch?"

"I don't think so," she said. "I'd offer you a drink, but I see you've helped yourself. Mind if I pour myself one?"

"Go ahead," he said. He did not take his eyes off her. "You paid the cop a lot of money to kill me. I suppose I should be flattered."

She did not reply, content to sip her bourbon.

"I'm a wanted man, and I have nothing to lose by killing you. You deserve it, anyway."

"We play a very dangerous game, don't we?"

"You said that already." Charlie grew impatient. "Talk or I'll find a way to make you talk."

"The Americans...they have decided you are not useful any longer, or worth the trouble. They seem to believe you are better off dead. They evidently don't like rogue spies running around Central Europe killing people," she replied. "Because they don't know anyone else to ask, they approached me to take care of the problem."

"The Americans? CIA?" he asked. "So, they're in the murder business, too."

"Agents with too much money. The CIA, probably. They're all worried that you know too much. That's the worst thing that can happen to you. It's always better to know too little."

"What about the American Army? Do they want me dead, too?"

"I don't know anything about them. They operate their own show, and they have never contacted me since the end of the war. So...," she said, looking him over, "You have escaped both the MGB and the assassin. His orders...by the way, American orders...were to kill you. Strange, I think."

"Why?"

"I would have thought the Americans would have made a rescue attempt first."

"He wasn't interested in the details of your plan. He needed the money. I hope you pay him well with the American money."

"Failure is not something I reward," Marta replied.

"Who? I want a name."

"I think it would be wiser for you just to disappear. Go back to Asia, anywhere, and lay low. Their memories are short, and now that you've killed the Russian Pavlov, your chances of having a life have improved greatly."

"Keep going. A name. Give me the name of the person who is paying the assassin."

"Jon Grey, CIA Station Chief at the Embassy," she replied.

"I was prepared to torture you for that information."

Marta shrugged and smiled, winking at him. "You know how much I like torture."

"Contact him. Do it now."

"Charlie, don't be foolish. Going after him will do you no good."

"What the hell do you care? You just tried to kill me." He was amazed that she would be offering him advice. "Send word to this Grey. Ask for a meeting."

"You're crazy."

"Do it now!" At that moment, he realized how tired he was. The revolver suddenly felt very heavy in his hand, but he had to settle this. "I have to get them off my back, and you're going to help me."

She watched him. Finally, she stood, disregarding the weapon pointed at her.

"Where are you going?"

"I'm getting paper and a pen so we can compose something, something that will motivate him to meet with you. Then I will telephone him. He gave me a number where he can be reached."

"Get it." He stood and followed her to a small desk where she retrieved the items.

When they were finished composing the message, she turned to look at him. "You look dreadful. And I know you must be famished."

"This morning you try to kill me, and now you want to feed me? You are a very strange--and dangerous--woman," he said. He had earlier stuck the revolver in his belt. "I will eat."

"Like you, I am a survivor who does what she must." She got up and walked into her kitchen. He followed, hungry, and determined not to let her out of his sight.

She saw the bread on a counter and smiled.

"I took it upon myself to get lunch but was interrupted," he said.

She watched him devour half a loaf of bread, cheese, and jam. He washed it down with a liter of beer. "That was good," he said. "Now make the call. Read the message and tell him the meeting will be tonight just after dusk in the old Jewish Quarter...in the cemetery."

Marta looked surprised. "It is dangerous to call the American Embassy. Someone may be listening, and they could set a trap for you."

"Make the call. I'll take my chances."

Marta made the call. She reached Grey at his desk and explained that Charles Stanek had survived and wished a meeting for this evening. Then she slowly read the message Charlie had composed.

"Yes, twenty thousand American in small denominations. You must bring the money with you," she said twice for clarity. "He's not bluffing. I believe he will reveal the entire Rasputin network in Eastern Europe to the highest bidder." She hung up.

"He will be there at seven."

Charlie looked at the clock on her mantel. "I have two hours. Get me money for a taxi."

She obeyed. "You're too recognizable," she said when she returned. "Get rid of the beard, and your hair is too long. I have scissors and can easily cut it."

He stood, looked in a wall mirror. "Where?"

"In the bath," she replied. "And while you're in there, you may want to take a bath." She wrinkled her nose.

"Let's go and do it."

Charlie sat on the edge of a large tub while Marta shaved him. Her blades were not sharp, but slowly she shaved his beard and trimmed his hair.

"Make it shorter."

Marta obeyed, clipping his hair shorter around his ears. "There," she said. "You look like a Slovak peasant."

"Perfect," he replied, looking in the mirror to appraise the job she did. He ran his hand across the top of his head.

Now the bath?"

"Yes, but you're going to get in the tub with me. That's the only way I can keep an eye on you. So, strip."

"If you want, but there are other ways." She was naked before he turned off the water. Looking her over, he had another idea. "Hair dye. Do you still have the dye you use on your hair?"

"How did you...? Then she looked down where he was looking. "Yes, I have it."

Marta dyed his hair in the sink. They both splashed in the tub, but the revolver was close, and she knew it.

"If I gave you the gun, what would you do?" he asked.

"I would throw it out the window."

Charlie laughed. "Why? You just hired someone to kill me."

"I'm not an assassin. I just do what I'm ordered to do."

"I see. You think that makes you a better person?"

"I'm not a killer."

"You think I'll kill this Grey?" he asked. "You don't think the bastard deserves to die?"

"Revenge is a waste of time," she said. "And gets people killed who can help you later. Understand?"

"You threatened the cop. Payback from another time, and with interest. Is that how you got him to do it?"

"You are in my country for revenge as much as rescuing your child. Grey—your Americans--tried to have you killed. So yes, I think you will kill him," she said. "There may be many reasons to kill someone, but revenge should not be one of them, especially when they can be of some use, eh?" She repeated her suggestion that he should not kill the diplomat.

Charlie said nothing.

Charlie arrived at the cemetery fifteen minutes early. He wanted to check out the place and make sure Grey did not bring along another assassin. *After all, he tried to have me killed once. What's to keep him from trying a second time?* After walking the grounds searching out advantage points for snipers, he settled in behind a mausoleum, checked the revolver, and waited. The cemetery was dark, no artificial lighting anywhere, but the light from a rising moon was enough to provide a sufficient view of the entrance. The light, reflecting off old stone crypts, cast shadows that seemed to dance and move about, adding another dimension to the scene. He smiled, knowing he had chosen a perfect place to meet with an adversary.

He considered who this Grey was and wondered how long he had been in the intelligence field. He was curious as to what kind of background he brought to this particular assignment. He had already decided the man was a reckless coward. *Probably some Ivy League little prick,* he decided.

Charlie did not have to wait long. A few minutes after he sat down, he heard footsteps on the concrete walk. Looking in that direction, he saw that it was one person. He stood carefully and walked circuitously toward the rendezvous location to ensure Grey had not positioned someone nearby. Then he waited until Grey sat down on a bench. Seeing no one, he walked out of the shadows, careful to stay behind him.

"Mr. Grey." He held the revolver against the back of Grey's head, pressing just a little to let the man know what it was.

Grey did not move. "Major Stanek, so we meet."

"Are you disappointed that I'm still alive?"

"Nothing personal. Just following orders."

"I thought I was one of the good guys. What's the deal?"

"You are an independent operator who knows too much. We're worried that you will work a deal with the MGB.

"We?"

"I work for State."

"What about the others?"

He shrugged. "We are on the same page."

"CIA, also?"

"I am following their orders," he replied. "I only know that if you are compromised, it would destroy the most important espionage network we Americans operate in Eastern Europe. Rasputin still operates, and Raindrops is our..." He suddenly realized he had said too much.

Charlie caught the slip and carefully filed it away. "Your attempt was very unprofessional. Was a poor Czech cop the best you could do?"

"On short notice."

"That brings us to why we are here, Mr. Grey. Twenty thousand dollars. Do you have it?" *Raindrops? Something about that name sounds familiar.*

"One question remains. How do we know you won't give up what you know to the Russians anyway? Or worse for you. They will torture it out of you."

"It's a risk you will have to take, Mr. Grey," Charlie said. He immediately saw that they were taking too much time.

"I would like to propose that you come with me to the Embassy. We'll give you a new identity, money, and get you safely out of Europe," Grey said. "From there you can go anywhere you want."

"A most interesting proposal, especially in light of the fact you just tried to kill me," Charlie said. "How do I know you won't try again? Regardless of whether I come with you or not, I still have, and will continue to have, the information in question. So, I guess the answer is no. I'm safer on my own."

"We thought you'd say that," he answered. "Here's the money you requested. Count it if you wish."

Charlie felt the large bundle in the envelope, opened it, and pulled a couple of bills from the middle. He held them up to the dimming light. "They look real enough."

"I'm happy you approve. One final thing." Grey produced a small capsule and handed it to Charlie. "Take it and use it if they capture you."

Charlie looked at it. "What is it?" But he knew what it was.

"Cyanide. Not nice, but it still beats torture."

"It's much safer for us that way," Grey said unemotionally and much too casually.

"Thanks for the sensitivity." He dropped it in a shirt pocket, hoping he would never have to use it.

"I guess I'll be running along then."

"Not so fast, Mr. Grey." Charlie pulled the man up from the bench by his shirt collar.

"I've given you what you want, and my safe passage is part of the deal."

Charlie felt Grey's fear, and that made him smile. "We're going to walk a little and talk some more." When the younger man was standing, Charlie walked around the bench to position himself immediately beside him. "Through the cemetery. Walk nice and slow."

Charlie walked him into the middle of the medieval cemetery and stopped. He turned to look Grey square in the face. He held his eyes, neither man blinked. "If the Americans continue to hunt me, I will find you and kill you. Do you understand, Mr. Grey?"

At first, Grey said nothing. He looked down at the brick walk. "I only follow orders," he repeated as if that could explain his actions.

"That's not an acceptable answer. You are an educated man who knows right from wrong. I'm tired of hearing the 'I'm only following orders' line of bull. Please, for all our sake, find the courage to do what's right. Good-bye, Mr. Grey." Charlie turned and disappeared into the eerie darkness. He walked a few meters and stopped, discreetly stepping into the bushes.

He watched Grey disappear down the walk and through the gate. Oddly, he felt at peace, even knowing both the Russians and the Americans wanted him dead—the CIA more than the MGB. *The Russians want what they think I know. Since I don't have the information, maybe it's time I get it...*Charlie knew the cards were stacked against him, even of getting out of the country alive, but he decided he had few viable options but to continue with his plan.

Charlie stood in the dimly lit hallway. Only a small window at the far end allowed in any sunlight. He knocked softly on the door. No answer, but he thought he heard movement from inside the room. He was taking a significant risk coming here, but he felt he had to. He wanted Louisa to understand who he really was, and he needed a hideout.

The door opened slightly. "Who is it?" a voice asked.

"Edvard," he replied.

She stared at him through the narrow opening. "You look different. I don't recognize you."

"I'm Edvard," he replied again. "I dyed my hair and shaved the beard. That's all."

"Liar," Louisa said. "You're Stanek, the American spy."

"Please," Charlie said. "Let me in so I can explain what happened. Don't believe MGB lies. Please."

She opened the door wide for him to enter. She wore a heavy robe, loosely tied around her waist. "No tricks or lies," she said.

"May I sit?" he asked.

"Sit."

They both sat, she on a wooden chair and Charlie in the one stuffed chair. "I'm not a spy," he said. "I've come here only to get my daughter," he said. "Oh, thanks, by the way, for creating a diversion in the lobby. You may have saved my life."

"You said your daughter?" She was visibly surprised by his admission.

"You see...during the war, I served with your partisans against the Nazis as a member of the American Army. I had to work with the Russians as well as Czechs, Slovaks, Poles, and Ukrainians. Our job was to rescue pilots and monitor the Germans."

"I don't understand."

"I worked with NKVD agents, one of who was a double agent working for us. I brought him to the United States and debriefed him. The MGB wants me because they believe I know who the American agents in Eastern Europe are. To get me to return, they kidnapped my child."

Louisa said nothing at first. "Your story reminds me of spy novels I read as a child."

"Would you believe it if I told you I am now an Australian cowboy, and not at all interested in European politics?"

"That seems wilder than the spy story."

They both laughed.

"What is your real name?"

"Charles Stanek."

"Like the police said."

"Do you believe me?"

"I want to."

"Will you let me stay with you for a night?"

"I will," she said. "I should just scream, but I won't."

He lay in the narrow bed under a home-stitched quilt. The mattress was lumpy and sagged in spots. Charlie decided it was probably older than he was. Louisa turned out the single light and walked to the bed. She reached the foot of the bed and dropped her robe to the wood floor. She stood naked in the darkness, staring at Charlie.

He watched her. "Come, we live tonight like before. Tomorrow, who knows?"

"Yes, tomorrow," she replied and crawled in beside him. She pressed her body hard against his. "Oh, Edvard," she said. "I've decided I will always call you by that name."

"Here, it is my name."

"I've thought of you every night," she said. She reached down to feel for him.

"You can call me anything you want, but you must give me my passport. The one I left with you. You still have it, don't you?"

"The one that says you are Edvard Konachek. Yes, I have it."

"I must have it back."

"I will give it to you in the morning, but now, please, hold me close. I feel cold and so alone."

He wrapped his arms around her, and they embraced. Only twenty-four hours earlier, he had slept naked and bruised on the cold, damp stone of a sixteenth-century dungeon.

Chapter 22

Relieved that Anna and her father were safe in the mountains of Slovakia, Marie returned to Prague determined to find Charlie before the Russians got him. When she arrived at her work in the government offices, she learned that recent events had overtaken her. "An American spy killed two important MGB agents and escaped from captivity" was the talk on everyone's lips. "Many worry that a killer is on the loose in Prague," someone told her. Others were concerned that the incident might provoke the Russians to intervene militarily in Czechoslovakia.

Marie marveled at Charlie's keen sense of survival, but she also realized it was only a matter of time before they captured him. She sat at her desk. The only thought on her mind was finding him. Papers and documents were stacked up before her, but she could not concentrate on her work. Although some were marked "Top Secret" and "Classified," she focused only on how to assist Charles. But she could not come up with any answers. *I must speak with the MGB*, she finally decided, with that, Marie got up and left the building.

When she entered MGB offices nearby, a soldier who introduced himself as Major Malinowsky immediately greeted her. He explained that due to the loss of General Pavlov and Major Andropov, he was temporarily in charge in Prague. "We will search until we capture the American," he said. "That is my mission."

"I was working with the general to capture him," she replied. "Now I need an update."

"Marie Benes...Yes, I have heard your name mentioned. You are Czech intelligence?" He looked her over carefully.

"I am, and I am our liaison with Karlshorst." Marie could tell that he found her attractive. She had her hair pulled back tightly to highlight the natural beauty of her features. She wore a simple cotton skirt and blouse and made sure the top buttons were unfastened. *I must use every asset I have*, she thought, feeling his eyes on her.

She smiled sweetly and hoped he would reveal some new bit of information on Charlie.

"Please sit," the major said, "so we can discuss the current situation."

"Where do you think he is now?" Marie asked. The Russian sat behind a large steel desk where she remembered Pavlov had once sat. She sat across from him and crossed her legs slowly.

He looked at her without speaking. She guessed he was trying to decide how much to divulge.

"We believe he is still in the city. With assistance from your government, we have posted men at all border crossings, at rail and bus stations, and throughout the public places in the city. It is just a matter of time, comrade."

"Where could he be hiding?"

"I suspect the American has contacts, enemies of the state willing to assist, and even agents here. One of them may be helping him. Here, you could be of great service to us."

"How can I assist?" she asked.

The major held up a manila file. "I've read that you and your father worked with him during the war. What do you know that may be of assistance?"

Marie expected that question would arise. "I knew him and had a child's crush on him. He is very handsome, as you may know. We had intimate relations. It was war, after all, and we all do foolish things. My father spent more time with him, as well as other partisans who Stanek led, rescuing downed American and British pilots. I have spoken to my father about him. Although he holds Stanek in the highest regard, he swears he has not attempted to make contact with him. Anyway, my father lives like a hermit somewhere in Slovakia and refuses contact with everyone, even me."

"That is not what your agents have reported."

"What do they say?"

"They say that you've recently returned to Bratislava. To see your father, perhaps?"

"Did they also tell you that I have a daughter, a child who has been kidnapped by my father?"

"A child... Yes, I read that. There is some question about that child's lineage. That the father is Stanek. The result of your friendship?"

"It was war."

"It was war, but he was an American spy even then. Did you know that?"

"Of course not," Marie replied. "I have devoted my life to my country and my party. I refuse to sit here and listen to your nonsense." She stood and prepared to leave.

"Please, comrade. I am only doing my job," he said. "I do not wish to offend you, but you must admit things are somewhat clouded and complicated."

"They are not. We have a spy loose in my country. We must hunt him down. That is very clear to me."

"Agreed," the soldier replied. "I would like for you to work closely with me and assist in coordinating efforts between our two countries so that we can apprehend this dangerous criminal once and for all."

Marie left wondering how much she had accomplished. She walked back to her building but decided to take the long way. She needed to think. Charles seemed to have disappeared, according to the MGB soldier, anyway.

For two days, he had eluded the police and the Russians. His ingenuity amazed her. Where could he hide? He must know someone, but who would protect him? She considered all the people in Prague he might know and concluded there were very few.

When she returned to her desk, a message awaited her. She looked around. "Who?" she asked a clerk sitting at an adjacent desk.

"A Russian soldier delivered it only ten minutes ago," her desk mate replied.

Marie quickly unfolded the note and read, "Have a new lead. Please return to my office at once. The message was signed 'Major Malinowsky.'"

"I must go." She grabbed her coat and headed for the door. Before she got out of the room, a young man who, unlike others in the room, was impeccably dressed, wearing a nicely cut suit and polished shoes, approached her. He caught her just as she left the room. "I am departing for Berlin and Karlshorst. What do you have for the diplomatic pouch?"

She looked at him, startled. "Follow me, Carl," she said, reacting quickly. When she got back to her desk, she handed the young man a sealed envelope marked "High Security, Top Priority."

"This is a very important letter from the Prime Minister to our ambassador. It must be delivered today."

"Yes, Comrade Benes," he replied.

"Remember," she said. "Keep your eyes and ears open. Our government is young and very vulnerable. We have enemies everywhere."

"I understand," he replied.

When Karl had departed, Marie left the building immediately to return to the MGB offices, hoping to gain more information the Russian may have on Charlies. She flashed her ID and a Russian guard waved her through security. She entered the office where the major was waiting.

"I just received this." He handed her a note written in Russian.

"I can't read Russian well," Marie said. "Can you translate?"

"Of course. An old babushka reported seeing a strange man in her apartment house. She said he acted out of place among her guests, is not one of her tenants, and is about the right age." The Russian smiled. "She said he has the look of a dangerous criminal."

"Is it worth investigating?"

"We must investigate all leads," he replied. "Shall we go?"

Marie walked beside Major Malinowsky. She fought desperately to mask her concern for Charles, but she knew she also had a job to do.

When they arrived at the old brick apartments, Marie recognized it immediately. She had stayed there when she first arrived in Prague for her job. Czech security police were already there. "We have the place surrounded," the man in charge said.

"Search the building, floor by floor. Force him to make a move and we'll be waiting for him," Major Malinowsky replied. "We will be right here."

"Yes, sir."

A dozen armed men moved into the building.

"And remember," he called after the Czech police officer. "We must have him alive. He is useful to us."

Slowly, men and women, mostly young, trickled out the door. Marie and the Russian inspected each as they passed by. An hour later, they heard a commotion, then yelling, from inside the three-story building.

Malinowsky looked at Marie and smiled.

The cat thinks he has the canary, Marie thought, returning his smile with a professional nod. Her feelings about this whole affair were complicated, and she knew she could not betray them to this man.

Soon four police officers came out the door with two others behind them dragging a tall man who was struggling against his captors. He cursed the cops. "I wish damnation on your eternal soul, you commie pig!" he said to the man who held a pistol to the back of his head. The Czech police had bloodied the man's head.

They dragged him to where Marie and Malinowsky were standing. "This is the man," the cop in charge said. "The landlady has already identified him." The man was barefooted. His hair was short, but he had an uncropped blond beard.

The man saw the Russian uniform and realized he was in deep trouble. "Please," he said. "I am just a bus driver. I've done nothing wrong. I only stayed one night in this house with my friend. I have nowhere else to go. Please."

The Russian turned to Marie. "Is this man Charles Stanek?" he asked.

Marie now knew why he had taken the time to bring her along. She looked the prisoner over. "No, this is not Stanek."

Major Malinowsky looked at her. "You are positive?

"I am positive this man is not the American, Charles Stanek."

He sighed, turned to the security police officer. "Let him go."

Chapter 23

Charlie felt restless and could not sleep, so he decided to use the single, shared bath in the hall before the early morning risers. That completed, feeling more refreshed, he returned to Louisa's room, where he finally settled into a chair in front of the window. He checked the old revolver, but mostly he thought. *I must have a plan to get out of Prague and back to the mountains. There I stand a chance, and I must get Anna.* He hoped that Marie was there also, but he did not know.

"Edvard," he heard in the dark room. "Come to bed."

He tore himself from the window and walked to the bed. "I can't sleep," he said.

She watched him. "You must escape from Prague, go back to America," she said. "It is the only way for you to survive. The MGB will keep hunting for you here."

"I can't take you with me," he replied.

"I know," she said. "I will lose you, but I have already lost so many of my people. I have learned how to live with that pain."

"I have money and I want to give some of it to you before I go. It is American dollars. Do you have a place where you can change it?"

She got out of bed and walked toward him. She wrapped her arms around him and pressed her naked body against his. "I know a place. First, lie with me a little longer. I need to feel your strength."

They lay together until the first rays of sunlight broke through the window. Then Charlie departed.

He walked south and east toward the newer section of the city. He knew the police would be watching the rail and tram stations. So, he had to find another way out of the city. Getting out of Prague was the most difficult part, he knew. Once he got that far, he believed his chance of making Bratislava would be very good.

In addition to walking, he had two options left to him— flying and driving. No airplanes were available, so finding a car had to be his best way out of town. He began searching for an auto, a truck, even a scooter that was unattended. He had been walking for more than an hour when he spotted an old sedan, a Mercedes-Benz, on a back street in a rundown section of the city. He saw that little here had changed since the war. Many homes were boarded up, while others were in a state of disrepair. The old sedan was the only vehicle he saw on the street.

Charlie looked around and saw no one. He walked to the Mercedes, looked around again, and tried the door. It was unlocked, so he opened it and slid in. Just as he suspected, there was no key in the ignition. He reached under the dash. *I think I can still do this*, he thought, fumbling with the wires. He became completely absorbed in jump-starting the vehicle.

"What do you think you're doing there?" a voice said behind him. "I saw you from the window.

Charlie jerked his head and turned toward the voice. The long barrel of a rifle confronted him.

"Come out of my car," the man ordered. He did not lower the rifle. "It's loaded, so no funny stuff."

Charlie did as ordered. "That's a Mauser, isn't it? I recognize it from the war."

The man, Charlie saw, was as ancient as the automobile. His head was completely bald. He was slim and wore coveralls and a light shirt. "Will you sell it? I can pay for it with cash—American dollars," he said. "I have an emergency and need to go east fast."

"Not in my car," the old man said. "Where you from?"

"The mountains," he replied. "Came for work but have a family emergency."

"Start walking," the old man said, "to that house over there. It's mine."

Charlie complied, the rifle barrel poking in his back. They entered a dilapidated brick house. Inside were few furnishings--a table, chair, and an old kerosene stove sitting in the middle of a large room? Icons and pictures of different religions plastered the walls. He saw a Jewish menorah on the table, a large, partially damaged picture of the Virgin Mary, and a statue of Buddha painted bright gold. *Who am I dealing with*? he wondered. *A religious lunatic?*

The smell of cooked cabbage seemed to permeate the room. A thin layer of dust covered everything. The place gave Charlie the creeps. It seemed as if more than memories haunted the place. He smelled the presence of death.

"Sit there," the old man said. He pointed the rifle at a single chair.

"What are you going to do?" Charlie asked. "Call the police?"

"Haven't decided. You wanted by the police for something? That why you're running?"

"The Russians want me. Probably will kill me when they're finished with me. The bastards think I'm a spy." By the look of the old man, something told Charlie he could level with him.

The old man stared at Charlie. "That right? And that isn't no Czech or Slovak accent."

"I'm an American—Czech American—here to rescue my daughter."

"Don't like the Russians much myself, and don't know anything about the Americans," the old man replied. "I did see some American soldiers here at the end of the war. Friendly bunch."

"The Russians took her and I'm getting her back," Charlie said.

"You speak good Czech."

"I was in Slovakia during the war, rescuing downed British and American pilots. I lived in the mountains, spied a little on the Germans. I can lie in three different languages," Charlie told the old man, trying for humor. He smiled but got no response from the old man.

At first, the old man just stared at him. "One man's truth is another man's lies. Did you learn that during the war, too?" he asked. "Nothing is real, everything is just words, and I get tired of hearing them. How do you know the Russians?"

"During the war, in the mountains near the borders. That's when I met the Russians, their secret service."

"Killers, aren't they?"

"I could tell you stories."

"They're as bad as the Gestapo. See this?" The old man pulled up his sleeve and showed Charlie a long scar. "They did it, but I was the lucky one. They killed my wife and son. Sent them to Auschwitz." He lowered the rifle. "I escaped into the mountains before they could stuff me in that train car."

"I worked with Jürgen Benes, Czech partisan. By chance, you ever hear of him?"

At first, the man did not respond. He only stared at Charlie. His misty gray eyes looked through him, but not vacuously.

Those eyes captured Charlie's attention. They seemed on fire, as if some alien force drove the old man. Charlie watched him for a sign—anything that indicated his thoughts.

"Yes, I know him," the man said with a strange smile. He turned his head to look up to the ceiling, at the cracking and peeling paint.

Or perhaps beyond the ceiling. The strange behavior puzzled Charlie. His musings made no sense to him. *The man is possessed,* he decided.

"You've been sent by the creator...," the old man's thin lips shaped each word as they rumbled from his mouth, "...to take the chosen one." His eyes finally rested again on Charlie.

"Look," Charlie replied, trying to ignore his gibberish. "I'll pay you a lot of money to drive me east toward the mountains. I have American dollars." He waited for a response.

The old man seemed not to have heard him.

"I need to get out of this city."

Again, the man looked up and nodded. Finally, he turned to Charlie. "Your mission in my country is not complete. I can see this."

"What the hell are you talking about, old man?" Charlie had no time to deal with such insanity. He had to get moving somehow. "I must go. If you can't help me, I'll leave."

"Return to the old city and talk to the woman. She looks for you," he said.

"What? You're crazy. You don't know anything about it." The old man had unnerved him.

"I've been ordered to help you."

"How?" He was becoming more confused as the conversation dragged on.

"I will drive you to her."

"How do you know where to go?" Charlie asked. "I can't accept this."

"Trust in providence and the Lord will guide us to her." The old man smiled at him, his eyes still ablaze. "Let's go now." Still carrying the Mauser, he grabbed Charlie by the arm and ushered him out the door.

Two passersby turned and looked when the two men came out of the house. One of them, an old woman smiled and greeted the old man. "Good morning, Enoch," she said in passing, as if carrying the old rifle was a regular sight in the neighborhood. "Are you hunting tonight?" she asked.

Charlie decided that the old man was well known.

Enoch smiled back to her without uttering a word, but when she passed, he whispered to Charlie. "Foolish old Gentile. She knows nothing about the great apocalyptic events that confront us in our old city."

"What do you mean?"

"We are being invaded by the godless heathen from the east. They are worse than the Mongols and the Nazis. They want to control our minds. That's worse than killing us in death camps."

Charlie gave in and went along with Enoch. He was making some sense, and Charlie knew he probably did not have much to lose anymore. With the police expecting him to make a run for the mountains, he decided to cooperate with the crazy old man.

"We go. Before I take you to the woman, I will show you the mountains. Beyond them is Germany. You must remember this." Confused and a little intimidated by the man's ramblings, Charlie still got in the old Mercedes. Enoch started the engine and they were off. They passed through several villages before reaching the foothills, and the old man drove several miles further. The Mercedes ran well, which impressed Charlie.

Finally, Enoch stopped the car and got out. "Out," he ordered. "Follow me."

They walked to the top of a rise, seeing the tree-covered mountains rising before them. Enoch led Charlie into a thinly wooded area not far from the car and pointed.

"Germany is on the other side of those peaks."

On the walk back to the car by a different route, they came upon a cabin. "Here...at this spot. Don't forget it," he said. They stopped and walked around the cabin. The old man seemed to be looking for something or someone, while Charlie was merely going through the motion of appeasing him.

"Why are we here?" Charlie asked. He looked in the cabin window and saw a few chairs, a table, nothing else. No one appeared to be living there.

"When you have the child, come to this spot, exactly this spot, at sunset on the Sabbath."

Charlie said nothing, trying to understand the old man's logic.

"Then and only then, an angel will come to take you away beyond the mountains to your freedom." He again pointed to the west. "To the Promised Land, eh?" He began to laugh, but as suddenly turned serious. "Do not forget what I've told you or the forces of evil will have you, and they will never let you go. Worse than hell."

"The angels will take me to Germany?"

"Yes, Western Germany...the American sector."

Charlie understood. "How do you know about this route?"

"Smugglers have used it for years, even during the wars."

"How am I to get here?"

Enoch looked at him. "The Lord helps those who help themselves. That is your problem." He suddenly laughed again and then patted Charlie on the back. "Don't worry. It will happen."

"I'll be here."

"Now, we go to get petro."

"I didn't notice any gas stations along the way."

Enoch looked at him as if he were a slightly disoriented or addled child. "Ha! You think we're in America. No, no, but there are always ways, ways the Lord has provided me." They walked back toward the Mercedes. "Here, take this and put it in your pocket. You will need it."

"This is gum, chewing gum."

Charlie looked at the old man, confused.

"It is good Czech chewing gum."

When they reached the car, Enoch opened the trunk and showed him a ten-gallon can and two feet of narrow-gauge hose. "You will need these."

It was becoming clearer to Charlie what Enoch had in mind.

Approaching the outskirts of one of the small villages, Enoch drove the car off to the side near a military truck park. "Grab the can and follow me." Charlie went to the trunk and pulled out the items, and then did as ordered. They crept along between vehicles, and soon they stopped in the shadows between two ten-ton trucks.

Russian, Charlie thought. He saw the Czech markings on the doors but knew the Russians had supplied them.

"Give me some American money, and then try that tank." He nodded to one of the big trucks.

Charlie did as Enoch told him. He unscrewed the cap, smelled it—definitely gasoline. He stuck one end of the hose into the fuel tank and sucked on the other end. Soon, he spit hard on the ground, and as quickly as he could, stuck the hose into the can. He heard the trickle of fuel. He spit again. He quickly opened the wrapper to get at the gum, and chewing feverishly, he looked up to see the old man laughing.

An approaching figure cut short their levity. "Hey! You there. What are you doing? This is military property," a young soldier called to Enoch.

Enoch walked over to greet the soldier before he could see Charlie. "I've come to trade," Charlie heard him say. "I have American dollars. What are they worth to you, my young private?"

"Let me see them," the soldier said.

"See?" Enoch showed him the bills.

Charlie quickly capped the tank and his can, rolled up the hose, and steadily crept back toward the road. He reached the Mercedes, set the can down beside the rear tire, and kneeled out of sight. Soon he heard footsteps. He pulled the old revolver and peeked through the glass of a side window. It was the old man. Charlie breathed a sigh of relief.

"Put in the fuel and we'll get out of here," Enoch said.

The drive back to Prague was less eventful. Charlie did not speak, but Enoch seemed to be having a running conversation with himself. Charlie wondered how the man could be crazy as hell one moment and so lucid the next.

"I will take you to a taverna where the woman has dinner each evening, but I will not go in. It's wiser that way."

"You know Marie Benes?"

"I am her godfather, but now it is better if we do not speak," he said. "You will tell her nothing of your plans. Then she cannot betray you."

"Because she works for the government?"

"Because she works with the MGB," he replied. "I know their methods. They treat Czech security like their dogs and think they are all paid off by Americans and British."

"What then?"

"What then!" Enoch looked to the heavens and launched into a tirade against the Germans and Russians. "You will see, my friend. Her actions will surprise you, but not to worry. Yahweh has plans for you...and the chosen one."

Charlie did not ask what he meant. He was learning not to ask the old man too many questions.

"Give me your pistol," Enoch said.

Charlie pulled the revolver from his belt and with great hesitation, handed it to Enoch.

Enoch took the pistol and immediately threw it out the window. "Junk," he said. "Take this automatic." He pulled a weapon from inside his coat and handed it to Charlie. "It's a Walther P38. The best. It cost me fifty dollars American. That soldier back there drove a hard bargain."

Charlie took it, slipped out the magazine, checked it, and reinserted it. He stuck the weapon in his belt. "Thanks."

Enoch parked the Mercedes in an alley, about a block away from where he told Charlie Marie had dinner each night. "We are early," he said. "Find a spot in the shadows and wait. Make sure she's alone."

Charlie did not bother to ask why he knew so much about Marie's nightly routine. "I need some of my money," he said.

Enoch looked at him. "Money? You want money from a poor old Jew?" He smiled. "Here, take this and only drink the lager. It's kosher. The other is sinful for you." He handed him Czech currency.

Charlie got out of the car.

"Oh, one more thing. If she is with a Russian, shoot him and save us some time."

Charlie did not reply, just turned and walked toward the taverna.

Inside, he ordered a lager—the one Enoch recommendedand walked to a far corner to sit. The room was full of people and cigarette smoke. He looked around and saw workers, soldiers, men in suits, women in dresses. *A good cross-section of Prague,* he thought. Sipping his beer, he waited quietly. Much of the conversation he overheard was political—the new government, the Russians. Charlie found talk of the American and British airlift to Berlin to be the most interesting news.

"Let the Germans starve. They deserve no better," he heard a man say.

Marie entered before he had finished his beer and she walked to the opposite corner of the room and sat down in a booth. She spoke with a waiter and quickly began reading something. Charlie, looking hard across the wide, smoky room, saw it was not a newspaper but a document of some sort. She did not seem to take much interest in it, as if it was a prop.

He prepared to walk over to her, but before he stood, a tall man was at her table. They shook hands and the man sat down. She obviously was expecting him. The man wore a suit and heavy coat, with nothing on his head. He shed the coat before he sat. Charlie could only make out the back of the man's head—a dark head of hair with no gray.

The two began to converse. It did not appear to be lively and light, like two lovers on a date, but much more somber and hush-hush.

Charlie, from the shadows, continued to watch. Marie's soft, gentle smile was gone. He was seeing someone else, someone tough, cold. Her eyes seemed distant. She was not looking at the man while he spoke; she was looking through him.

He ordered another beer, hoping the crowd would stay to continue his cover. If the cigarette smoke lifted, he knew Marie would see him.

The man quickly perused the document Marie was reading, then stuffed it into his shirt, close to his chest, Charlie observed. They both ate but drank very little. Soon, before Charlie had finished his second beer, they got up. The man paid the bill.

Charlie watched as they left separately. The man left first through the front door. Marie waited until he was out the door and then departed by the side door. Charlie ran outside to try to catch her, but she had disappeared into the dark night. He ran around the building to follow the man, but he also was gone.

A clandestine meeting of some type? Charlie looked into the darkness, walked to the end of the block, and finally returned to the tavern. He paid his bill and left.

Enoch was snoring when he got to the car. "Hey," Charlie said, leaning in the window. "Wake up."

The old man opened his eyes with a jerk. "Seen her, eh? Talk much?"

"No, she met with a man, and then they left separately." Charlie looked around, and then he got into the Mercedes. "Let's go."

Enoch stared straight ahead for a moment. "You did not recognize the man? Young? Old? Czech or foreign?"

"Young and well dressed. Why?"

"You must remember. She is a Bolshevik now. Life is serious—deadly serious."

He turned the ignition key and the old Mercedes roared to life. "Now, the war against the Sodomites will begin," he said pleasantly as if it were a sporting event. "I wish the plagues of Egypt upon them, slowly, one at a time. Blood, frogs, eternal darkness—until they beg God for mercy."

The car jerked forward, and within seconds was roaring down the old brick street.

Chapter 24

Soon, they were in the country. Charlie rolled down his window to take in the fresh night air. He inhaled deeply. It felt good not breathing the polluted, soot-filled air of the city.

Enoch looked at him and smiled. "The great god of Moses and Akhenaten watches over us."

"Who?"

Enoch looked at him, surprised. "You know Moses, don't you, my boy?"

'My boy?' What kind of bull is that? Charlie thought. "Yes. Do you think he's concerned about us?"

"Of course," Enoch replied. "I think, my boy, you do not understand. Moses was a follower of the pharaoh, Akhenaten. A later pharaoh, Ramses, the one who ruled during Moses' time, drove Moses and the Israelites out of Egypt for following the true religion of the one single god--Aten. He was the God of Akhenaten. We're all followers of Aten, even the Muslims. For us, he is called Allah or Yahweh. You just need to understand your religious history. When we have time, I will teach you about the true religion."

"I see you've been giving it a lot of thought."

"Since the war, I've thought about it, wondered why things happened the way they did, why God ignored our suffering. I can't forget that...ever." He stared directly ahead.

Charlie watched Enoch, more confused than ever. "I understand why you feel that way, but what's all this Aten stuff?"

"An old man thinks a lot, tries to understand. I must believe, yet I want to reason it all out, but I refuse to give up what I believe. I think Yahweh is old like me. He doesn't always see everything and missed our terrible suffering. I must believe that."

"I don't believe in God," Charlie replied with a shrug. "I can't accept that God —any God—would allow something like that to happen. I decided that we're alone and we should make the best of it."

Enoch looked long and hard at the younger man. "Don't be foolish, my boy."

"I've learned to live in a world where nothing is certain, not God, not anything." He looked at Enoch and saw he was listening intently, as if pondering Charlie's words.

"You sound so certain," Enoch said, then laughed.

"Is that funny?"

"You are certain about uncertainty? I think you are very confused."

"Perhaps."

"I think you believe in many things, my young friend," the old man replied. "Like a fish, I believe everyone should swim, and you are swimming very well, but in very dangerous water, surrounded by hungry sharks."

Charlie thought a moment. "I've learned well how to swim with my beliefs."

"Then you swim alone, my young friend."

"I believe in myself and my ability to get out of trouble."

Enoch smiled. "That's good. For a while, I believed God had abandoned us, and I searched for a sign, some type of meaning from all the death and suffering I saw. Then one day, I decided I had to keep my faith. God would reveal his plan when He was ready, and who was I to challenge his way."

Charlie was quiet.

"Religion is about many things, but mostly, I believe it is a way we try to make sense of the world we live in," the old man said.

Enoch impressed Charlie with the clarity of his views.

"It's about our need to wonder and marvel at how great the universe is, and it's about our struggle to find our place," Enoch continued. "We are small, like bits of sand on a beach. When you look up at the stars, see that our problems are very small. Remember this, my boy."

Charlie looked at him. "Religion oppresses and reduces that universe to simple laws and rules," The conversation was beginning to bore him. "I thought you were angry at God."

"Angry yes, but I can never disrespect someone so much greater than myself."

Charlie was impressed with his strength and, at the same time, he pitied him for his time-consuming battle with himself over an idea.

"You must have faith," Enoch said again, as if reading his thoughts. "Only through faith can we have hope. Not only for ourselves, but also for the salvation of humanity.

"Even for the sodomites?" Charlie chuckled.

The latter statement made the old man smile. "Laugh, my friend. That is important, too."

"You're right," Charlie managed to say.

Czech police stopped them twice before they were able to get out of Prague. They looked for Charlie. The police description had Charlie wearing a beard with much longer, lighter hair. Both times, they checked their passports. Charlie was using the one given him by Marta and returned to him by Louisa, stating he was Edvard Konacek from Pilsen.

At the first checkpoint, Enoch told them he was a rabbi who had lost his flock during the war. "Himmler destroyed my flock but couldn't hurt my religion. Now, I am a simple carpenter. This man is my assistant," he told them. They asked to see his tools. Enoch opened the trunk, and there laid out neatly were the tools of the trade. "We are going to Bratislava to build furniture," he said. If they had searched under the tools, they would have found Enoch's old Mauser, neatly wrapped in an oily sheet.

Outside Prague, on the main highway to Slovakia, police stopped them again. Czech soldiers assisted them. "Are we at war? Have the Nazis returned?" Enoch asked a military officer who appeared to be in charge.

"No, we are looking for an American spy," he replied.

"What do we have that the Americans want?"

The soldier smiled. "The Russians want him, so we help them."

"Don't help them too much."

The soldier laughed.

They arrived in Bratislava before nightfall. Charlie was ready for a break after listening to the old man the entire trip. Enoch tried hard to convert him, but for the life of Charlie, he still did not know to which religion. The man talked about Moses, then Jesus, and at other times, he spoke of the ancient Egyptians again. He even heard Muhammad's name mentioned.

"How do you know the Benes family?" Charlie asked.

"During the war against the Satanists," he replied.

"Were you in the mountains?"

"No." He parked the Mercedes a block from Jürgen's house. There were no lights on anywhere. "We wait and watch," Enoch said. He switched off the ignition and slumped down in his seat.

"Then you knew him before the war?"

"Yes, and we found each other again after it ended. We all lost someone, but he found her—his daughter. Almost at the gates of hell, but she was saved from the fire. Mine had already disappeared into the raging inferno."

"Jürgen is still in the mountains with the child."

"I know this," Enoch replied. "We wait. They will check his house again. I know their ways. The devils."

The two men sat in the car as first one, then two hours passed. Finally, around 10:00, a nondescript gray car stopped in front of Jürgen's house. Two men dressed in long overcoats got out and walked to the door. When there was no answer at the door, one man walked alongside the house, apparently looking for a way in.

"The Satanists have come," Enoch said loudly. "It is time. Come." He reached under the seat and pulled out a hammer.

"What are we doing?" Charlie asked. "I think they're Czech security."

"They're all the same," Enoch replied. "Follow me." He got out and ran toward the police car.

Charlie followed him even though he was confused about what the old man planned to do.

When Enoch reached the car, he began to pound on the windows with the hammer. With each swing of the hammer, he yelled, "Kill Sodomites! Kill Satanists!" When the rear window collapsed, he ran around the car to the windshield.

One of the police officers ran toward him, pistol drawn. "Stop! I order you to stop!"

"Yahweh commands it!" Enoch answered.

"Stop, or I'll shoot you crazy old man," the police officer said. He aimed his weapon. The other police officer ran from the Benes house to join him.

Charlie instinctively pulled the P38 from his belt, even though he had no idea what was happening. "Don't shoot him," he yelled, running across the street toward Enoch.

With a final blow of the hammer, Enoch shattered the windshield. "I demand that you surrender and beg forgiveness," he said. "The Lord commands it." His deep voice resonated across the dark night.

The first police officer answered with two shots from his revolver. One struck Enoch in the chest but did not seem to slow the old man. He continued swinging the hammer at the sedan.

Charlie returned their fire. "Enoch, get back," he called. He fired again and kept up firing until he could get to the old man. "We've got to get out of here. Back to the car."

"Messengers from Stalin, sent from hell," Enoch replied. He held his hand over the wound. "Bastards!"

"Stay down," Charlie said. He saw that Enoch was bleeding heavily. The thin shirt he wore was a deep red.

"Sofia, no. This is the only way. Soon the country will rise up," Enoch said. He was beginning to mumble and whisper nonsense.

Charlie dragged the old man down the narrow brick street. With his arm wrapped tightly around him, he ran toward the car with all the strength he could muster. Bullets zinged overhead.

Charlie swung the driver door open and threw Enoch in. "Start the car. I'll cover us." He returned fire until the magazine was empty. He pulled another from his pocket that Enoch had given him—his last--snapped it in, and continued firing. Enoch turned the key and the engine roared to life.

"Go!" Charlie dived in the passenger side.

Enoch floored the gas pedal and the old car shot down the street. They slid across the corner, smashing over a lamppost, as Enoch barely made the turn. A single bullet penetrated the rear window but lodged harmlessly in the backrest.

"Soon, every security agent in the country will know where we are," Charlie said.

"They already do. It was only a matter of time before they came here."

"Who were you talking to back there?"

"Talking to?"

"Who is Sofia?"

"She's my wife. We still talk when it suits her. Doesn't matter to her what I'm doing."

"She's gone. Don't you understand?" Then, Charlie noticed blood oozing from the wound. "We've got to take care of that. Or you'll bleed to death."

"I can't die until my mission is finished."

"Right."

Enoch continued to drive while Charlie tended to his wound. He tore off part of his own shirt, exposed the area around the small-caliber hole, and stuck a piece of the cloth into it. "When we get out of town...in the country, stop. You hear me?"

"I will get you and the child out of the country. She has demanded that."

Charlie looked at him. "Don't forget Marie."

"She won't be going with you."

They drove east, the road taking them higher into the Carpathians. "Stop, and I'll dress your wound," Charlie said.

Enoch pulled the car over, opened the door, and crawled from behind the wheel.

Charlie got out of the sedan holding a canteen of water and walked to the driver side. "Get in the backseat. We'll use this." He held it up.

"That's all the water we have."

Without responding, Charlie poured water on the wound. "Drink the rest." He saw that there was no exit wound, so the bullet was somewhere in his chest. *Not good.* He tore another strip from his shirt and wrapped it around Enoch's chest. "The bleeding has slowed," he said, more to reassure him. "Lie back in the seat and hold your hand against the wound."

Enoch did as Charlie told him without question. "They will come. Eventually, they'll come. You must be prepared for it."

Charlie ignored him. "I'll drive. I know the way."

They returned to the narrow road. Charlie figured they were still more than an hour away. He looked in the rearview mirror at his wounded passenger. Enoch stared at him but said nothing.

Forty-five minutes later, he turned off the road onto a rutted, one-lane path through the woods. "Almost there," he said. "Jürgen can tend the wound."

Enoch became agitated and began to weep. He started rocking back and forth in the seat, and the motion caused the bleeding to increase.

"Lie still," Charlie ordered.

"The light has gone out. Darkness is descending on the Czech lands." Enoch sat straight up. His eyes were on fire. "I cannot stop it."

"Lie still," Charlie repeated.

Enoch fell back into the seat. He gasped, fighting for breath. Then he was silent.

"You okay? Talk to me," Charlie said. He looked into the rearview mirror and saw that the old man was not moving. He could not hear breathing.

Charlie immediately slammed on the brakes, jumped out, and opened the rear door. He bent over the old man to check his breathing, pulse. Nothing. Enoch was dead.

Chapter 25

Charlie stood in the meadow with Jürgen and Frank, all three bowing their heads out of respect for their friend and comrade. Charlie was holding little Anna in his arms. A strong wind blew out of the northeast, mixed with a cold rain that stung their faces. They stared into the grave where they had just laid Enoch.

Jürgen said a few words in Czech. "He was Jewish, you know? A real survivor." His voice quivered. "But I don't know any Yiddish. I'm sorry."

"He was a brave man who served his God in every way," Charlie said. "He saved my life, fighting against oppression until the very end."

"His wife and child were murdered at Auschwitz. He was my best friend since the early days in Bratislava before the other war," Jürgen continued. "He was Marie's godfather, and he never took the honor lightly. May our friend and compatriot find peace, a peace he never had in this life."

"Amen," the three men said together. Charlie, with Anna still in his arms, and Jürgen turned and walked slowly back to the cabin. Frank stayed to cover the grave.

Back in the cabin, they warmed themselves in front of the old wood-burning stove. "What will you do now?" Jürgen asked. He looked at the child.

"I have a plan to get us out of the country, but it's a long shot," Charlie replied. "Enoch showed me where I can cross the frontier into the American sector of Germany. The area is heavily forested and guarded lightly."

"That's a long way. And you'll have a child with you."

"We must speak about that." He sat down. "Have you heard from Marie?"

"I don't think she should be part of any plan you make."

"I could never separate a child from her mother. Never."

Jürgen stood and paced the room. He said nothing.

Charlie watched him. "What's bothering you, my old friend?"

Jürgen stopped and looked at Charlie. "Marie and I have talked. We both feel that Anna should have a life with you in America, and it is worth the risk. Today, things are much worse. With Soviet tanks ready to storm Prague, we have lost our chance at freedom. You must take the child."

"But..."

"There is something we have not told you," Jürgen said. "We lied to you, but now you must know since Marie will not come with you."

"What are you talking about?"

Jürgen sat next to Charlie. "Anna, go and see Frank."

The child put on her coat and left the cabin.

"The child is not yours...nor is she Marie's."

His statement hit the creaky wood floor like a concrete block. "What?"

"She was an orphan. In the final days of the war, Marie found her as a baby in the streets, abandoned, forgotten, or simply lost in the chaos of war and destruction. We believe the Nazis killed her parents or perhaps sent them to the gas chambers, and they overlooked the child. We will never know what happened to her or her relatives.

Marie said ash and dust covered the child, as she just sat in the smoldering debris. Still, she had the brightest blue eyes. She did not cry, and when she saw Marie, the child smiled, her eyes sparkling like stars in a deep summer sky. It was then that she decided to take her as her own. 'If I don't, she will die,' is what she told me when she brought the child to me. To give her proper lineage, she said you were the father. Marie was proud to tell people that the American soldier, Charles Stanek, was her baby's father. I think the wrong ones heard her."

Charlie was stunned. "Pavlov found out, and he threatened to harm them if I did not return to Czechoslovakia. That's it, isn't it?"

"I'm very sorry, but once the MGB discovered you were her father, the situation was out of our hands. That Russian, Pavlov, seemed obsessed with finding you."

Charlie stared at the wood beams crisscrossing above his head. He said nothing.

"Does this change things for you?"

He looked at Jürgen, stood, and began to pace about the small cabin. "This whole damn nightmare could have been avoided. A little lie has almost cost me my life and placed everyone here in grave danger."

"No, my friend, your past placed you in danger. Your attempt to escape it was futile. I think it was your destiny to return here and settle things."

"Enoch believed Anna is chosen by God for some special purpose. That she is free, unburdened by history."

Jürgen smiled. "He was a crazy old man. Can anyone really escape their past? Germans did terrible things to the Czech people. Can we ever forgive or forget those atrocities?"

Charlie nodded, thinking about his escape to Australia. "I just try to focus on the job at hand."

"Then your past came back to haunt you," Jürgen said. "Enoch was mistaken. His beliefs were those of an angry man who felt betrayed by God. After he lost his wife, he began to question his beliefs and searched for answers. 'Why did God allow such horror?' he often asked me. I had no answers for him. I can only hope he found his way at the end of his life."

"He believed Moses followed some Egyptian god that had become unacceptable to the next Pharaoh. He escaped from Egypt and Ramses' wrath to be free to practice his religion—based on monotheism. He spoke of it."

"Are you comparing Hitler to an Egyptian pharaoh?"

Charlie looked at him, through him, to the outside world as the door opened wide.

Anna entered the cabin with Frank. She held his hand and smiled, a picture of innocence.

"She is my child and will always be mine," Charlie said finally. "We will make the trip together. If I am captured, you must state that I took her from you, kidnapped her."

"I understand."

"Come here," Charlie said. He held out his arms.

Anna hesitated. She seemed frightened and was standoffish.

Her behavior is understandable, he thought, but he felt hurt, believing she feared him.

They began to prepare for Charlie's escape with Anna. He would drive Enoch's Mercedes after they packed weapons, food, and clothing for the child. Jürgen would go with them as far as the border. Frank would go to Bratislava and stay in Jürgen's house to divert the attention of Czech security. If they arrested and interrogated him, he would tell them that Jürgen was in the mountains, held hostage by Charlie. They figured that might stall them long enough for Charlie and Anna to get away.

They had not heard from Marie. Charlie knew she was the missing part of his plan, and he understood he had come between her personal feelings and her commitment to Czechoslovakia. But what he did not understand was how she was willing to give up Anna for her cause.

The trip out of the mountains was without incident. They saw no police or soldiers. Soon, they stopped at a dilapidated roadside inn where Jürgen knew the proprietor.

Frank stayed in the car with Anna while Jürgen and Charlie went into the inn. The two old men greeted each other with emotion.

"It has been a long time," Jürgen said. "So much has happened."

"Too long," the proprietor replied. "Who is your young friend?"

"This is Charles, a friend from the war." The two men shook hands.

"I am called Josef. Please sit."

All three sat in a small room, surrounded by dry goods.

"Every day I read about new events, and the Russians get closer," Josef said. "What will happen to us, old friend?"

"We are like an apple caught in a vice. We can only hope we won't be crushed."

Charlie did not speak.

"That is so," Josef replied. "Now, what can I get you? I don't have much, but what I have is yours."

"We need petro for our old car. Do you have any?"

The old man frowned. "Petro, a very rare commodity." He sighed. "I can get you maybe twenty gallons. Will that help?"

"That will help," Jürgen replied. "Thank you." He touched the other man on the arm. "What are the rumors from the city? Have you heard anything interesting?"

"I hear only that our government is making a close alliance with Stalin. Farmers have reported seeing Russian soldiers to the east. I worry."

"We have seen Russians in the mountains," Jürgen said. "Other news?"

"The police search for an American who they say killed a Russian." His eyes searched the faces of Jürgen and Charlie. "I say good for him."

All three men laughed, but there was a hollow ring to it.

"I will also buy food for us, and then we must go."

"I understand," Josef replied. "Be careful. I hear the streets of Bratislava have police on every corner. They are security police who work with the MGB."

Jürgen and Charlie stood. They both shook the old man's hand. "Pump the fuel. I'll get the food," Jürgen said.

Charlie nodded and left.

"We must change our plan," Charlie said. They were nearing the outskirts of Bratislava. "We cannot risk driving into the city."

Before they could change their route, they came upon a roadblock. Two police officers standing in the middle of the road stopped them. Both were armed.

"Do we try to run it?" Charlie asked. He looked to Jürgen.

"Stop. We can't risk a chase in this old car."

Charlie downshifted and brought the Mercedes to a halt. A police officer stood at each of the front windows. "IDs," the police officer at Charlie's window said. "Everyone's."

"Even the child?" Charlie asked. He felt for the automatic under his coat.

"No."

Charlie collected the IDs, added his passport, and handed all three to the cop. They watched as he read the documents while looking at each face carefully.

"Edvard Konachek. That's you?"

"Yes," Charlie replied.

"Only a passport. Where's your ID?"

"I'm only visiting here. I live in Pilsen. I've recently returned from the Soviet Union, where I studied engineering. See the stamps?"

"Please get out of the car." He stepped back from the vehicle. "Everyone out of the car, including the child."

"May I ask why?"

"There's a dangerous criminal on the loose. We must check everyone out." He looked Charlie over, and then slowly opened the passport again. "Your hair. It's different. Why?"

"That was during the war. A snapshot in Moscow by the Army."

The man nodded. They stood on the road, their backs to the car. The other police officer looked Jürgen and Frank over. "Your child?" he asked Frank.

Other vehicles began to line up behind theirs, but there was no honking or yelling. Everything was very orderly, very patient, and extremely anxious.

"No...his," he replied.

"This your car?" he asked.

"I got it from a Nazi general just before the war ended. I've been driving it ever since."

"In Russia?"

"Parked it for a while when I was in Moscow."

The cop walked to the back of the Mercedes. "A bullet hole...how'd that happen?"

"The German didn't want to give it up. He needed some persuading."

The cop laughed. "Where were you during the war? In Pilsen?"

"Hell no. Fought as a partisan during the war...with him, up in the mountains." He nodded toward Jürgen. "We blew up Nazi trains." He could tell the cop was impressed and did not seem to notice the different accent. "I figured they owed us this car. It might be old, but it runs good."

"Let them pass," he ordered. "Sorry for the delay."

The four got back in the Mercedes. Charlie started the engine and idled slowly through the barricades. The two police officers stepped aside and waved them through. Two others standing by the barricade waved back. They lowered their Russian PPS43s to allow the car to pass.

"That was close," Charlie said. "How many more of those can we expect?"

"We've got to change routes and avoid Bratislava and Brno. They'll be waiting for us in both cities." Jürgen looked back to Frank. "We'll take you to Prague and drop you off. Near the train station. You will contact Marie in her office. Tell her only that we will meet her after dark at her godfather's house. She must make sure she is not followed."

"I will do as you ask," Frank replied. "What about Anna?" They both looked at the child, now asleep in his arms.

"We'll make sure nothing happens to her. I'll surrender before she is hurt in any way," Charlie said.

"I'm going with you. After I speak with Marie, I'll go to Enoch's house. You could use an extra gun, Uncle," Frank said.

"If that is what you choose," Jürgen said. "But remember... your mission to speak with Marie is very important. She must decide whether she goes with Charles or stays."

The old car roared down the graded road, making up for lost time.

"Stop!" Jürgen ordered. They had passed two old women walking along the road. "Pick them up. They will help us through the next roadblock."

Jürgen extended an invitation, and the women accepted. They got in the back with Frank and Anna.

"Oh, such a beautiful child," one of the women commented. "Who is the father?"

"I am," Charlie replied.

"How far do you travel?" Jürgen asked.

"To Prague," the same woman said.

Chapter 26

Trapped with the Russian MGB agent on a trip to Slovakia or anywhere was the last thing Marie wanted. She had to avoid any future trip there. *But I need an excuse to get away from him,* she told herself.

Marie really did not know where Charlie was, but she knew she had to find him, and she could not do that with the MGB officer with her.

"Major, I will deploy the police, inform them of the importance of catching Stanek, and have them establish barricades on all major highways around Bratislava. I can do that from my office. It's easier that way, so it's not necessary that we go."

Major Malinowsky looked at her. "Yes, you're right. I should also stay in Prague to coordinate my men. We will establish a command post here with your people. You will send everything you discover to me. Any report or incident, no matter how minor."

"I will do it immediately," she replied.

Malinowsky accompanied Marie out of the building, and there they parted. The Russian got into a vehicle and sped away while Marie walked back to her office. She was relieved, but still, she did not know what her next move to find Charlie would be. She suspected her father was with him...and Anna, but they could be anywhere. *I must contact my godfather, Enoch,* she decided. *He will know what to do.*

When she returned to her office, Frank was there to greet her. Marie was shocked to see him. "Frank," she said. "So long...what brings you to see me, and how did you know where I worked?"

He smiled, and they embraced. "Your father...I bring a message," he whispered.

She looked around. "Not here. Come with me." As they left the building, she introduced Frank to the guards as her cousin to satisfy inquiring minds. The eyes of the state were everywhere. She felt them. *Things are changing quickly,* Marie thought with growing concern.

She led Frank to a small café near her building. It was crowded with patrons, mostly young people she worked with. She decided it would be safe to talk there. They found a small table in the far corner inside and out of the way.

She ordered tea for both of them. "Now, tell me."

"Your father and Charles are here. They want to meet with you."

"And Anna?"

"She is with us."

Marie smiled. She was again hopeful that things would work out. "The message."

"Meet us tonight after dark at your godfather's house. Make sure no one follows you."

A young male waiter brought tea. "Thank you," she said and paid immediately.

Frank stood. "I must go. It's not safe for us."

"That's the entire message?"

"I must go."

"I will come," she replied.

* * *

A fog covered much of the cemetery, limiting visibility to only a few meters. Jon Grey saw no one as he sat at his usual place on the concrete bench. "Adolph Spelcher," he said, reading the name off a mausoleum a short distance away. He heard footsteps on the walk but did not look away from the name.

Marta sat down several feet away from Jon. He looked at her but hardly recognized the woman. Her hair was no longer dark, and she had pulled it back tightly to wear it under a large floppy hat. Glasses shielded her eyes, and she wore no lipstick.

"What do you want?" she asked bluntly. Marta did not look at him, but stared straight ahead, instead. "Times are very bad. The Russians are sending more soldiers here. There is talk of a big war with the Americans."

"Where is Stanek?" Grey also did not look at her. "I must know."

"Why? So, you can kill him?"

"He's a dangerous man."

"I won't help you." She prepared to stand.

"Wait! That's not what I want," he replied, and finally looked at her. "I just need to know where he is."

"How much is it worth to you?"

"Ten thousand dollars." He pulled an envelope from his coat.

"Jürgen Benes has a friend who lives in Prague. They are there, but you must hurry. He prepares to leave the country soon. Here's the address." She handed him a folded slip of paper with directions already written down. "Now, give me my money, and I will go."

Jon handed her the envelope. She opened it and examined the contents to ensure the full payment was there. "Good, it is as you say," she replied. "Do not contact me for a while, until the latest crisis blows over. It's much too dangerous, and my contacts are worried the MGB will discover them."

"I understand," Jon replied. "About the other... can you help?"

"No, I don't know anyone in the politburo or Central Committee. Find someone else." She got up quickly and disappeared into the mist before Jon could reply.

He sat there, contemplating his next move. He looked at the slip of paper and thought, *I cannot jeopardize my career. I will follow orders.* He had little problem making that decision while forcing issues of right or wrong to the back of his mind. He stood and walked slowly into the mist, going in the opposite direction from Marta.

Chapter 27

The last time Marie had visited Enoch was just before the war ended. She had brought Anna with her. She remembered that he was enthralled with the child. He told her Anna possessed his dead daughter's spirit. "A new world order shall arise from the death and destruction of the camps. It will be a world filled with young survivors like this child, and will be a kingdom of God," Enoch had ranted. His outburst did not surprise her. His beliefs were complicated. She knew that because her father had often told her of Enoch's complex and ever-changing philosophy.

Enoch had been a rabbi before the war. That was before the Nazis had carted off his wife and daughter to Auschwitz, lost to him forever. She remembered that he had said Yahweh had abandoned him and his people. Had he remained loyal to his God? Marie decided that in his strange way he has.

She saw the light inside the house from the street but kept walking. She had to make sure no one had followed her. She walked slowly around the block. Certain no one was behind her, she knocked on Enoch's door and waited. She could hardly contain her excitement at seeing Anna and Charlie again.

The door swung open. She entered and the door slammed close. "Marie," Frank said. He stepped out from behind the door. "Come." He led her into another room in the far back of the house. She walked past the religious icons on the walls.

"Papa," she said, seeing Jürgen standing there ready to greet her. Charlie stood behind him.

"My beautiful daughter," Jürgen replied. They embraced.

"Marie," Charlie said. They also embraced.

"Anna?" Before anyone could reply, the child ran to her.

"Mama," she cried.

Marie raised her up in her arms and hugged her. "My darling girl, I love you so." She set the child back on the floor, still marveling at her. "You've grown so much."

Anna blushed and grabbed hold of Marie's hands.

Marie looked around the room. "Where's Enoch?" she asked.

At first, no one replied, then Charlie answered. "He was killed."

"Oh, my God! In Bratislava?"

"In a shoot-out with Czech security police," Charlie said. "We got away, but he died on the way to the cabin. I couldn't save him. He bled out."

"I'm so sorry." But Marie did not have time for sorrow. "The MGB is everywhere with the police. You must get out of the country now."

"You must come with us," Charlie replied. They both looked at Anna.

"Come, child, you must sleep. Tomorrow, you have a long trip." Jürgen picked Anna up to carry her into another room.

"No! Mama!" She began to cry.

Marie looked at Anna, tears welling up. "Come, Anna, we'll get you ready for bed, and I'll sing you your favorite Slovak lullaby."

Jürgen handed the child to Marie. "Sing the one I sang to you when you were a child, like Anna."

"I remember." With the child in her arms, she went into the next room. Soon, they heard singing from the room:

Raindrops a-falling from the skies,
Tired and sleepy, close your eyes.
Tired and sleepy,
While the skies are weeping,
Weeping and singing you their lullabies.
Tired and sleepy,
While the skies are weeping,
Weeping and singing you their lullabies.

The men were quiet. Jürgen smiled, remembering when he sang the lullaby to Marie.

Charlie also smiled. Then, like something jumping out at him, he remembered. In the woods--it was during the war--Marie would sing that song when they were alone. *Yes, "Raindrops." I'm certain,* he thought. Everything suddenly made sense. Marie could not leave with them, nor could she keep Anna here in the country with her. It was far too dangerous.

A short time later, Marie returned, a bright smile on her face. "Thank you. That was wonderful," she said. She wiped the tears away.

The three sat on the floor in Enoch's parlor. Frank kept a watch at the front window.

"Poor Enoch," Marie said. "He was a strange yet wondrous old man. I loved him."

"A great friend," Jürgen said.

"We leave tomorrow. Or our escape route closes," Charlie said, other things on his mind. "I have no choice."

"I understand," Marie replied.

"Will you go with him and Anna?" Jürgen asked.

"No, Papa, I cannot. I have a mission here in Prague, and it is too dangerous for Anna to stay." She held his hand. "Did you tell Charles about Anna?"

Jürgen nodded, tears flowing easily down his grizzled cheeks.

"I know, and I understand enough about your mission, and I don't want to know more. It's too risky. Anna is now my child, too," Charlie said. "Someday, we will meet again under happier circumstances. I'll still be in Australia." Choked with emotion, he had to force each word out. "I will never forget you, nor will Anna."

Charlie and Marie embraced again, this time more passionately. He held her long, unwilling, or unable to release her. Sadness gripped them. "I will always love you," he said, both resigned to never seeing the other again.

Jürgen stood behind them, his head bowed.

"I love you, Charles. Father, we will see each other in Bratislava when all this blows over. Good-bye." Wiping the tears away, she turned and left. The men silently watched as she left the house. Marie did not look back.

* * *

Walking back to her room, she wondered if she had made a mistake giving up Anna and letting go of Charlie. *I trade them for a life of solitude and loneliness,* she thought sadly, *but if I do not fight for my country, who will? I am responsible for what happens here, and that must drive my actions. My love for them would only be a refuge from my duty, nothing more.*

"I must go on. I will not change my plan," she said into the darkness, but her cries of resolve into the night did little to mask her heartache.

When she got back to her empty room, she quietly undressed and crawled into bed. Tears graced her cheeks. *Life is so tragic.* She began to sob.

* * *

In the predawn hours, a single figure made its way through the narrow yard to the back door of Enoch's house. He tried the door. It rattled but did not open. He moved to a window. Unlocked. He carefully and quietly slid it up. Holding his weapon--a U.S.-issue automatic—tightly, he stepped into the room and looked around, but saw no one. He crept through the open doorway into what looked like a parlor.

He saw two men sleeping on the floor. He walked to the nearest of the two and kicked him in the side to make sure he was the right one. The man raised his head. He looked at his face. Yes, he was the same man from the cemetery. Grey clicked off the safety and prepared to fire.

Charlie reacted quickly. Rolling onto his back, he looked hard at the intruder and recognized him. "You're not a very good burglar, Mr. Grey. I've been listening to you since you tried the door. Put the gun down. You are covered."

"I've been ordered to kill you." Jon pointed his weapon at Charlie's head, and his hand trembled slightly from the weight of the .45, and fear. He had never killed anyone.

"Drop it, or I'll shoot you dead," a voice said. "Now!"

Jon looked over to another man, surprised. "Who are you?" He had not anticipated another man with Stanek. Sturnburg had said only him and a child.

"Drop it," Jürgen said. "I won't say it again."

Jon dropped his weapon—Charlie picked it up and jumped to his feet. Frank grabbed the man and pushed him to a chair.

"Who is this man?" Frank asked.

"An American bastard," Charlie replied. "Shall we shoot him?"

Frank and Jürgen looked at him. "You know him?"

"He works for the American spy service, assigned to the American Embassy here. They were worried I'd talk to the Russians, so they ordered me killed."

"Wait! Don't do anything hasty," Jon said. "I'm only following orders."

"Unless you talk, this will be the last order you ever try to carry out," Charlie said.

"You wouldn't kill an agent of the United States Government." Jon sounded surprised that they would shoot him—him, an American.

"Without hesitation," Charlie replied. "Who gave the order to kill me? Specifically? Name?"

Jon was silent.

Charlie walked over to him and threw a hard right into the man's face. The blow forced Grey back against a wall. Blood flowed from his nose. "We'll start there."

Jon was more shocked than hurt. He raised his arm to cover the blood flow.

"Find a towel," Jürgen said.

Frank walked into the kitchen to find a cloth.

"Now, one more time. Who gave you the order?"

"The Directorate...in Washington.

"Who in Europe?"

"An operative with special orders from the Directorate to terminate."

"Name?"

"I can't."

Charlie planted a left and a right into Grey's midsection. The man bent over in pain.

"I'll ask one more time. His name."

"Johnson. He calls himself Robert Johnson."

The name seemed familiar. "Tell me about him."

Jon looked at him. "Old hand. I think he said he worked for Donovan during the war. In Washington."

"Why is he in London?"

Jon shrugged. "He's not in London. I met with him in Frankfurt. He's assigned to find you and terminate you. He ordered me to assist. That's all I know."

"Then orders to terminate didn't come directly to you from Washington?"

Jon looked at Charlie. He paused to consider. "No, they came from Johnson."

Got a current location for him? Is he still in Germany?"

"You plan on paying him a visit?"

Charlie backhanded him. "Wrong answer, asshole."

"I only have the address where we met." He gave it up to Charlie. Blood from his nose splattered across his face. He tried to stop it with the old cloth Frank handed him.

Charlie conferred with Jürgen while Frank handed Jon another cloth, and sympathetic, tried to help him with the bleeding.

"Here's the plan, Jon. We're going to tie you up nice and secure. Then we're going to leave and, you'll never see any of us again," Charlie said. "You being a smart college boy, I'm sure you'll figure a way to get loose before starving to death."

"But..."

"Or, I could just shoot you and be done with you." Charlie looked at Jürgen and Frank. "By the way, don't tell Johnson you gave up the info on him. It probably wouldn't help your career any."

They were gone within the hour. Before departing, Charlie had tied Grey securely and placed him in a back room. Charlie figured the ropes would hold at least until evening, and he did not expect the American agent would report them to the cops or the Russians. Charlie decided getting to the rendezvous site early was a good idea. That would give them time to check out the place.

Arriving at the cabin without incident, Charlie and Jürgen decided to search the area before they entered the dwelling. They split up. Charlie walked around the cabin to a wooded area, while Jürgen walked down the path a short distance, looking for uninvited guests.

Frank carried Anna into the cabin. Charlie walked deeper into the woods. Fifty meters in, he discovered a well-worn trail that went west into the mountains. If their contact did not show, he would follow that trail. He did not have many other options.

It was a bright sunny day, and the weather was balmy. Returning an hour later from their walks, Charlie and Jürgen sat outside. Frank joined them with beer he had brought. "She's asleep," he said. "She has a long journey ahead of her. It's good that she sleeps."

"Jürgen, it's time for you and Frank to leave," Charlie said.

"I'm going with you," Frank announced. "I can take care of the child, and I want to be free of the Russians. My future is with you."

Charlie and Frank looked at each other, but neither spoke for a moment.

"Much danger lies ahead, and I cannot promise you anything, a job, or even a country."

"I understand, and I'm willing to take that risk."

"Jürgen?" Charlie asked.

"He is a man and can make his own decisions," Jürgen replied.

"I accept your decision," Charlie said with a nod to Frank. "I can use your help."

"I'm ready," Frank replied.

"I've found a good trail if Enoch's contact doesn't show," Charlie said. "We will take turns with Anna. We must bring water for three days...at least, I figure."

While they continued to plan for the trip, Jürgen stood and went into the cabin. Within minutes, he returned. "I've said good-bye to my granddaughter," he said. "Now it's time to go. I must reach the cabin today." He embraced Charlie and Frank. They escorted him to the Mercedes.

"Farewell, old friend," Charlie said. "Somehow, I will send word to you when we reach safety."

Jürgen and Frank shook hands, but neither spoke. Frank was tearful.

Jürgen slowly got in the old Mercedes, cranked the engine, and drove east as the sun rose higher in the sky.

Charlie and Frank spent the remainder of the day preparing. Darkness soon surrounded them. Inside the cabin, they packed and prepared to depart with or without assistance. They divided weapons, ammo, water, and food among the two of them. "You have your documents?" Charlie asked.

"I have a passport, an ID," Frank replied.

"Good," Charlie said. "I have the Edvard Konachek passport. So, for now, only refer to me as Edvard."

Frank laughed.

They packed warm blankets for Anna and rigged a way to carry her. The terrain would be rough, and the trip would be difficult, but they felt prepared.

"How long do we wait?" Frank asked.

"One more hour then we go."

* * *

Jon Grey was badly bruised, and worse, humiliated, by his encounter with Charles Stanek and his gang, as he thought of them. It had taken him almost four hours to get free and back to his small flat. He knew they were long gone. *Probably along the frontier somewhere,* he thought. He showered and ate but decided to wait until evening to go to work.

Darkness had fallen when he arrived at the American Embassy, passed through security, and entered his small office. He saw a cryptogram on his desk waiting for him. He decided it had to be a message from London and Fredericks. He deciphered it and read:

```
Rosebuds has informed us that
Outlaw in Prague. You are ordered by
Washington to provide full assistance
to get Outlaw to west. Repeat: Assist.
Ensure he crosses the border into
Western Germany safely.
```

He immediately saw that the message was from Fredericks, forwarded from the Directorate. Jon was confused and surprised. Johnson had initially ordered him directly to terminate. He had to consider recent events. "Robert Johnson...the bastard has set me up," he blurted out angrily and tore the message into a thousand pieces. *If Stanek disappears, meets with an accident, or the Russians finally capture him, they will blame me*, he thought furious. *Perhaps even accuse me of being a Russian agent. I have no witnesses to my meeting with Johnson, nothing in writing where Johnson orders me to terminate Stanek. I'm certain Johnson sent a message to London and on to Washington, informing them he is prepared to intercept and assist Stanek, IF HE SHOWS. Whose side is he on?*

He duped me, Jon thought, as everything became clear. My word against his. I'm done. Jon stared at the wall, paralyzed.

Chapter 28

Major Malinowsky sat in his staff car, waiting for Marie to exit the building. He had driven as far as the edge of Prague checking roadblocks, and he was insistent that everyone was briefed on the importance of capturing Stanek. No one had reported any encounters or incidents. Stanek had managed to avoid the ten roadblocks his men had painstakingly set up, or they had never left the city. But he also knew that the Czech police and their secret police were notoriously unreliable, and they resented the Russian presence in their country.

Malinowsky wondered if Benes had deceived him. Or, had Stanek successfully escaped? He considered. The terrain would be extremely rugged regardless of where they chose to cross. He thought that fact greatly reduced the odds of Stanek traveling through the densely forested mountains and risk getting lost. All border crossings were on high alert. If Stanek entered Austria, the major believed they could capture him before he reached the American sector. The commander of the Red Army division there had already assured him they were prepared.

He watched Marie come down the stairs of her office building. When she was in front of the car, he called to her. "Comrade Benes."

Marie turned to look. She recognized the Russian and walked briskly to the driver's side. "Major."

"Please get in," he said.

Marie nodded and walked to the passenger side. She opened the door and slid in. "Any news?" she asked.

He looked at her. "I was hoping you had information to share with me."

"I have received no information," she said. "My father has not replied to my correspondence. I suspect he is hunting high in the mountains. He usually does this time of year."

"Nothing?" He found that difficult to believe. "No sightings by police or neighbors?"

"Nothing."

"What about your child? Who is caring for her?"

"Anna?"

"Your child...where is she?" He had caught her off guard, which he easily noticed by her response.

"My Anna is cared for by our neighbor in Bratislava, a babushka who I trust completely."

"Then you've spoken with her? Talked?"

"Not recently."

"I think you should call her immediately," the major said. "Perhaps she has information helpful to us. And I'm certain you're worried about your Anna."

"I will do that when I return to my office."

"I think you should do it now. And I will accompany you." He watched her for some reaction. There was none. "Sergeant," he said. "We will escort Comrade Benes back to her office. A soldier from the rear seat got out to open the door for Marie. He then reached in to grab her arm tightly. He was not polite.

Major Malinowsky got out and walked around the car. "Come." The two Russians flanked Marie, one on each side. They walked back into the building.

The guard passed them through, and they briskly walked up the steps to her office area. When they reached her desk, Marie sat down. The major stood over her while the sergeant remained at the room's entrance. Marie's coworkers watched them.

"Make the call," the major said.

"I will call her son. The old woman has no phone," she said while dialing. "Hello." She got a reply from the other end. While they spoke, the major listened.

"Then my father has Anna?" she asked. "Yes, still in the mountains. Thank you." She hung up and turned to Malinowsky. "I was mistaken. My father still has her, so he has not gone hunting."

"I think you must take us to this cabin in the mountains," he said. "We will depart immediately." He motioned for the sergeant. "Take her to the car. I will be along shortly."

He sat at her desk and, as unobtrusively as possible, went through the documents he saw there. Malinowsky was beginning to have serious concerns about the loyalty of Marie Benes. However, he found nothing that would incriminate her.

The Russian sergeant drove all the way. They passed through the many roadblocks without any delay. Marie sat in front with him, while the major rode in back. They stopped several times for food, fuel, and to relieve themselves. They reached the end of their journey just before nightfall. "Take that turn onto the trail," she instructed.

When they arrived, Marie saw another car parked at the trail's dead end. They carefully approached. The car was empty. The sergeant looked it over closely, to see if it had been driven. "Engine is warm. It was driven maybe within the last hour," he said.

"Whose car? Do you recognize it?"

"The car belongs to a friend of my father's," Marie replied. "He is not a threat."

"I'll be the judge of that. Take us to the cabin." They began to walk, following a well-worn path through the woods. After a distance of about three miles, they reached a meadow. On the far side, they saw a small building, smoke rising from its chimney.

"Do you think your father will mind three more guests for dinner?" the major asked. Both Russians pulled out their pistols. They walked through the meadow toward the cabin as if they were preparing to assault it.

"Is that necessary?" Marie asked.

"Stanek is dangerous, and if he's there, we must be prepared."

"But my father...and Anna. They could be hurt in the crossfire."

"We will be careful. With your assistance."

"Of course. What do you want from me?"

"You'll enter the cabin first. Then I'll follow. The sergeant waits outside. He'll enter when I give the word."

"An ambush?"

Marie walked in, and Major Malinowsky followed. Jürgen greeted them from the other side of the room. "Marie," he said. He did not mask his surprise at seeing Russian MGB with her.

"Papa," she said. "This man is MGB. We have come looking for Charles. Is he here? Please, he must give himself up for your sake."

"No, I have not seen him or your child. I worry they have fled into the mountains...to Austria."

"You're lying," the major said. "I've had enough of you people lying to me to hide a spy and a murderer. Sergeant, come in."

The sergeant entered, pistol drawn.

"Your car is still warm. Where have you been, old man?" Malinowsky asked. "I demand that you tell me."

Jürgen leaned to finish building his fire. "I have been below for provisions. I have been alone."

"Whose car?"

"The car belonged to an old friend who recently passed. He gave it to me. Do you wish to see documents?"

"Tie up the old man," the major said, losing patience. "We'll find out quickly what he knows...and where he's been."

"No, stop! My father," Marie said. She tried to intervene, but the sergeant pushed her away. "Please," she said. "He doesn't know anything."

The Russians ignored her pleas. The sergeant grabbed Jürgen and threw him down in a nearby chair. "Rope. I need rope."

Major Malinowsky looked around the room and saw twine in a far corner.

"Please, Major, not this. He is old. Please."

The major turned to Marie. "Do your duty, comrade, or I will speak to your superiors." He began gathering up the twine.

Marie saw her father's weapon behind the door. It was a German MP44 assault rifle from the war. Avoiding suspicion, she picked it up slowly. She knew her father would keep a round in the chamber and the magazine full for just this type of occasion. His habit from the war. She released the safety.

"Stop, you cannot do this!" She held the weapon tightly, one hand on the grip and the other on the stock. She pointed the barrel at the sergeant.

Everyone turned to look at her.

"Papa, get back toward the door."

"Marie...." He stood and did as she ordered.

"Give me that gun. I order you to give it to me," Major Malinowsky said.

The sergeant made a move, raising his pistol toward Marie. "Drop it, woman!" he said. "Or I will shoot you where you stand."

Marie looked at him with eyes that screamed with rage. "Go to hell!" She opened up with a full burst from the MP44. Its velocity threw the sergeant hard against the wall, bullets stitched across his chest. She turned the weapon on the Russian officer before he could draw his pistol, killing him instantly with a single burst across his midsection.

"It was the only way," she said, looking at her father coldly. "We would both be arrested soon. We will get rid of them and their car." Smoke and the smell of cordite permeated the room, mixing with the smell of death. Their ears rang from the loud crack of the weapon in the small cabin.

Jürgen said nothing.

Chapter 29

Charlie and Frank were preparing to leave on their journey west when they heard a noise from outside the cabin. They grabbed their weapons. Charlie moved Anna to a far corner behind a chair. Then both men took positions at the windows.

"Enoch," they heard from the darkness. "Enoch, it's Henry. Are you ready for the trip?"

"Come closer...in the light where we can see you," Charlie called back to them. He motioned for Frank to cover him, and slowly opened the door. He stood in the doorway, the light behind him. He knew he took a risk by giving them a target.

Two men stepped out of the darkness. Charlie saw a small, slight man, and he thought he made out another, much larger man standing in the shadows. He was prepared just in case it was a trap. He saw that both intruders were bundled up in warm clothes and that they were armed.

The small man smiled. "So, it is you, Stanek. I expected you when I received a message from Enoch. Where is he?"

"He was killed by Czech state security several days ago."

"I'm sorry to hear that. We were friends from the war against the Nazis. He was a good man."

"And a very brave man to the end," Charlie added. "I remember you from Istanbul. Henry. I heard that you were going to Palestine." Henry still wore the old fedora he had worn in Istanbul.

"Yes, someday. Next year, perhaps. For now, my work is here rescuing people like you from the Bolsheviks." He walked toward Charlie and Frank. "How many are you?"

"Two of us and a child. This man is Frank."

"A child?" Henry replied. "Yes, I remember from our meeting, and Enoch said there would be a small girl—Jürgen Benes's granddaughter."

"That's correct. Anna, come here," Charlie called.

Soon Anna appeared in the doorway. She was frightened but did not cry. She stared at Henry.

"She is as he described her," Henry said to his companion, who now stood beside him. The other man smiled. "This man is called William. He is our guide who will take us into Germany. Are you prepared for a three-day trip?"

"We are," Charlie said. "What's the cost of this trip?"

"I'm getting you out as a favor to Enoch. We expect no payment," Henry replied. "I can do this because I'm an independent operator." He smiled broadly. "I help Jews get out of Europe, and fools get in." The men stood outside the cabin, with moonlight pouring down on them. He carefully looked each of the three over.

"Enoch had many friends, Charlie replied."

"We were partners," Henry stated. "If they had money, we always found a way to get them out. Business has been good since the war ended. Enoch will be missed by many."

"We're ready."

"Get your packs and we'll leave. Prepare to travel at night until we cross the frontier. We will enter the American sector, but we won't encounter any outposts until we are several miles inside Germany. The terrain is rough, but we must avoid using any roads."

"I understand."

"When we get inside Germany, William and I will leave. You are Czech refugees fleeing the Communists. Do not tell them you are an American. They will learn your identity soon enough. Do you all have papers?"

"Frank and I have Czech passports. Anna only has an ID."

"Good. We can take care of the child," Henry replied. "Let's go."

Charlie and Frank gathered up their packs. William picked up Anna. "You will travel in front with me," he said. She was not frightened of the large man with the bright blue eyes. She nodded and held on.

The group soon disappeared into the woods. The full moon guided them as they began their ascent into the mountains.

The travel became increasingly difficult as the mountains rose higher. William carried Anna throughout the night, and neither she nor William ever complained. Periodically, he stopped to show her a deer, bird, even a wild boar he spotted in the dark. She was enthralled. When the sun rose, Henry called a halt. They built a small fire to prepare a meal.

"Keep the fire small," he said. "Rest. You will need it. The climb becomes steeper before getting better." The four men stretched out beside the fire. Anna was already asleep under a large oak that loomed over the campsite.

"Enoch said the child was special. He believed God chose her to live when others around her did not. She has a special purpose, he said." Henry looked at the child. "I think she belongs in this new state called Israel."

Frank and William slept. Their snores echoed through the small clearing.

"I don't know if she's Jewish or Gentile," Charlie said.

"What does it matter? She is a survivor of the Nazis." He watched Charlie. "What do you think about taking her to Israel?"

"She is my responsibility and mine alone."

"You are mistaken," Henry replied. "God will take care of her."

"I don't believe that," Charlie answered. "We are alone. I must take care of her now. She is my responsibility," he repeated.

"God protects me because I work for Him. He protects her because he must. But you, my friend…" He shrugged and then smiled broadly.

"He is not a part of my world," Charlie said. "And I don't expect any help from him."

"Yes, but the child…She needs a family who will love her and raise her."

"I'll find a way to take care of her."

"Enoch believed that God has a special purpose for her. That is why she still lives."

"I don't believe such things."

"She must be made safe, protected. That is most important. Can you do that?" Henry asked.

The heat from the embers cooled.

Charlie did not answer him.

Finally, the fire died. Neither spoke, both thinking private thoughts.

During the morning hours, as the sun rose higher in the sky, the five travelers busied themselves with small tasks, waiting for the shadows to return. The men watched the sky, always alert to planes while Anna played with sticks. Henry assured Charlie that no patrols from either country would venture this far. "Too much work," he told him.

Late in the afternoon, they broke camp and departed. William took the lead with Anna on his back. He seemed to enjoy her presence and she his. They walked carefully through narrow, heavily wooded valleys and picked up different trails, all the while moving westward. Charlie figured they were more than halfway across and were probably already in German territory. *Was that a good thing*? he wondered.

Around midnight they stopped to rest. "Tomorrow we will reach the first American checkpoints. Then you are on your own. I must take your weapons, or they'll find them when they search you," Henry said.

"Will we see you again?" Frank asked. He did not like the idea of giving up his weapon.

"They will send you to a refugee center to be processed. After...? Probably moved to a camp where you can stay. Speak no English to them. Only Czech."

"But we don't have to stay there?"

"You can leave after they process you and determine you pose no threat to security. At that point, I will make contact. If you want your pistol, I will return it." Henry admired the Walther P38.

"I understand." Charlie paused to consider. "What about intelligence agents? Will we be interrogated?"

"Possibly," Henry replied. "Say little and stick to your story, Edvard."

"What do you know about American spy operations in Europe?" Charlie asked. "I need information to know we aren't walking into some trap. They are looking for me and probably have the word out that I'm crossing."

"I worked with Allen Dulles and the OSS at the end of the war. Knew him personally. But I know nothing about the new boys in the CIA." He looked at Charlie. "We know they are searching for you just like the Russians are, but with thousands of refugees to deal with, we must gamble that you will be missed. That is your only chance, I'm afraid."

"That's not too reassuring, but at least, Anna will get to safety."

"Sorry, Henry replied. "I have contacts, mostly from the war. This standoff between the West and the Russians creates new problems. My business is to provide safe passage not to spy."

"Have you ever heard of Attila? He is a double agent for the Russians, working the game since the war. I don't think the Americans have found him yet."

"Yeah, brutally efficient and ruthless. I've heard of him... from the war."

"That, but mostly just smart, I'd say."

"That's all I know about him except that the Americans and the Brits are still looking for him. He's got great cover to stay in business for so long. During the war, if there was any question about someone's loyalty, he terminated him. Several British operatives in Germany behind Russian lines at the time were killed, and the deaths had his MO. That was after the Germans had already surrendered. That's all I know about Attila." Henry shrugged.

"How do you know this?" Thinking of Attila brought back his memories again. He knew his path had crossed with that of Attila at some point during the war. Charlie had met many of his OSS colleagues. He wondered about the double agent's tenure in Eastern Europe. *Had he been turned there?*

Zerenowsky had warned me of Attila when I had debriefed him. He even claimed he had given the agent his moniker. But what else did he tell me of the man? I have to remember, Charlie thought, closing his eyes.

"Like Enoch, I've been around a long time and heard the stories," Henry continued. "I've worked with the British and Americans here since 1938. Their networks were small, and during the war, I recruited many of their top agents, several still operating."

"Like Raindrops?"

He paused. "I don't know anything about that one. He work in Russia?"

"I don't know," Charlie said. "Thanks for the information."

"Let's go," Henry said. "We must reach the checkpoint at dawn. It's easier to get across then. The Americans aren't awake yet."

The group slowly began to move out.

At dawn, they saw the lights of the first checkpoint covering the road below them. Henry and William collected the weapons and disappeared into the trees. Charlie led the way down the mountain, about twenty meters ahead of the others, while Frank carried Anna. When they were on the road, near the crossing, Charlie stopped. He raised his arm to alert the small band, and seeing the signal, they moved slowly forward.

American soldiers at the checkpoint saw them. Four walked forward with their pistols out.

"Halt and identify yourself," one of the soldiers ordered, speaking in English.

Charlie and Frank stopped and waited without speaking. Frank set Anna on the road and held her hand. She pointed at the Americans and smiled.

Soon the soldiers were upon them. Pointing their weapons, they surrounded the refugees. Two searched Charlie and Frank, patting them down and rifling through their packs.

"Where do you come from?" a sergeant, the highest-ranking soldier, asked after they had completed the search.

"No English," Charlie said. "Refugee, help."

"They're unarmed, Sarge," a soldier said after rummaging through their backpacks. "Clothing, some food, water. Nothing else."

"Come on," Sarge said, He motioned them forward, and Charlie and Frank followed with Anna in tow. She turned and waved at the three soldiers who followed behind.

"Cute kid," Charlie overheard one of the soldiers say.

When the group reached the checkpoint, an officer stopped them. "Who are they?"

"I think they're refugees, probably from Czechoslovakia," Sarge said. "No weapons found, but they have identification."

"Load 'em up."

The soldiers took them to a camp outside town, several miles from the checkpoint. In a large green tent, a soldier fed the three a hot meal. One of the guards played with Anna while Charlie and Frank ate. "Your daughter?" he asked Charlie. "Where is mama?"

Charlie looked at him, feigning ignorance, but when he heard "mama," he reacted. "No mama," he said. "No, no. Nazis."

The soldier acted as if he understood.

"Let's go," the soldier who appeared to be in charge said. "In the truck." He pointed to the open back of an Army truck. "Get in, get in now."

Charlie crawled up and then helped Frank and Anna. When the child was in, she ran to the front and looked in the cab window.

Two soldiers got in with them, and within minutes, they were moving. No one spoke. One of the soldiers offered cigarettes, but both Charlie and Frank refused.

When they finally arrived at a large open, grassy area with rows of tents, they disembarked from the truck. A young soldier led them into some type of processing center. Charlie was cautious. He looked at the soldiers standing in front of him. Then he looked at Frank. "I will do the talking," he said, whispering in Czech. "They want intelligence on the Russians, I'm certain."

A higher-ranking officer accompanied by a civilian female approached Charlie.

"Your passport," the soldier said.

Charlie handed it to him.

The woman began to speak to him in Czech while the soldier slowly reviewed it.

"Where do you come from?" she asked.

The woman spoke a dialect from the Prague area, Charlie noticed. "Slovakia in the mountains," he replied.

"Why do you leave your country?"

"The Communists now run the country. We see many Russian tanks," he replied. "We wonder if another war is starting. We decide to leave because we have no future there."

"I understand." She looked at Anna. "Your child?"

"My child," Charlie replied. "Her mother was killed by the Nazis." Charlie could tell the woman was sympathetic.

"Let them through," she said in English. "Later, the Americans will want to speak to you...about the Russians."

"I understand," he replied.

The Americans soon loaded the three of them into a truck with two women and several small children and drove them to a nearby village. The truck stopped in front of a large concrete building, and the MPs escorted them inside, but not under armed guard.

Looking around at the barracks-style building, Charlie thought the German Army had built and used it during the war. Inside, he saw men, women, and children milling about. *Obviously, refugees*, he thought.

"You can stay here for several days or until you have a place to go. Do you have money?" the soldier asked.

"Money?" Charlie asked.

The young soldier pulled out a German mark and showed him. "Money."

Charlie shook his head. "Money, yes," he said in English. "We sleep here?"

"Yeah, right here, and don't go nowhere," a private replied sternly.

The two men relaxed on the cots provided. Anna immediately fell asleep. Charlie gave Frank several thousand American dollars. "Just in case we're separated," he told him. "You will need it."

"Charles," Frank said. "Maybe Israel is not a bad idea. It is a new country, and Henry said that he would make sure Anna is a citizen. He believes she is special. Many opportunities, I think."

"A place to start over?"

"I think, yes."

"Edvard Konachek?" The female translator called from the entrance. "Come with me." Two military police flanked her.

"Trouble," Charlie said. "If I don't return, take Anna to Israel. I will try to find you."

Frank nodded.

The two MPs walked stiffly to their cots and waited for Charlie. "Come with us," one said.

Charlie did not resist. The three joined the translator, and they all left the building. The MPs escorted Charlie to another, smaller building. They took him down a hallway that led into a small windowless room. He knew what that meant.

He sat in the hard-back chair for what he decided had to be several hours without anyone speaking to him. Finally, a soldier entered, accompanied by the translator. Charlie saw that the man was a major, and by the insignia on his collar, Intelligence.

"You are Edvard Konachek?" He held Charlie's passport. "Your birth date?"

The question surprised him, but he was prepared. "October 21, 1919."

The soldier sat down. "I am Major John Korning. We have several questions that we need answered before you can enter this zone, which you should know is the American Zone of operations."

The woman continued to translate. She never gave her name.

"I will answer your questions," Charlie replied in Czech.

"You have stamps that show you were in the USSR for more than two years. Please explain."

"I was selected to go to Moscow for training as an engineer. When it was complete, I returned home."

"Are you a communist?"

Charlie expected that question, and he was prepared. "I was asked to join the party, but I refused. It was then that they sent me home."

"Your passport indicates you were born in Pilsen, but you told one of the MPs that you were living in Slovakia."

"My wife was Jewish. We fled to the East early in the war, to the Carpathian Mountains, but they eventually found us. They sent me to a work camp while my wife went to Auschwitz, where she died. We hid our child with relatives."

"And following the war?"

"Yes, following...we were liberated by the Russians, and I was offered training in Moscow. I studied for two years. My daughter stayed with family in Pilsen." Charlie stared into the major's eyes, with his hands limply at his side. "I hate the communists, but I know nothing of their operations."

"I'm sorry for all that's happened to you," the woman said.

The soldiers watched the prisoner. Charlie knew the major was trying to decide whether to believe him.

"I am not a Communist," he repeated. "When the new government was installed in Prague, and I saw that it closely allied with the Russians, I knew we had to leave. I cannot live in a conquered land any longer, and my child deserves better."

The officer unfolded a piece of paper, looked at it then back to Charlie.

"What is the problem," Charlie asked.

"An attempt was made on an American employee of our embassy in Prague."

"Successful?"

"I have a description of the suspect, although it's very brief, it matches you in weight and height. The Czech police are saying he was a foreigner, presumably a man with ties to Russian intelligence. A rogue agent. Information we have suggests the man is trying to cross the border somewhere to escape the manhunt. This has become an international incident as you would expect, and all militaries in Central Europe, especially the Russians, are searching."

"I know nothing of this."

"The man is said to be an American by the name of Charles Stanek, an international outlaw."

"I've never heard of him," Charlie replied. "Please, you must believe me."

The major stared at Charlie as if trying to decide something. "You will stay here tonight. Tomorrow we will decide your fate."

"You can't send me back. Please...my child and my nephew...what of them?"

The two rose to leave. "For the time being, they are safe in the barracks."

One day passed, then two. Finally, on the third day in lockup, the major entered with the interpreter in tow. "Bring him to the second room," the major ordered two MPs. One man on each side of Charlie, they marched him to the room, positioned him in the middle, and then stood at the door.

The major and interpreter entered and sat at the desk. Charlie stood in front of them. He had not cleaned up in days. "Let me go!" he said. "I'm a refugee, and I must see my daughter."

"Your appearance only vaguely matches that of this Stanek. We've found no evidence to support your story, but we cannot dispute it either. We have looked through our lists and have found that your name and description do not match any lists we have of felons, so we, by established policy, cannot send you back as you are claiming refugee status," the major said. He observed Charlie closely.

"You have a small child who is much better off with a parent. That is in your favor," the interpreter added.

"You are free to leave," the soldier said. The woman translated.

"I can see my daughter and nephew?"

The two looked at each other. "A man arrived this morning, and they left with him. We believed he was a relative of yours."

"What did he look like?"

The woman listened as the soldier explained. "He was a small man, very polite. He wore an old fedora. Here. He gave me this to give to you." He handed Charlie a folded slip of paper.

The woman interpreted. Her cold, empty smile began to irritate Charlie. He felt like slapping her, but when she finished, he humbly thanked her. He read the message written in Czech: "Meet us in Munich at the Hotel Bavaria. We will wait for you." He was relieved but said nothing to the soldier or the interpreter.

"The hotel is easy to find. We have a bus that will take you to the city later this morning. There are shower facilities in the barracks. You will be given toiletries."

The bus stopped in front of Hotel Bavaria as darkness set in. Charlie departed and made for the entrance. Days earlier, before the Americans, he had hidden dollars in the bottom of his boot. They had taken his boots when they locked him up, but no one bothered to look inside. He figured he had a thousand remaining.

Inside, a crowd of men, all wearing American Army uniforms, swallowed him up. He looked around and decided to head for the front desk. He walked slowly through the crowd, smiling and nodding. "No English," he said if someone tried to speak with him. He felt uncomfortable as if someone was watching him.

At the desk, he described Henry, Anna, and Frank in Czech. The clerk looked at him, not understanding. He retreated to speak with a woman, and they conferred in German. Charlie understood bits and pieces of the conversation. "He's the man, Konachek," he heard the woman say.

Charlie waited, and the man returned to the counter.

"Room 234," the man said and handed him a key.

He picked up the key and left. *Something isn't right*, he thought, climbing the stairs to the room. *Did Henry take care of all my accommodations?*

Just before reaching the room, he saw a table with half-eaten food and silverware on it. Charlie picked up the knife. *Just in case*, he thought. He knocked on the door, wondering if he would find Frank and Anna inside.

There was no answer, so he opened it and entered. It was a suite of two rooms. The first room was dark, so he went to the window and opened a curtain. He walked toward the second room. He was finally beginning to relax.

Suddenly, a tall man dressed in a dark suit and holding an American .45 automatic stepped out of the shadows to confront him. Charlie turned to run for the door but saw that he could not outrun a bullet. He was trapped. He turned to the sound of the voice.

"Mr. Stanek, I've been waiting for you," the man said.

"Who are you?" Charlie replied. "My name is Konachek."

"Ha! I know different."

"Where is my child?" Charlie asked.

"I wouldn't be concerned about them. And the name is not important," he said.

In the growing light, Charlie stared hard at the man. *He's so familiar. Yes, I know him.* "Attila! You are the one called Attila, aren't you," Charlie said, seeing the pieces fall together. "I remember your face from the war—the men you killed. German or partisan, it didn't matter, did it? I saw it in your eyes."

"Couldn't be helped. Collateral damage. I'm sure you understand." Attila looked hard at Charlie. "War, after all, is hell." He smiled grimly.

"Ruthless bastard," Charlie growled under his breath.

"Before I ask you to sit, I want you to strip one item at a time, beginning with your coat. Drop it on the floor and kick it over to me."

Charlie complied, undressing slowly.

"Hurry, damn it!"

Charlie began with the boots. One at a time, he slid them over. "You...you're the traitor," he said. "Zerenowsky warned me about you. 'You must find him and terminate him,' he said."

"I figured he did, and it was just a matter of time, wasn't it, Stanek? You would have remembered our meeting in '43 on the flight to Moscow." He checked the boots. When he tipped the right boot, the knife fell out. "Nice try," he said.

"How did you know I would be here?"

"I got the information from the Army. Do you think we're so incompetent that we don't communicate? Especially when we find someone crossing the border illegally." He held up the passport and looked through it. "Edvard Konachek, eh? Henry does very good work, doesn't he?"

Charlie watched him while he looked through the passport. "Know him?" he asked.

"Only by reputation."

"I'll tell you what I told your stooge in Prague, the one you ordered to kill me. Fuck you," Charlie said defiantly.

"It doesn't matter what you know or don't know about agents in Eastern Europe that you may have told Pavlov," the man said. "You know about me, don't you? That is your death warrant. My only question is, why did you not tell Donovan?"

"I remembered you only as another mad dog with the scent of blood on his tongue. Only now am I able to connect you with that bastard, Pavlov." Charlie smiled. "Now I know— the mole in Washington. You were the man keeping the MGB informed of Donovan's business. Pavlov turned you, but sadly, Zerenowsky could give me no information on your identity. Smart. He never met you in person, did he?"

"No, but I always suspected he knew much more about me and passed that on to you. You would put two and two together and have me."

"I got out of the army and tried to put it behind me. That is, until the Messenger contacted me," Charlie said.

"Yes, memories of the war you tried to forget, and so, forgot about me, too, but you didn't, not really. Things don't always work the way we want, do they?"

"They'll figure out who the traitor is and come for you," Charlie said. "Worried about losing a good Washington job?"

"It's all about politics."

"Why didn't you just take care of me in Prague instead of sending this runny-nose kid to do the job?"

"When you came out of hiding, I decided I had to take care of you. I could not risk you blowing my cover. You see... unlike Pavlov, I have the utmost respect for your skills. I've read all about them. It was just a matter of time before you remembered me. That, I'm certain of."

"Thanks for the compliment."

"The Army boys have been using you as bait. They hoped you would uncover my identity, or you would figure it out on your own. Did you know that?"

"I had an idea."

"Did you think they needed you, a used-up agent out of the game for two years, to spy on the Soviets?"

"I wondered."

"That's why you have to die," the man said. "I can't allow you to ruin my career or damage my retirement."

"You're a traitor to your country."

"I betrayed my country for a better cause. But you...why did you sell out your country?"

"I've always served my country honorably, unlike you."

The man smiled. "A man without a country who will die silently and anonymously, somewhere in Europe. Too bad," he said. "When it's dark, and the soldiers have returned to their barracks, we will go. Somewhere nice and dark, eh? So, sit down. We have an hour."

"Where's the child?"

"I don't know anything about a child." The man quickly looked out the window, but still kept his eye on his prisoner. "Soon, Stanek, very soon, I will be rid of you for good, and can continue my work not bothered by the likes of you." He pulled a pack of cigarettes from his pocket, forced one out, pulled a Zippo from a trouser pocket, and lit up. "Want one?"

"What name do you go by? That would be nice to know and nothing you'll have to concern yourself with any longer."

"Oh, sorry." He said. "Johnson, Robert Johnson, Major retired, U.S. Army."

"Why didn't you stay in the Army. There's certain to be another war."

"My work is much more important."

"Your work? Killing me and men like me?" Charlie mocked him. "Don't you commie spies talk to each other? The MGB, your boss, still wants me alive. General Pavlov wanted to interrogate me personally."

"Before he killed you or sent you to a gulag? I'm just saving them time and effort," he replied. "Pavlov, the senile old fool. He was obsessed with getting you to Germany so he could identify Raindrops and get his revenge on you for humiliating him in Hanoi." Attila chuckled. "He was risking everything I had built in the States to capture you. I hoped you would fall off the radar—disappear into obscurity--but Pavlov insisted on finding you in '46. He sent a young agent across the world chasing you."

"Wallenski," Charlie added. "He found me in the middle of the Pacific."

"He had orders to get the information Pavlov wanted and terminate you," Johnson continued. "I never heard from him again, but your trail seemed to have gone quiet, so I left it alone. Pavlov was also quiet, but I didn't know that the old man continued to search for you. He refused to give up until he got confirmation on your death. Of course, he never did. Then he found you. He had great resources."

Charlie, still standing, listened as Johnson told his story.

"I had no choice but to intervene to finally get rid of you. If only to protect my cover, an identity that took seven years to build. Did you know that? Through the entire war."

"Donovan needed agents, even asshole traitors like you."

Johnson smiled, thinking he is going to enjoy terminating this bastard. "Pavlov's death was very fortunate for me. Thanks for that, by the way."

"Blame it on cancer."

"Zerenowsky knew too much. Pavlov should have terminated him much earlier...before the war ended."

"Zerenowsky didn't want me to put it in his debriefing report that he knew about you. He knew his life would be worthless. It was anyway," Charlie added.

The man shrugged. "I directed them to his hideout in Wisconsin. A good clean hit. And we almost got you." He smiled and sat down to wait.

"They'll discover you eventually," Charlie replied. "You'll hang, and your buddy Joe Stalin won't be able to save you."

"Shut up. Put your clothes back on." He still held the gun on him.

Charlie dressed slowly, again trying to buy time.

"Here, put these on." Johnson threw him a pair of handcuffs. "We leave soon."

Chapter 30

Jill counted the days since Charlie left. Twenty-two, but it seemed like forever. What concerned her most was that she had not received any word from him—not a telegram, card, nothing. She was beginning to fear the worst had happened. She did not understand his purpose in traveling to Czechoslovakia, but she knew it had to do with a woman and small child—his child. His past during the war was murky and filled with danger. She knew that. He had told her a few things about rescuing flyers in Eastern Europe, but the other stuff, the spy stuff, he left out of his stories.

They had just completed the roundup and shearing of a thousand head of sheep. They had culled and separated the lambs and corralled those going to market. She had to relearn everything about running a large sheep station. Once she did, she adapted quickly. Jill had forgotten how hard this life was, but there was something good and exhilarating about it. The work was honest, and it was a free, open life without the distractions and demands experienced by city people.

Jill knew she was lucky to have a hardworking crew and an excellent foreman in Rusty. He ran the operation but was always careful not to overstep his position. Rusty spoke highly of Charlie and often told her he would make a good bossman. While she has babies," he said. "Tough man, smart man, I think."

Jill knew that Rusty and Charlie had worked together for several years, so she constantly pumped him for more about Charlie. However, Rusty did not seem to know much. "An officer in the American Army," he only told her. "Who fought the bad man, Hitler."

Five days after Charlie had left, while she was preparing for the roundup, which would involve long days in the bush, a dark sedan drove up the long lane. Rusty and Jill stood on the porch, watching. Two men got out when the car reached the house. Rusty eyed them suspiciously. Jill was curious. They did not get too many visitors out there.

The only real visitors she had were men from around Alice Springs who came courting her. As the owner of the largest sheep station in the area and the most attractive woman in Central Australia, Jill had begun to receive proposals as soon as word got out, she was back.

"Rusty, go and get your shotgun," she said. Jill was not taking any chances.

"Yes, boss," he replied. He turned and went into the house.

The two men slowly walked to the porch. "Jill Russell?" the tallest man asked. He was in short sleeves, while the other man wore a dark suit.

"Who's asking?" she said. *Anyone wearing a jacket on such a day out here is certainly not from the area,* she decided.

Rusty stepped out on the porch with the shotgun. He pointed it down but, in their direction, making sure the men noticed, but not threatening them too much.

"What do you want?" she asked.

Both men looked hard at the weapon. "We're just looking for information," the suited man said. "No need for that." Both men looked in the direction of the shotgun.

"Where you from?" she asked. He sounded like a Yank. "The States?"

"The American Embassy...in Canberra."

"I know where the embassy is," she replied. "I'll repeat myself for your benefit. What do you want?"

"We just want to talk to you about an American by the name of Charles Stanek."

"What about him? What has he done?" Jill asked. She did not miss the fact that the other man had not spoken. "And who's he?"

The American looked at his partner. "Criminal services in your government. National Security."

"You still haven't answered my question. What has Charles Stanek done?"

"There was a shooting out here, and a foreign national was killed. We need to know more about it. The Soviet Embassy demanded an investigation, and we're conducting it."

"Since when does Australia need the assistance of the U.S. to investigate a crime?"

"The United States considers Stanek a person of interest, and we have been looking for him for several years."

"Stanek break any laws?"

"Not according to the constable."

"We mind our business and have too much work to do to get on with your kind of business," she said. "We obey the law—Australian law." Her appreciation for Rusty and his shotgun was growing by the second.

"We know that," the Aussie finally said. "The man killed was a Russian from the consulate, and they are demanding answers, more than they've received."

"You want more information on that man? He murdered my father. Killed him in cold blood. I say, 'to hell with him.'" Anger scorched each word from her mouth. "What more can we tell you about the bastard? He came to this station and shot my father with no provocation. Didn't even know him. I think he deserved to die."

"We read from the report that it was self-defense, and we're not challenging that," the Aussie said. "We need to hear the story. The Russians are upset. They demand more information on Stanek."

"I wasn't here, so I can't answer your questions."

"Is there something you're not telling us...about Stanek's role in the shooting? Did he know the shooter?"

"The Russian can rot in hell for all I care," she replied, still fuming. "He pulled a gun and was shot. I'd say that was good. Charles Stanek was one of my father's hands. I don't know if he knew him or not."

"We think that's why the Russian was here...to bring Stanek back to Russia." The two men looked at each other. "You must understand that Stanek is not a citizen in Australia, and lives here only because we permit it," the Aussie said. "And I must remind him that his visa expired long ago."

"Where is he?" the American asked.

"Don't know. He left about five days ago, and I don't expect he'll return."

"I represent the United States Army, and Major Stanek did work for us, but all that is, well, classified. Top secret, you know, and can understand such things, I'm sure. An educated woman like yourself," the American said.

"Don't patronize me."

"Sorry. Major Stanek has been missing for several years, and we want to find him, to help him."

"Well, good luck," she said. "Now get off my land." She turned and marched back into the house. The screen door slammed behind her. Rusty stayed on the porch until the dark sedan drove off down the long lane in a cloud of dust.

For the first time, Jill felt queasy and unsure about Charlie. She knew he was a man with a dark past, but now...now, she began to think she would never see Charles Stanek again. She had decided the night of her father's funeral that she loved him. Just her luck to fall for a man with a dangerous past.

She flopped down in her dad's chair to think, but there really wasn't much to decide. She had a sheep station to run, and that was that.

Rusty walked in, set the shotgun in the corner behind the front door, and looked at her. "Don't worry, boss," he said. "Bossman, Charlie, come back. He come back when his business done." He smiled. "We go now."

For the next few days, Jill felt like someone was watching her. She could not put her finger on it, but her intuition told her the men were still in the area. Rusty reported that his people had spotted strangers around Alice. "Just hanging out," he said. "Not doing nothing. Mostly staying at the hotel and drinking at the bar." Soon her suspicions and the reports from town stopped. Jill figured they got tired of the heat and boredom and had returned to Sidney, Canberra, or from wherever they had come.

The days passed, turning into weeks, without any word from Charlie. Her life moved on, and she became much more deeply involved in the day-to-day management of the station. She had to deal with paying bills, hiring and firing, fixing machinery, marriage counseling, and more. At night, when she was alone with her thoughts, she thought about Charlie, wondered if he was still alive. She dreamed about how he had touched her during their one night of lovemaking. In Jill's remote part of the world, she had to hang on to something. Meanwhile, while letters and phone calls came each day from prospective suitors, she heard nothing from Charlie.

Chapter 31

"**D**ig it longer. Another foot, I'd say, and two feet deeper. I don't want you found for at least ten years," Robert Johnson, a double agent for the Soviet Union, said to his prisoner. "I want you to fit just right in there, Stanek." He leaned against the tree, flashlight in one hand and .45 in the other. A cigarette hung from his lips.

Charlie looked up at his captor. Perspiration streaked down his cheeks. His shirt was damp where it had soaked through. "Go to hell. I think I'll stop right now."

"You want to die fast or real slow? Your choice," Johnson replied dryly. "I don't want to do this. You're probably a real nice guy with friends, a girl, but I have to do it. Understand that? That's how the game we play works."

"Is it mostly psychopaths like you and Pavlov who work for the Russians? Probably all they can find to do their dirty work," Charlie said. He threw the dirt as far from his grave as he could. *I'll make the bastard sweat just like me*, he thought. The mound of dirt continued to grow higher.

Charlie dug as slowly as he could without Johnson noticing. With his back toward him, Charlie punched at the wall of hard clay with the shovel. During the last hour, he had made the hole about three feet deep, cutting through tree roots and hitting an occasional rock. His mind worked feverishly to think up some plan of action, but the deeper he dug, the less his chance of escape, he knew.

Suddenly, from behind him, he heard a loud thump, then a crash. He spun around to see the tall man bent over, blood running from the side of his head. "What the hell?" He turned to look in the shadows beside the tree where Johnson was leaning. He saw a large man standing there, looking down at him.

"William," Charlie said. "How...?"

Johnson recovered quickly, surprising William. He thrust his arm out to retrieve his weapon from the ground in front of him.

Charlie saw the .45 lying there. He also saw Johnson reaching for it. From inside the hole, Charlie stretched to get it before the other man.

Johnson grabbed at it, but the weapon was just beyond his fingertips. He crawled toward it, exerting every ounce of strength he could muster. His fingers wrapped around the grip, and slowly he pulled it toward him and away from Charlie.

Charlie refused to give in to the traitor. He knew if he did he was as good as dead. In one swift motion, he rose to jerk the weapon away from Johnson. Not hesitating, he clicked the safety off. "Give it up or die, you son of a bitch," he whispered, barely forcing the words out. He looked into the other man's eyes and saw a grim determination to kill him. He knew Johnson would not hesitate to pull the trigger.

Johnson, with every ounce of energy he could muster, wrestled the weapon away from Charlie and took it firmly in his hand.

The two men in their life or death struggle took no notice of William, who finally intervened. Leveraging his large hands around Johnson's neck, he pulled his head back hard just as Johnson tried to aim and fire. Johnson's face turned red. He began to gasp for breath, but still, he managed to pull the trigger.

The weapon barked loudly, but the bullet shot harmlessly into the night sky.

Charlie saw his opportunity to end it. As the spy struggled with William to get free, Charlie, with his remaining strength, grabbed and turned the weapon, shoving the barrel into Johnson's face.

The gun fired again. Johnson was thrown backward by the close impact of the bullet. He collapsed into the mound of dirt. A bullet had penetrated the front of his head, above the eyes. He was dead instantly.

"Thanks," Charlie said. He looked at Johnson—Attila, at the man he had just shot. The man was unrecognizable to him, as he had been since their brief meeting four years earlier. Charlie was numb and exhausted but relieved to be alive. He stared into the long hole Attila had forced him to dig. *It could have been me easy enough,* he thought. *And I would never be heard from again, a man without a family, without a country.*

William nodded without saying a word. He also looked relieved.

"You know him?" Charlie asked.

William did not respond.

"We knew of Attila," a voice said from behind Charlie. "The Americans just needed you to flush him out."

Charlie turned to see Henry standing behind him. He wore his fedora and a long, dark wool coat, the collar pulled up to his chin.

"I'm glad I could be of service to the United States Army," Charlie said. "How did you know?"

"The Americans were alerted when they discovered someone had sent an unauthorized message to Jon Grey at the embassy in Prague, and also a coded message to a friendly, someone working both sides—another independent operator. The messages were about your whereabouts." He chuckled. "She figured out who he was and betrayed him by immediately getting word to the Americans that Attila was loose in West Germany.

The clerk at the hotel saw you leave with a man whose actions the woman said reminded her of Gestapo. She grew suspicious and tipped me off. At that moment, I didn't exactly know who we were dealing with. I routinely stay at that hotel, so she knew me well enough to confide in me."

"How did he know I had crossed the frontier?"

"Attila monitored the Army reports on refugees from the east, took the chance that one of them was you. Smart guy. No wonder he was so dangerously effective."

"Yeah, I met him once during the war, but couldn't remember anything about him," Charlie said. "But the worse was no one could believe that I couldn't remember enough to finger him, or that Zerenowsky did not tell me who he was. I guess I was the most vulnerable link that had to be plugged."

"Bad luck, eh?" Henry replied. "I had a suspicion he would take you to the nearest grove of trees for a quick termination. We found the car parked along the road and started searching in the woods. Then we heard your voices."

"You saved my life," Charlie said. "As you can see, I was digging my own grave." He tried to smile. "What about Grey?"

"Attila's fall guy? I think he's being reassigned to other work. I don't think his career in intelligence is working out, and I don't think he wants any part of the business. I understand Attila's order for him to terminate you was his undoing. Life in a gray world, having to operate between right and wrong was the kicker." Henry smiled. "Sure, scared the hell out of the young man. I think he will want to transfer back to the safety of the States real soon, or so the Brits tell me. He, evidently, has become a great cocktail story among Europe's diplomatic set."

"Good. The bastard tried to kill me."

"Then Johnson set Grey up after he failed to terminate. You suddenly disappear, and the Americans in Washington want to know what happened. Attila points to Grey who ordered the hit, to take the blame for your death," Henry said. He kneeled to examine the rectangular hole that was to be Charlie's grave. "For a man who wears the mark of Cain, you're damn lucky, as lucky as I've ever seen," Henry said. "Should be long dead or in some MGB torture chamber." He smiled humorlessly. "I think you could survive standing in the ashes of hell. God must have a special plan for you, my friend."

"I don't feel real lucky."

"Let's get out of here. Take all his identification--wallet, money, lapels off his coat and jacket, everything that can identify him," Henry said. "Then drag him into your grave and cover him good...with leaves and brush. William, take his car and dispose of it. No trace. You know what to do."

William turned and disappeared, again without a word. Charlie began searching the body while Henry leaned against the same tree and lit a cigarette. "Want one?" he asked.

"No."

When Charlie had finished his unsavory task, he turned to Henry, then on his second cigarette. "What do we do with these?" He showed him everything he had taken off the body.

"Keep the money. I'll send his ID to Army Intelligence with a note that says something like, 'Attila found and terminated. Reward expected,'" Henry replied. He smiled. "You don't need the money, do you?"

"It's yours," Charlie replied quickly. "Too many bad guys running around Europe. You'd think the war was still going on. I hope you find a few more," Charlie said.

"They had to find this man and silence him. He was doing too much damage."

Charlie stared at him. "Donovan never gives up, does he? He's determined to get his money's worth out of me."

"They knew you didn't know enough to threaten operations in Europe, but you could draw out a spy. They bet on that."

"The bastards. I can't seem to escape them."

"The car is parked along the road. Let's get out of here before it's sunlight." Henry walked into the trees toward the road.

Charlie followed him. He had completely forgotten about the time, and it had passed quickly.

"How did you know Attila met me in the hotel room?" Charlie asked on the ride back to town.

"The woman told me you had gone upstairs, and that the other, Gestapo-looking man had flashed an American intelligence credential when he asked about you earlier when I inquired about your arrival. We waited. I posted William at the back door just in case."

"You saw us leave?"

"Things didn't look right. I put two and two together, and it equaled trouble. I didn't figure Attila was your visitor until now, but it all makes sense."

"What took you so long? He was about ready to shoot me dead in the damn hole."

"We almost lost you on the last turn, but we doubled back and found the car parked along the trail."

"Where's Frank and Anna?"

"A friend's house. We're going there now. It's not too far," Henry replied. "They're safe. I got an associate lining up documents. Everything should be ready in a day."

"Then what?"

Henry looked at him. "You need to get out of Europe. The longer you stay here, the better your chances of getting caught."

"Caught by whom?"

"Take your pick. You got the Russians, the Czechs, Brits, and the Americans looking for you, and I probably missed someone."

"I think I'll head east to Asia. I kind of like it there, and people leave me alone."

"That's not what I heard."

"Damn Russians and Americans are everywhere. I just need to stay out of their way."

"I hope your luck doesn't run out," Henry said. "What about the child? You taking her with you while you run and hide?"

"Like I already told you, she's my responsibility."

"She belongs in Israel."

"With the chosen people?"

"That's right," Henry said. "We can offer her a life and a future in a world a helluva lot safer than yours."

"How's that? They just fought a war. How safe is that?"

"We won, and now we are free and independent. No more trouble."

"I'll think about it."

"Think fast. Time is running out."

Inside the small, stone house where Henry had parked Anna and Frank, a hot meal awaited them. William was already at the table, sitting with Anna, Frank, and an elderly woman. With her gray hair pulled back tight, a pale, wrinkled face, and trembling fingers, the woman got up and scurried around her kitchen, acting as their hostess. Charlie felt her eyes on him as he washed.

Looking around, he saw a sparsely yet comfortably furnished room, with few signs of the recent war.

"You the father of this child?" the old woman asked as soon as he sat down. Her English was very good.

"Her guardian," he replied. "Where did you learn such good English?"

"I lived in America before the war with my husband. He was a college professor, and we returned in 1938, just before the war. We hated the Nazis and one day they came and took my Otto away. He died in Buchenwald."

Famished and exhausted, he reached for a chunk of bread. "I'm sorry."

"Where are her parents?" the old woman persisted.

"Dead. Killed in the camps. She was left as an infant to survive on her own when she was found."

The old woman made the sign of the cross.

"In this community, we lost many good people in the camps, not only Jews but Catholics, intellectuals, and trade unionists too. Almost as many as killed in the fighting. Hell came here and took them away. I spit on Hitler's ashes." She got up from the table again and hobbled to the stove. She ladled two bowls of soup, handing one to Charlie and the other to Henry. She saw their hunger and had plenty. "You are American?"

"I am."

"Take her to your country. That is good, I think."

"I'm not going back there."

She looked to Henry for some explanation.

"Don't ask any more questions, Emma," he told her.

Anna slid her chair back from the table, crawled down, and walked over to Charlie. She stood in front of him, looking up into his eyes as if waiting for something.

Finally, Charlie, finishing his second bowl of soup, lifted her onto his lap. Their eyes locked together. She touched his face with her hand, and he smiled softly.

"I love you," she said in perfect English.

Charlie began to weep. Tears streaked down his face.

Chapter 32

December 1, 1948

The old Ford pickup wildly swerved as it roared down the rutty dirt road. The rocking, side-to-side motion sent freshly picked watermelons rolling downward onto Charlie. He moved quickly, but several still managed to land on his outstretched legs. "Hey! Slow down," he yelled to get the driver's attention.

"Can't mate," the driver called over the engine noise. "I gotta deadline."

"Yeah, Mike, I get that, but...," Charlie said. "How much further to the Russell station?" He knew from before he could not argue with a man as committed and dedicated to his job as Mike. He let it go. His back had experienced worse than bumps and watermelons from a hard ride in the back of a pickup truck.

"'Bout five-mile." The older man turned his dark-bearded head sprinkled with gray to Charlie and smiled. "Don't ya like the ride?" Parked beside Mike on the torn leather seat, sat Roosevelt, Mike's aging Border collie. When asked why he named him Roosevelt, Mike replied, "He saved ur arses, did he not?"

The dog sat back on his haunches staring through the windshield. When Mike downshifted the old Ford, Roosevelt howled loudly. Charlie did not know if from exhilaration or simple fear. He had earlier declined Mike's gracious offer to sit in the front with the two of them.

"Love it," he replied. Charlie had known Mike for two years. He was one of the first residents of Alice Springs he met. Mike kept all the stations supplied with fresh produce and he took his job seriously. Mike never sold bad produce, and he was never late. Charlie considered him a good friend, one of only a few he had off the Russell station. Mike was his number one drinking mate.

Although still early in the day, the summer sun in a dazzling blue sky was already heating up the dry, parched land. Charlie wiped sweat from his brow and tried to stand to get a view of the land. Mostly to get his balance, he had to grab onto the tailgate to pull himself up, but he still held on tight to the side rail.

Finally, balanced, Charlie gazed out over the wide-open range and smiled. *Home,* he thought. *But would Jill still be waiting?* He had had no contact with her since leaving. He did not even know if she had kept the station or had decided to sell. He figured she was getting good offers from surrounding owners eager to expand their holdings.

The trip from Europe had been long and arduous. Henry had negotiated passage for the four of them on a freighter steaming to Suez. William did not make the trip. The ship was packed with refugees, survivors of Hitler's reign of evil, all looking for a future in a new land—Israel. He was mostly concerned about Anna. Taking her from the only home she had known, as horrible as her childhood had been, and traveling to a strange and different part of the world had to have been traumatic.

The travelers were very fortunate. With calm seas and sunny skies, their trip was uneventful, and it helped that the other passengers left them alone. They disembarked in Haifa, before Suez, and relatives of Henry met them at the dock and took them in.

When that day had finally arrived, Charlie hated parting with Anna, but he understood that leaving her in Israel was probably the best thing he could do. His future was uncertain, dangerously so. He was responsible for killing MGB and CIA agents, so he could expect some type of retribution. He had to face the prospect of spending the rest of his life on the run, or at best, always having to look over his shoulder. That was no life for a child.

Henry and a woman he knew at a kibbutz near the Golan Heights assured him that they would take good care of Anna and Frank. His brief, weeklong experience at the settlement, where he met wonderful people, soon convinced him that he had made the right decision. He was saddened that Marie would never know that Anna was safe, but deep inside, Charlie believed someday they—Marie, Anna, and he--would be reunited.

Charlie went to Czechoslovakia to rescue Marie and his child from the clutches of Andre Pavlov. *Funny how things turned out*, he smiled. *Pavlov is dead, never to bother me again, and Marie and Anna are free to pursue their lives without his interference.* He found that very reassuring. *As for my future*, he thought hopefully. *All I know is I'm prepared to confront it head-on.*

His ride across the Indian Ocean and the Bay of Bengal was quiet and uneventful. His ship, named Quiet Seas, docked in Singapore. Loaded with military supplies for the British Army, the ship made its first stop after leaving Suez two weeks earlier. In Singapore, the ship picked up textiles and headed for Melbourne. Charlie had disembarked in Darwin.

He was one of only five passengers on-board, and he had made it a point to meet and speak with each one of them—all British traveling to Singapore and Australia. He had decided he had to feel them out. He wanted no Wallenski-type surprises. Three were businessmen, and two were laborers from Liverpool. All were war veterans hoping to start a new life. Charlie told them he was a Czech refugee who hoped to find a new life in Australia. They appeared to believe him. Still, he had decided to stay vigilant.

It was good for him to be a little paranoid. When he slept, the P-38 pistol, that Henry had returned to him, was always under his pillow. He never ventured far without it. He spent most evenings pacing on deck topside thinking and wondering who would be waiting for him when he finally reached Australia. Will it be MGB or CIA?

Jill was always front and center in his thoughts. It had been seven weeks. *Have I accomplished what I set out to do?* he constantly asked himself. He thought of his friend and employer, George Russell, and his tragic death. *That too was my fault. He* ruminated over whether he could have saved his friend from the assassin, a bullet meant for him. *Can I make a life with his daughter? Will I have to continue running?* He recalled Henry's prediction. That would be no life for her, either.

"Hot as hell," he growled to himself, bracing against the bumps and potholes. He wiped the sweat from his brow.

"What ya say, mate?" Mike asked, downshifting the old truck to make a bend in the road.

"Nothing." He smiled, flashing back to Jill with her blond curls, soft skin, and pouty lips. Charlie knew they were getting close to the station. His head buzzed with anticipation.

Without warning, the old truck screeched to a halt in front of a long lane, almost throwing Charlie forward into the watermelons. Roosevelt howled with delight.

"You here," Mike called. "Say howdy to Miss Russell. A real beauty, that one."

Charlie grabbed his duffel and jumped from the back of the truck. "Thanks, Mike. See you in town, at Dowdy's Pub, eh."

"You got it." Mike waved, put the truck in gear, and roared off, creating a swirl of dust as he headed west.

Charlie walked—ran—up to the house. Not unlike two years earlier, he jumped up onto the front porch and looked in the screen door. Seeing no one, he knocked but heard no answer, so he called into the house: "Jill? Anyone here?"

On the third call, a voice called out from the kitchen. "I'm coming, mate. What's your hurry?"

Hearing the sound of her voice again was music to his ears. He smiled when he saw a beautiful young woman coming toward him. She wiped her hands on her apron while walking toward the door, obviously distracted.

"Hi, Jill!" He called through the screen, barely able to control his excitement. She was dressed in tight dungarees and an old cotton shirt. She wore George's old, grease-stained apron. Her hair was long and unkempt, with blond curls falling to her brow. Still, she was the most amazing thing he had seen in a long time.

"Hi, Jill," he repeated. "Remember me?"

She looked up, froze, and then burst into tears. "Charlie, I can't believe it's you. My prayers are answered." She rushed to the door.

Charlie opened the screen door, and she jumped into his arms, crying. They kissed and held each other tight, neither wanting to move from the doorway.

The day passed quickly, with Charlie explaining what had happened to him. Jill listened quietly, not wanting to disturb the flow. She then told him of the work at the station and the many proposals she had received for marriage. They laughed and cried together. The evening grew late.

In the early morning before sunrise, Charlie lay in Jill's bed—the same one in which they were together before he had left for Europe. He was thinking while Jill slept soundly beside him, her head resting comfortably on his shoulder. She was the best thing to have ever happened to him, and he knew it. He touched her cheek and smiled.

Have I emerged a better, wiser person for having gone to Czechoslovakia? he asked himself. But he already knew the answer: *I accomplished much in Europe, but I solved nothing,* he concluded.

He kissed Jill on the forehead and tried to sleep, knowing that in several hours, they had a business to run.

THE END

We hope you have enjoyed Robert Tecklenburg's novel, *PRAGUE: Darkness Descending*. You are encouraged to look through the other titles available through BluewaterPress LLC by way of our website at www. bluewaterpress.com.

www.ingramcontent.com/pod-product-compliance
Lightning Source LLC
Chambersburg PA
CBHW031953120726
47898CB00002BA/419